I0763336

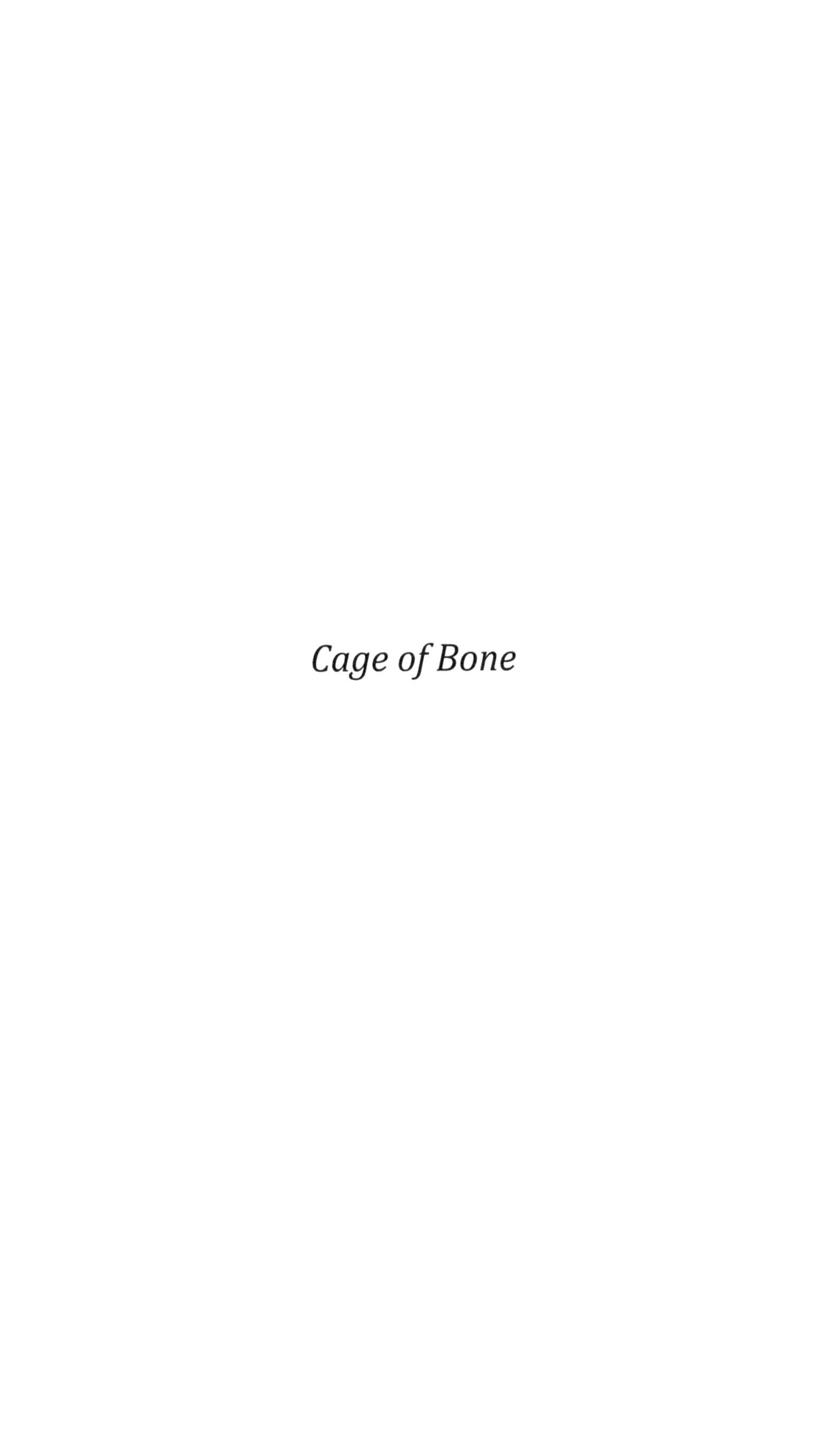

Cage of Bone

Books by David Dvorkin

Fiction

The Arm and Flanagan

Budspy

Business Secrets from the Stars

Cage of Bone

The Cavaradossi Killings

Central Heat

The Children of Shiny Mountain

Children of the Undead

Damon the Caiman

Dawn Crescent (with Daniel Dvorkin)

Earthmen and Other Aliens

The Green God

Pit Planet

The Prisoner of the Blood series

- *Insatiable*
- *Unquenchable*

Randolph Runner

The Seekers

Slit

Star Trek novels

- *The Trellisane Confrontation*
- *Time Trap*
- *The Captains' Honor* (with Daniel Dvorkin)

Time and the Soldier

Time for Sherlock Holmes
Ursus

Nonfiction

At Home with Solar Energy
The Dead Hand of Mrs. Stifle
Dust Net
Once a Jew, Always a Jew?
Self–Publishing Tools, Tips, and Techniques
The Surprising Benefits of Being Unemployed
When We Landed on the Moon: A Memoir

Cage of Bone

David Dvorkin

Editing, print layout, e–book conversion,
and cover design by DLD Books

DLD Books

www.dldbooks.com

Editing and Self–Publishing Services

ISBN: 978-1-7362886-5-8

1

His world began in agony.

Squealing brakes. An impact. He floated for a moment and crashed onto a hard surface. Bones splintered, and he screamed. Cramps folded him over.

He was lying on his back on a cold, hard surface in bright sunlight. For a moment, he saw a baby lying beside him in a pool of blood, kicking its legs and screaming in impotent baby rage.

Lights flashed, red and blue, and the baby disappeared. A man in uniform rushed toward him, leaned over him, did things to him, mouthed words meant to comfort. The agony of being torn out from inside himself intensified.

Blows thudded against him. There was a man with a red face, shouting, throwing punches.

He stumbled backwards and tripped over a chair and fell, turning, landing hard on his stomach on a carpeted floor. He floated in pain. He examined memories that meant nothing to him. He stored them away and tried to scream as cramps doubled him up again, but his mouth was filled with liquid. He was being torn in two, expelled from himself. He couldn't escape. It wouldn't end.

Exhaustion.

He had no strength left, no will, no life. Everything was

fading away. Darkness waited.

He pushed the pain, the fear, the dying away from him, put them behind a thick, hard wall, and became himself. Alone. The wall protected him.

No man remembers his birth. The pain and confusion remained buried behind that wall for forty years. And then Max Iverson went to a movie and was torn open again.

2

The phone rang as Max was moving drowsily around his tiny kitchen, preparing his morning coffee.

It was Anton. "I need you on graveyard for a couple of days. I'm switching Suzy to days. I'll shift things around when I can, and then I'll put you back on days."

Made incautious by sleepiness, Max said, "She's willing to fuck you just to get moved to the day shift? I bet it's not worth it."

Anton said, "You're fired, dickhead. I'll mail you what I owe you." He hung up.

Max was now fully awake without needing any coffee.

"Shit," he said aloud. "Now what?"

Now you have to find yourself another job, he told himself. Again.

Fortunately, there was no lack of the right kind of job available in Piketon at the moment—meaning work where the pay and status were both low, where little experience was required, and where he would not have to deal with other people on more than the most superficial level.

I'll give myself a few days' vacation before I look for another job, he decided. I'll take a couple of days, and I'll...do something.

Mechanically, he continued with coffee, breakfast, shaving, and showering as though he were getting ready for work. Then, all dressed up with nowhere to go, he went downstairs and down the block to a vending stand and bought the morning edition of the *Chronicle*. He took it back up to his apartment and read it as slowly as he could, killing as much time as possible.

Any day now, the *Chronicle* would discontinue its print edition and be available only online. That was happening everywhere. The *Chronicle* was one of the last holdouts. Max understood why newspapers were going digital and discontinuing print editions, and he knew he would adjust to the change when he had to, but he was glad it hadn't happened yet in Piketon. Right now, he needed the distraction of handling a physical newspaper.

He read the national news and all the trivial items from surrounding states. He read about the machinations of state legislators and city politicians. He looked at every word in the summaries of the night's burglaries and bar brawls.

He studied the unsolved murder of a young woman at a gas station.

The murder was a week old, and the newspaper implied that the police had no leads at all, despite their vague hints that they were hot on the trail of the killer. The victim was an eighteen-year-old girl working alone in the cashier's booth at an all-night self-service gas station. As far as anyone could tell, she had been held up, had handed over all the cash she had available, and had been shot and killed anyway.

Only eighteen, Max thought. Just like Suzy. Maybe Anton wants to shift her from nights to days because of that murder. Maybe he's just trying to protect her, and there are no sexual favors involved.

The article included a request from the police department

that anyone with information about the crime call the police tip line. Anonymity was guaranteed.

It better be, Max thought. Who would be willing to risk exposing themselves to a brutal killer?

He wondered if such tip lines ever worked. He knew he wouldn't be able to call that number even if did have useful information. It wasn't in his nature.

The article tangentially mentioned Deputy District Attorney Grady Jacobs, who had some connection with the investigation.

Grady Jacobs, Max thought, turning the name over in his mind. The name appealed to him. Grady Jacobs. He repeated the name to himself. He felt confidence in the man, although he could not have said why.

This isn't paying my bills, he thought. Maybe if I call Anton and apologize, I can get my job back. I could grovel. That would earn me points with him.

Then he remembered that, unlike the young cashier who had been murdered in the gas station, Suzy had not been working graveyard by herself. There were always at least two clerks on duty in the store, even in the middle of the night, and often three. So it was about sex, after all.

Sex with Anton, he thought. Jesus, Suzy. No job is worth that.

That any woman, especially a young and pretty one, would ever consider sleeping with Anton was beyond Max's understanding, but the workings of other people's minds generally were.

When Max finished the newspaper, the morning was still only half over. The day before at work, he had borrowed a copy of a Dick Francis novel from the racks, intending to return it as soon as he was done. Now it belonged to him.

He spent the rest of the morning and the first part of the afternoon lost in horse racing and murder in the misty English countryside. He could not have traveled farther from the climate and terrain of Piketon without buying a plane ticket—and now that was even more out of the question than usual.

Engrossing as the novel was, Max emerged from it suddenly.

Exercise. Something physical. He had been sitting in one place for too long, and he was feeling jumpy and nervous.

I should work out, he thought. Use that gym membership while I still have it.

He wouldn't be renewing it unless he found another job soon.

No, not the gym. He wanted the outside world—traffic, movement, people, the city with all its life. It was a life he was always cut off from, never able to connect to, but he loved its presence, the feel of it.

He put on a light jacket and went out.

Instead of English mist, old buildings, green meadows, and a quiet broken only by hoofbeats, the world outside the apartment building was filled with noise and sunshine. The autumn air was chilly and dry. Traffic moved steadily along the street. Horns blared. People walked past him, all carefully avoiding eye contact. This was the anonymity of the city, and he welcomed it. Don't talk to me, and I won't talk to you. Don't look at me, and I won't look at you.

He strode along the sidewalk, stretching his legs, trying to imagine that he had a purpose and a destination even though he had neither.

A block ahead of him was one of Piketon's two remaining old-style neighborhood movie theaters. This one, The Baron, had been renovated a couple of years earlier and was being used to show an eclectic combination of foreign films and restored Hollywood classics. Big red letters on the marquee spelled out SPARTACUS.

Max headed for The Baron to check the times when the revival of *Spartacus* would be showing. The first showing of the day was due to begin in less than five minutes.

He hesitated when he noticed a sign that read FOR THIS SPECIAL EVENT THERE WILL BE NO REDUCED MATINEE PRICES. Since his morning telephone conversation with his then-boss, finances had assumed a larger role in his calculations.

Why not? he asked himself. Spartacus had had a purpose in life, a great, grand, noble purpose. He had also had the ability to connect with large numbers of his fellow humans.

To hell with the bustling life of the city. Maybe watching the movie would do him some good.

He bought his ticket and went inside. The smell of fresh popcorn awoke his hunger and reminded him that he'd had no lunch. He bought the smallest size bag of popcorn—small but nonetheless absurdly overpriced—and went into the auditorium.

To Max's surprise, despite the movie's fame, there was only a handful of people inside. He chose a seat in the middle of a row about in the middle of the theater and settled down with his popcorn just as the lights dimmed, the classical music on the speakers stopped, and the screen lit up.

Max found himself as engrossed in the restored print of the movie as he had earlier been in the Dick Francis novel. Despite that, he was aware of someone coming in late, making a fair amount of noise as he stumbled in the dark. The latecomer finally sat behind him. Max twisted around. In the glow from the screen, he made out a young man in the row behind him.

"What are you looking at?" the man said.

Jerk, Max thought, but he said nothing and faced forward again.

He turned his full attention back to the action on the screen and tried to suppress his annoyance.

He managed to become absorbed in the storyline again.

Every now and then, during particularly violent moments on the screen, Max sensed excitement from the man behind him. It wasn't that the man was moving around or making noises of some kind. The Baron wasn't that kind of movie house. Rather, Max was aware of something indefinable, something intangible, something radiating somehow from the other man.

Max shifted uneasily.

It's your imagination, he told himself. Watch the movie.

He realized that he had been holding popcorn in his mouth without chewing it. He chewed and swallowed and tried hard to imagine himself in ancient Rome.

On the screen, a huge black man, a gladiator, stood over the fallen Spartacus, whom he had just defeated in the arena. The black gladiator stood ready to plunge his trident into Spartacus. The Roman aristocrats in the stands yelled at him, urging him to kill.

The black gladiator changed his mind, turned, threw his trident at the stands. Then he ran across the arena, leaped partway up the wall and began to climb, trying to get his hands on the bloodthirsty aristocrats. Just as he reached the top of the wall, within very reach of his quarry, one of the aristocrats leaned forward and slid a dagger into the black man's neck. For a long moment, the dying gladiator glared up at his killer, at the camera, at the movie audience, defeated but still defiant. Then his grip loosened, and he slid back down the wall to the arena floor.

As the gladiator hung on the wall, mortally wounded but refusing to give up, staring his hatred into the camera, his face suddenly vanished, replaced by that of a young girl. The hatred in the gladiator's face became fear in the girl's.

"Don't," she begged. "I gave you everything. Please, don't."

Max was staring at her over a gun. There was glass between them. He could see his own face reflected in the glass. But it wasn't his face. It was the face of the man seated in the row behind him. He knew that the man's name was Al Thompson, and he knew where Al Thompson lived.

The gun fired.

Max's hand jerked, shaking popcorn onto his lap.

Glass exploded in front of him. The girl's face disappeared in a shower of blood. She was flung backwards.

Max watched his own hand move forward carefully, through the hole in the glass. His point of view moved forward, tilted downward. Now he could see the girl lying on the floor of the small booth, moving slightly.

The gun pointed down, fired again. The girl became the gladiator again, sliding down the wall with Laurence Olivier's dagger in his neck and the glaze of death in his eyes.

Behind him, Thompson chuckled and whispered, "Yeah, bitch, yeah!"

Max sat unmoving, scarcely breathing, trying not to think. His bag of popcorn slid from his hand, spilling the remainder onto his lap.

Thompson chuckled again. The young woman's murder replayed itself in Max's mind, this time without any prompting from the action in the movie.

Max closed his eyes. He shivered. He felt close to throwing up. He tried to close his mind to Thompson's thoughts, but he couldn't keep the murder out of his mind. It ran through yet again, from beginning to end, a horror movie that would not stop repeating.

Max was faintly aware of Thompson getting up and leaving. Thompson's memory of the murder of the young woman left with him.

Max sat perfectly still, breathing shallowly, doing what he had done as a young boy when he had lain in bed, unmoving and scarcely breathing, afraid of invisible monsters.

This time, the monster had a name: Al Thompson.

Max waited until the movie ended and then pulled himself to his feet. For a moment, he thought his knees would buckle. He felt dizzy and even more nauseated than before.

He could not give in to weakness. For the sake of Thompson's victim, he must find the strength to move.

How did he know that any of what he had seen in his mind was real? Al Thompson, the gun, the girl, Thompson's address—it might all have come from his own unconscious, some sick thing lurking inside him, triggered by the violence on the screen.

But what sickness in him had added those terrible details, not mentioned in the newspaper story—the girl's face exploding, the killer leaning in over the counter and shooting her while she lay on the floor still alive? What insanity was this?

He knew better. He didn't know how he knew, but he was as sure that he had been experiencing Al Thompson's thoughts and memories, that it had all been real and solid and from outside his own mind, as he was that his feet were touching a real, solid floor and that his hand was resting on the back of a real, solid theater seat.

He walked back to his apartment, shuffling, bent over, exhausted. He felt ill and old and used up. Climbing the two flights of stairs to his apartment door was almost impossible. He had to rest frequently, panting for breath, before he could continue.

Inside his apartment, with the door firmly locked behind him, Max collapsed into the chair in front of the small desk holding his laptop.

I should call the police tip line, he thought. They said it's anonymous. I can't do it. I don't remember the number. But it must be on their website. But I can't—

His hands were shaking. He fumbled at his laptop and finally managed to turn it on.

Not the police. Grady Jacobs. That was the office he needed, not the police. He didn't know why, but he knew it was so.

He found the number of the district attorney's office on the city's website. He was about to call the number on his cell phone when he realized that would be unwise.

He recorded the number on his phone and then left the apartment. His fatigue and shakiness were lifting.

Down the street was a drugstore with one of the few payphones still in existence. He entered, closed the door behind him, and placed the call.

When a receptionist answered, Max asked to speak to Grady Jacobs.

"I think he's probably left already," the receptionist said. "Is this important? Can it wait till tomorrow?"

"It has to do with a murder," Max said. His voice sounded thin and weak to him. "The girl who was killed at that gas station a week ago."

"I see. Let me get you the number for the police tip line."

"I don't want the police. I want to talk to Jacobs."

"Sir, the police are in charge of the investigation. You need to give them any information you have."

"No. I need your office, not the police."

"Sir, I have the tip line number right here. Do you have something to write it down with?"

"I'm going to hang up, and no one will get my information. The murderer will go free."

"Sir— Just a moment, please."

Max could hear a muffled conversation but could make out none of the words. Then a man's voice came on the line.

"This is Grady Jacobs. Who is this, please?" It was a smooth voice, well modulated, a pleasant baritone.

"My name's Max." He hesitated. Damn it, he thought. I should have made up a name. It's okay. He probably thinks I did. "Just Max. You're investigating the murder of that girl in the gas station, aren't you? The cashier who was shot?"

"Yes, that's right." Jacobs' sudden tension and alertness transmitted themselves across the wire. "What connection do you have with the case?"

"None. I mean, I'm not connected with the case in any way, but I do have some information you can probably use."

"That's great. I'm ready to hear it." The tone was neutral, conveying neither belief nor skepticism.

Maybe he gets crank calls about murder cases all the time, Max thought. Maybe he'll just ignore what I tell him. But what else can I do?

"The guy's name is Al Thompson." Max spoke quickly, before he could panic and change his mind and hang up. Now it was said, and he was committed.

Despite his attempt at self-control, the images he had picked up in the movie theater reemerged, brilliant and detailed. He began to shiver and to feel sick again.

He gave Jacobs Thompson's address and added a description of Thompson's face, watching it again reflected in the glass of the cashier's booth as he did so. He managed to keep the image in his mind frozen at that point, kept it from moving on to the next instant, when the glass had been shattered by Thompson's bullet and the cashier's face had exploded.

"That's very interesting," Jacobs said, still sounding neutral. "Would there be anything incriminating at that address?"

"I think—" Max thought again. "Yes, I'm pretty sure that some of the money is still there, at his apartment, and the gun he used to kill the girl."

"Mm hm. Now, you know, Max, the police have gotten a few other calls implicating other people. They can't get a search warrant each time. How do I know you're not just trying to cause trouble for someone you don't like?"

"Christ, he killed that girl, and now he's gloating about it! She handed him the money, and then he shot her. That wasn't good enough for him. She was still alive, so he stuck his hand through the hole in the window and shot her again while she was lying on the floor. You can't leave a man like that roaming around!"

"Tell me that part again, Max—about his sticking his hand through the window and shooting her a second time." Jacobs' voice was alive with interest now, all neutrality gone. "She was standing up against the far wall, you said?"

Max was shaking violently and crying. He heard someone walking by behind him. He turned his face to the telephone and huddled inside the booth, sheltering himself from view. He waited until the footsteps had faded away and he could talk without choking on his tears.

"No, no, I didn't say that! The poor girl! Jesus! She was lying on the floor of the booth, moving a bit, and the bastard put his hand through the hole and leaned forward so that he could see her and pointed his gun down and shot her again. She stopped moving. Oh, God, I can't stop seeing it!"

"You were there, Max?"

Max wiped his eyes and drew a deep breath, seeking control. "No," he said. "I wasn't there. I—I heard all about what happened and who did it. Isn't that enough?"

"Yeah, it's enough. This is a good lead, Max. Listen, do you have a number where I can reach you, just in case I end up needing more information?"

"No, I don't," Max said. "Anyway, I've told you all I know about it. I don't have any more information."

He hung up before Jacobs could say anything else.

Two days later, the local media carried news of the arrest of Alfred Thompson in connection with the murder of the young gas station cashier. Thanks to evidence police had found at his apartment, the case against him was said to be airtight. The *Chronicle* gave all the credit to the police, but on TV, the chief of police credited Deputy District Attorney Grady Jacobs, whose office had provided the crucial lead. Henry Fredericks, the district attorney, was quoted as speaking approvingly of Jacobs.

Max was happy to let Jacobs take all the credit. He felt well out of it. He hoped he could sleep again, dreamlessly, without the images from Thompson's mind intruding.

He had done what he could for the dead girl and for society. Now it was time to get on with his own life again. In particular, it was time to look for another job.

Within a week, Max was working again. Once again, he was the lone employee on the day shift at a convenience store. He interacted with strangers as a stranger. There were no other employees with whom he would have to pretend friendship. He was earning enough to cover his small expenses. He still had his gym membership and was working out regularly and hard.

The nightmarish memory of the intercepted thoughts faded. Most nights, he slept till morning, undisturbed by terrible dreams. It began to feel as if the awful incident with Thompson and the murder had never happened. How he had picked up someone else's thoughts, let alone the awful nature of those thoughts—all of that would remain a mystery. He was alone and safe, secure within the fortress of his own mind, looking out at the world and protected from it.

3

Contentment lasted for a month.

Max was riding home from work on the bus, more asleep than awake. Lulled by the swaying of the vehicle, the overheated interior, and the hum of traffic coming through the closed windows, he dozed. He was vaguely aware of the woman beside him getting up and leaving and of the man who took her place.

Minutes later, the images began.

The knife, the blood, the fading struggle to live. The body, with the knife still in it, disappearing under shovelfuls of earth. The feeling of satisfaction at a necessary task done well—and, even stronger, the pleasure. Then two or three faces, vaguely glimpsed, mentally tagged as the next to be eliminated. And then anticipation, something akin to sexual arousal.

Max sat rigid, staring ahead of him, concentrating on the coat collar of the man in the seat in front of him. Lights passed by through the window to his right, alternating with darkness—streetlights, bus stops, residential streets, store fronts. Max kept his eyes aimed ahead, afraid to move. He must not look at the man beside him, must not move and draw the attention of this killer whose hands were strong enough to drive a knife so far into a human body, whose mind could take pleasure in committing such horror.

In the images from the killer's mind, Max saw a cheap restaurant, now closed, then the bar next door to it, still open, the words GLENNS HIDEAWAY painted on its window, then the next door down, opening to a stairway leading up to the killer's apartment.

But he didn't see the names of the people, neither the killer's name nor the victim's. Nor could he see anything to identify where the killing had taken place or where the victim was buried. Before any of those details appeared, the killer stood up and left the bus, moving swiftly out of Max's mental range.

Max sat frozen in his seat, afraid even to turn to watch the man walk away along the sidewalk.

He rode the bus home, went to the same drugstore payphone, and called Grady Jacobs.

Jacobs said, "It's not enough."

"Why not? It's like the stuff I gave you last time."

"Because last time you also told me enough for us to get a warrant to search for real evidence. Silverman's a sympathetic judge in these matters, but even so, the police were only willing to go to him for a warrant because I convinced them that there was something there to find. I went out on a limb doing that, but you knew details about the crime that weren't available to the public, and that's what swayed me.

"This time, all I have is a guy on the phone insisting that a crime has been committed, but this is a crime we aren't even aware of. It's a murder I hadn't heard a thing about before your call. It's all vague and incomplete, and you're even telling me that there's nothing incriminating in this guy's apartment. And you don't know where his apartment is. How can we go to a judge with that?"

"You didn't believe me at first before, either," Max pointed out. "I had to prove myself. I had to give you those details. Then you believed me."

"Uh huh. That's true. So I'm inclined to believe you this time, too. But it's not a matter of you convincing me. It's a matter of me convincing the police and of them convincing a judge. I need to know where the weapon is, where the body is—something, anyway. Hell, at least I need an address where this guy lives! Call me back when you can give me the kind of information I need, okay?"

"Yeah. Okay."

Max was frustrated and angry—angry at himself for not having picked up the sort of details Jacobs needed, but even angrier at Jacobs for involving him in this way. He wanted Jacobs to take over and finish the work, the way he had the first time. Max was being drawn into someone else's tragedy, and he hated it.

You have to do it, he told himself. You can't let this slide. It's not just that the killer has to be caught and punished. He has a mental list of future victims. You saw that in his mind. You've got to give Jacobs what he needs so that he can stop the guy before he kills those other people.

He walked home, grateful that the dark sidewalks were almost empty. He had started to fear that the more people he was around, the more likely it was that one of them was a murderer, and he would pick up the murderer's terrible thoughts.

He wondered how he could get Jacobs the information he needed. This mindreading ability of his wasn't something he could control. If he could, he'd make it go away forever. It had happened twice, and it had been a complete surprise to him both times.

Then he realized that there was one important factor the

two incidents had had in common. He had been physically close to both Al Thompson and the new killer, the man whose name he had failed to pick up. Whatever this strange new ability of his was, it seemed to depend on proximity.

If that was the case, then to have any hope of getting more information for Jacobs, Max would have to get close to the new killer. He would have to risk exposing himself to a murderer who took pleasure in killing. He knew what Thompson and this new killer were capable of. He could imagine what they would do if they found out about him and his role in their capture.

I can't let fear stand in the way, he told himself.

No, he thought, be honest. Don't call it fear. Call it cowardice. I can't let my cowardice keep me from doing what I have to do.

Okay, he thought. Okay. Maybe it won't be so bad. There's that bar the guy was thinking about. It's next door to where he lives. I'll go there and see if that gets me close enough to pick up the additional details Jacobs needs.

Incongruously, Max looked tough. He was taller than average, solidly built, well-muscled from regularly working out, with a strong face that struck most people as dangerous. The truth was the opposite of the appearance, but his appearance had stood Max in good stead more than once. It had kept him safe and out of fights. He would have to count on it doing so again in the bar.

Or should he forget about the bar?

He had caught a mental picture of the outside of the killer's apartment building, gleaned during the quick flash of terrible, bloody images on the bus. He had seen the stairway inside it, leading to the killer's apartment. What he ought to do was go up that stairway and wait quietly in the hallway outside the killer's apartment. Sooner or later, he was bound to catch a glimpse of what he needed to know—the killer's name, the victim's name, the body's location, something that would satisfy Grady.

Max imagined himself standing quietly in the shadows of a hallway, listening with his mind, separated only by a thin wooden door from a murderer.

He shivered. The idea terrified him.

No, it would be the bar. That was his limit.

Max changed into blue jeans, running shoes, and a dark T-shirt with the logo of a rock band on the front. He put on a windbreaker and left his apartment, making for the bus stop two blocks away.

The bus was headed downtown and was half empty when he got on, but it filled up quickly. A few stops along, a young man took the empty seat next to Max. Preoccupied, Max was only subliminally aware of him.

Then an image came into Max's mind of the pocket in the side of his own windbreaker.

Money in the guy's pocket, the young man was thinking. Grab and run at the next stop.

Max turned and stared at the young man.

For a moment, he saw himself through the young man's eyes: big, powerful, angry, violent.

The young man quickly drew back the hand that had been near Max's pocket. He got up and moved to another seat. Max returned to his own thoughts, to the privacy and safety of his own head.

Max got off at the same stop where the killer had exited the bus earlier in the evening. He had a clear picture of the outside of the bar, but it was mostly an image of a window on which GLENNS HIDEAWAY was painted. He had no picture of the name of the street Glenn's Hideaway was on or the route to it.

He took out his phone and entered "glenns hideaway piketon" into the Google search bar. There were no results.

Must be the type of place that depends on alcoholic word of mouth advertising, he thought. I should ask one of the locals.

He shrank from that idea. What he had seen that afternoon on the bus had left him with terror at the idea of any human contact, especially here in the killer's own neighborhood, where someone might remember Max and tell the killer about him.

He put his hands in the pockets of his windbreaker and leaned against the sign marking the bus stop. He stood in a pool of light cast by a nearby streetlight—one of the few that still functioned in this part of town.

Pedestrians passed by, working class and never-working class, all of them white, but united more by their poverty and near-poverty than by their race. They looked at him incuriously for a moment and passed on.

Max ignored them. He stared into space, concentrating on the killer, on the idea of the man, the mental smell of violence and bloodlust. But it was no good. He caught not the slightest hint of his presence.

He had already learned that his talent was intermittent and unpredictable, and even when it came upon him, it required proximity. Either it wasn't working now, or the murderer was not within the required few feet. Or possibly both.

How many feet? Max wondered. How close do I have to be?

Even if he were to find the killer's apartment building and climb the stairs and stand outside his apartment, he still might not pick anything up. His talent might choose to remain absent. It might leave him standing outside the murderer's door, not one whit the wiser and naked before the man's need to kill.

GLENNS HIDEAWAY

The image of the sign floated briefly through his mind. Max snapped back to the here and now and looked around wildly.

The killer! He's here!

No, he would remember that man's mental presence forever, even if he didn't know what the man looked like. There was no one around who fit, who felt right.

There were people on the sidewalk, and cars still crowded the street. There was no way of knowing who had been thinking of the bar or where that person was now. It could have been anyone.

Max became aware of the noise of the crowd, the traffic, and the smell of vehicle exhaust. He also became aware of a small, stooped man standing in front of him, looking at him hopefully.

"What?" Max said. "Did you say something to me?"

"I said, I need eighteen cents more so I can take the bus to the north side to see my sick sister, who's laid up with arthritis."

Max stared at him, nonplused. "Eighteen cents?"

Sensing a possible mark, the panhandler added quickly, "And take my two little nieces to the circus, too."

Max laughed. "All that for eighteen cents?"

"Eighteen cents *more*," the panhandler corrected him.

That kind of creativity deserves a reward, Max thought.

He reached into his pocket and saw GLENNS HIDEAWAY again.

He stared at the small man before him. "Eighteen cents more, huh?"

The image of the window of Glenn's Hideaway appeared again, clearer and brighter—brighter and more inviting than it had been in the mind of the murderer on the bus. Max jingled the loose change in his pocket, and the image of the bar's window grew still brighter and yet more inviting.

Max brought out all the coins he had in his pocket and dropped them in the outstretched hand. "Have a real good time."

"Hey, thanks! Uh, God bless you, sir."

"That's okay."

Max looked away, concentrating on the image of the front of the bar. It had grown brilliant, glowing and beckoning like the gateway to Paradise.

The panhandler looked at Max for a moment. Then, satisfied that Max wasn't watching him, he walked away rapidly down the sidewalk.

Max followed.

Glenn's Hideaway was only three blocks away, but it was around a corner. Max knew he would never have found it by himself.

He watched from across the street as the bum entered.

The front of the bar was far drabber than the image in the bum's mind, drabber even than the picture in the mind of the murderer.

Despite himself, Max's eyes drifted along the storefront to the doorway beside the bar. He froze, staring at that doorway.

He shook himself.

Fixing his eyes on the door of the bar, he crossed the street and entered.

Inside, Glenn's Hideaway was a long, narrow, poorly lit room with a bar down one side and tables along the opposing wall. There was barely enough space between the tables and the barstools for a man to walk. Most of the tables were occupied, and there were few spaces available at the bar. The air was filled with the low hum of conversation. There was just enough light for Max to be able to tell that the floor was unpolished—or that any polish had long ago worn off. The place stank of stale beer, vomit, and urine.

Mental images flooded in suddenly, vague and ill formed, confused, tenuous. Max wondered if his talent had suddenly grown stronger. Or maybe it was some sort of critical mass, something to do with so many alcohol-dulled minds crammed into a small space.

Maybe it's my fear, he thought. Tension, terror, adrenaline. Something like that.

He took one of the few empty seats at the bar and ordered a beer. He sipped it slowly and concentrated, reaching for an image like the one that had terrified him on the bus. All he could sense was the fuzziness of the drunken minds to either side of him.

He grimaced and slid off the bar stool. He looked around the bar for a table that would give him some degree of privacy, some distance from the mental buzz. The continual assault by the meandering thoughts of others set his teeth on edge and made him feel queasy.

He saw one table with no one sitting at it. Better yet, it was the table farthest from the bar, up against a wall and even more dimly lit than the rest of the tavern. He picked up his beer and went to the table. He sat down and sipped his beer. He hoped he was blending in.

He drew in a mouthful of beer and choked.

The knife sliced into the victim. Blood sprayed everywhere. It was happening in front of him. Sunlight and the dappled shadows of a woods lit up the dingy tavern.

Max coughed and managed to regain his breath.

His apartment must be right above me, he thought. I must be close enough.

And the killer must be reliving his crime, reveling in the

details, in the memory of blood and agony and of depriving someone else of life.

Max sat at the table, grateful for the concealing darkness. He was shivering, he knew his face was white, and he felt close to vomiting. He tried to shut the images out and was only partially successful.

No, he told himself. You have to watch. You have to get the details for Jacobs.

Again and again he watched the knife slicing into the victim's flesh, the blood gushing, the agony and terror, then the body, the knife protruding from it, being pushed into a shallow grave and dirt being shoveled over it.

He didn't wipe the knife off, Max thought. If I can find out where the body is, wouldn't there still be fingerprints on it? That should be enough for Jacobs.

God, surely it would!

But maybe that still won't be enough. Maybe the guy'll get off somehow. He'll go free. He shouldn't. He should die. If I could make him kill himself, I wouldn't have to worry about getting information for Jacobs.

New images intruded. Knives again, but guns as well. Mangled bodies, blood, and death again, but the faces of the victims were new ones.

What is this? Max thought. Is he a serial killer?

Watch, he told himself, gritting his teeth. Listen.

He caught hold of a thought: All of them. I'm gonna get all of them. They're all traitors. Any one of them could turn me in. Gotta get them all. That's the only way to be sure.

A gun glittered in the overhead light of the killer's living room. The killer turned it back and forth. He saw and Max saw the gun firing bullets into the skulls of the cronies he feared would betray him.

So it's not what he *has* done, Max realized. It's what he's planning to do. It's what I saw on the bus. He has a list of people he's going to kill. Christ, now I really have to stop him!

He closed his eyes and concentrated on the man one floor above him.

Kill yourself, Max thought. Put the muzzle of the gun against your forehead and pull the trigger. Do it, he thought. Do it! *Do it!*

Over and over, he repeated that thought.

There was no change in the images of slaughter flooding into Max or the feelings of satisfaction and anticipation. Max's thoughts were having no effect on the killer. The talent was one way. He could receive only, and even that was haphazard. He could neither pluck thoughts at will from the minds of others nor insert thoughts into them.

He was overcome with shame. Even if he were to develop an ability to influence the thoughts of others, how could he think of bypassing the justice system? Who was he to pass sentence on a killer and carry it out?

All right, he told himself. Calm down. Listen for what you need. The place where that body's buried, that's the key. Concentrate on that. He's bound to think about it sooner or later.

But he didn't. The killer had passed from reveling in the details of the murder a few days earlier to anticipating the murders to come.

Max felt close to despair, and then the killer thought, very clearly, Martinez, Glade Avenue, and Max saw him in his imagination walking up to the front door of a brick duplex, knocking on the door, pretending friendship with the wispy young man who answered, going inside, and shooting the young man between the eyes.

269.

The killer had imagined glancing at the address as he knocked on the door, and the number was 269.

Max lurched to his feet, banging against the table and upsetting his beer. He didn't notice the glass toppling over and breaking or the beer running over the table and dripping to the floor.

He ran to the bar and shouted, "Telephone! Where is it?"

The bartender stepped back from the bar. "It's only for business use. Use your cell."

Max gritted his teeth, glaring at the bartender. "God damn it," he said through his teeth.

He couldn't afford the time to go to the only public telephone he knew of, the one near his apartment. He looked toward the front door, wondering what to do.

Someone passed along the sidewalk in front of the bar, visible as a silhouette through the front window. It could be the killer, already on his way.

"God damn it!" Max said again. He turned his attention back to the bartender, thinking there must be some way to appeal to the man.

The bartender took another step back. "Okay, okay," he mumbled. "Here." He lifted the telephone from a shelf behind him and put it on the bar, sliding it carefully toward Max. "Just don't tie it up too long, okay?"

"Right." Max knew both numbers by heart—Jacobs' office number and his home number, which Jacobs had given Max after his first call. This time, he dialed the home number.

Be there, Max thought. Please be there.

Jacobs answered almost immediately. "This is Jacobs."

Max said, "It's Max. Get the police over to 269 Glade Avenue right away. I don't know whether that's North or South, but there's someone named Martinez living there, a young guy, and the man you want is on his way over there now to kill him."

"You sure about that? I'll look like an idiot if you're not."

"I'm sure."

There was a pause. Then Jacobs said, "All right."

Max gave the telephone back to the bartender, who snatched it away and scuttled back out of sight.

Max leaned against the bar to support himself. His knees were shaking.

Suddenly, he realized that the bartender must have heard his side of the conversation.

And he can identify me, Max thought. By now, Jacobs knows where the call came from. He probably has men on the way here already.

He pushed himself away from the bar and left the tavern, heading back toward the bus stop.

I've done enough, he told himself. I've done everything I could. I've done more than anyone could expect me to. It's up to Jacobs now. It's out of my hands.

Max slept little for most of the night, dozing for a few minutes and then jerking awake. When he did sleep, he dreamed dreams derived from the memories he had picked from the killer's mind, but often with himself as the victim. When awake, he feared that the killer would escape the police and come hunting him.

Half an hour before the alarm was due to go off, he gave up and got out of bed. He made a pot of coffee and turned on the radio. It was always tuned to the local NPR station, and the morning news program was on. He waited, mentally tuning out the national news, waiting for local headlines.

Here it was: a visit to the state by a presidential candidate, an argument between the governor and the legislature over school funding, and then finally what he had been waiting for.

"This morning, Piketon police announced the arrest of a local man, Thomas Hughes, for attempted murder. Deputy District Attorney Grady Jacobs said he will also be lodging charges of murder against Hughes in connection with the disappearance of another local man, Frederick Berry. Jacobs has been working to crack the disappearance case for some time, he announced, and based on information provided by his office, police had had Hughes under surveillance. In a dramatic confrontation last night, police and Jacobs apprehended Hughes as he entered the home of a Gabriel Martinez, intending to kill him. Jacobs has promised that more details will be forthcoming in a press conference he will be holding this afternoon."

During his lunch break, Max walked about a mile from his workplace and found a working payphone inside a drugstore.

He was determined not to establish a pattern that could lead to him. Jacobs was no doubt keeping track of the locations Max's calls had come from. Max imagined a wall map with pins on it, one for each call. He wanted the distribution of those pins to look random.

Max punched in Jacobs' office number. He had a feeling that Jacobs was the type who usually ate his lunch at his desk, working all the time.

"Jacobs." The voice was crisp and energetic, the voice of a man in command of his life and circumstances.

It would be wonderful, Max thought, to feel that way. "I see you got him," he said.

"Ah, it's you. Yes. Caught in the act, and Martinez told us quite a bit about the other guy, Berry. After that, Hughes started talking and couldn't stop." He laughed in delight. "I really owe you for this one. You've done a real service to the city."

"You were on the scene. Being seen."

"I was there in case it didn't work out. There would've been a shit storm, and I wanted to be there to intercept it before it hit the people who work for me. Got anything more for me? I don't know how you get your information, but it's solid gold. From now on, anytime you feel like passing something on, just call me right away, either here or at home, and I'll run with it. Okay?"

"Yeah, okay. If anything more comes up, I'll pass it on."

Sensing that Max was about to hang up, Jacobs said quickly, "You know, I'd like to meet you so that I can thank you in person. And maybe you could tell me a little about your sources, too."

Max laughed. "No, not likely, Jacobs."

He could imagine the man's reaction if he told him the truth: I read people's minds. But it's unreliable, so I never know when I'll read someone's mind, or who it will be, or when it will happen.

"Grady," the prosecutor said. "Call me Grady, okay, Max?"

"I'll call you if I have anything to tell you, Grady. But I can't tell you when that'll happen again. I can't even tell you *if* it'll happen again. I never know ahead of time."

"Okay. Got it. Well, thanks again, Max. The whole city thanks you."

After he had hung up, it occurred to Max that the whole city would have trouble thanking him if it didn't know he existed—which, thanks to Jacobs' taking all the credit for himself, it never would.

But I really did do something very good for the city, Max told himself. I mustn't forget that. I guess I'm a hero.

He didn't feel heroic, though. He felt sleazy, a mental Peeping Tom who sneaked around the city eavesdropping on people's thoughts, looking for memories of wrongdoing.

Hiding within his own skull, he rifled the contents of other people's minds.

4

Max found himself looking at his customers with too much intensity. He would stare at them, wondering what was going on behind their unremarkable faces, what thoughts of blood and death floated through their brains, and wondering whether he would suddenly catch some of those thoughts. Then he would come to himself with a start and ring up their purchases.

When it finally did happen, it felt anticlimactic.

He was in the middle of making change from the cash register drawer. The orderly trays of differently denominated bills and coins vanished, replaced by the bruised and terrified face of an old man. Behind him were wooden cabinet doors. The old man was crouched against them, moaning in fear and begging for mercy. Along with that picture came a certainty that the twenty-dollar bill the young woman on the other side of the counter had just handed Max was one of a large number the old man had given her so she would stop beating him.

Max froze for only a moment and then finished what he had been doing. He placed the bills in her outstretched hand, counting up as he did so. "That's five dollars, ten, and twenty."

As he spoke, he kept glancing at her face. She was concentrating on the money, frowning slightly, but smiling at the same time.

She seemed so pretty and young and fresh. How could she have done what he had read in her mind? Perhaps she hadn't. Maybe he had picked up a stray memory of a movie she had seen.

But once again, he knew better. There was something about the thoughts, an indefinable flavor, that marked them as real. Al Thompson's memories of the murder of the gas station cashier had had that flavor. So had Thomas Hughes' thoughts. The twenty was tainted by its source, by the methods used to obtain it.

She was small and slender, this young woman. But she was young, and that must count for a lot when the victim was old and frail.

Max could hardly imagine committing such a crime. Now, though, he knew all too intimately how someone who had committed such a crime thought about it afterwards. She was satisfied with herself and happy to have the money. She felt no remorse.

This time, Max remained sufficiently objective and detached to concentrate on the details. He caught the victim's name and address and the fact that he lived next door to his abuser.

As soon as he had a break, Max telephoned Grady Jacobs and told him what he could about the old man.

"Not exactly big-time stuff," Jacobs told him. "I mean, I believe you, Max. I know this is solid information, and I'll act on it. But something like this sucks up resources without returning much on the investment, you know?"

Yes, I know, Max thought. You want something the press will latch onto. You want something that will make you a hero.

"I've read about this being like an epidemic," Max said. "Victimization of the elderly, or whatever they call it. Elder abuse. That's it. Jump on this one, and you'll be the hero of all the old people in the city. Hell, in the state." All the old voters, he thought.

"Hmm, you're right about that. This isn't just an isolated crime. It's a symptom of a deep and widespread social ill."

"Spoken just like the great social reformer you are, Grady."

The DDA laughed. "Believe it or not, Max, I am. By the way, how did you find out about this poor old guy being beaten up by his neighbor?"

"The same way I found out about the previous two crimes, okay? Just leave it at that."

He hung up abruptly and went back to the drugstore counter.

Later, he realized that he was hanging back from the customers, reluctant to touch their money and fearful of accidentally touching them.

You don't have to do that, he told himself. They're normal. Most people are normal.

Most people are normal.

He repeated it over and over, a mantra, or perhaps a spell to protect himself against monsters he had never before imagined existed.

Max saw the results of his warning on the local television news that evening. He also saw Grady Jacobs making what appeared to be an impromptu speech.

First came the news story.

Thanks to a tip from an unidentified source, an elderly man had been rescued from months of extortion and physical violence at the hands of a young neighbor. The victim was now being cared for by out-of-state relatives. The neighbor, a young woman, was in custody, and the Piketon District Attorney's office was preparing charges against her. The investigation had been prompted by Grady Jacobs, one of Piketon's Deputy DAs.

The screen filled with Jacobs' face. He looked earnest and concerned. His dark hair was brushed straight back, showing his high forehead. His suit was conservative, almost somber.

Handsome guy, Max told himself. Looks a lot better doing this than I would.

Jacobs spoke directly to the camera. "Abuse of the elderly is a crime that revolts us all. But it's even more than that: It's becoming an epidemic in America. Today, we rescued one unfortunate senior citizen from a pattern of physical abuse and extortion of his life savings by a greedy and heartless younger person. But how many more elderly people are still suffering from the same kind of treatment? I'm giving warning here and now that our office will not tolerate this crime in our county. If you are an elder being abused by a neighbor or a family member or a caregiver, or if you know or suspect that an elderly person is being abused, I want you to call this number with whatever information you have."

He read off a telephone number, which simultaneously appeared along the bottom of the screen.

"This crime is a scourge," Jacobs went on. "It's a blot on our entire nation. And I'm going to do everything in my power to erase that blot."

The vapid news readers reappeared briefly and then made way for a commercial.

I *did* do some good, Max told himself. I don't know how sincere Jacobs is, but I did rescue that old guy.

Perhaps Jacobs was using Max and his information for political gain, but Max was using Jacobs to eliminate evils big and small from Piketon. It was worth a great deal to Max to know that.

It kept getting easier.

The thoughts that flashed into Max's mind came more and more often. He might be sitting in a movie theater or on the bus or serving a customer, as with the earlier incidents, or he might be walking down the sidewalk or eating in a restaurant. Over and over, he was forced to relive other people's crimes.

The thoughts were often mild, not like the intense, terrible ones, the products of powerful emotions or fearful memories, that he had intercepted the first few times. Now the crimes were smaller, often just minor misdeeds, such as keeping extra change given by a careless store clerk. Sometimes, what he heard were details of purely personal sins, such as adultery.

But every now and then he was inundated by something awful, something bloody, something vile that sent him straight to the telephone to pass on to Jacobs everything he knew. Those were the images and memories that left him weak-kneed and shaking. They were the ones that invaded his dreams and destroyed his sleep.

He wondered what percentage of all the truly evil thoughts he was overhearing. If his talent were truly haphazard and the majority of what other people thought remained inaudible to him, then he must be picking up only a small fraction of what was going on in other people's heads. Therefore, the awful things he did hear must represent a far larger number of evil deeds. He must live in a world filled with monsters.

Or perhaps his talent was increasing in power and reliability. Power, certainly. The distance involved was not so small as it had once been. Was he also hearing a larger fraction of what went on within other people's skulls? That was a comforting thought, in a way. It meant that his fellow human beings were no more evil than he had always thought them.

But what could have increased the power and frequency of his talent?

It must be Thompson and Hughes, he thought. Maybe reading their minds kicked open a door in me.

It was a door into horror.

His augmented talent seemed to work exclusively with thoughts and memories and desires Max did not want to hear. It did not let him tap into other people's happiness. Where were the dreams of love, the memories of delight, the anticipations of wonder? He was as blind and deaf to those as anyone else.

Maybe I'll go through life surrounded by this filth, he thought. This is all I'll ever see of what's behind the mask of other people's faces—just the shit and the evil.

"I read about you in the paper. Congratulations."

"Hello, Max."

"You answered quickly. First ring."

"I always do when this number rings. You never know who it might be. I was hoping it would be you, though."

"Oh? And why's that, Grady?"

"Because you always have such fascinating information for me."

Max laughed. "Enough to get you named Chief Deputy DA, right?"

"That's right. I'm really enjoying my big new office, thanks to you. It's only been one day, but I already feel at home here."

"Well, gee, Grady, don't get to feeling too much at home. I'm sure you've got bigger offices in mind, right?"

"I'll worry about that when the time comes. So, Max, do you

have something interesting for me?"

"Nope, not this time. I really did call to congratulate you."

"Cocksucker," Jacobs said with a laugh. The anger he was trying to hide came across the telephone line. "Sometimes, Max, I feel as though I'm a fish, and you're just dangling bait out here for me, playing with me."

"Really?" The image surprised Max. "There's no hook, Grady. That's the difference between me and a fisherman." No malice, either, he thought.

This is going nowhere, Max thought. I should hang up.

But he had a strange feeling that he wasn't just talking to Grady, that he was talking through him to someone else, someone important. He felt again the odd connection he had felt when he had first heard Jacobs' name. He wanted to maintain that connection.

His voice calm and friendly again, Jacobs said, "So, Max, haven't you ever wanted to be in on the kill? Haven't you wanted to see your information being put to good use? I figure that's one of the reasons you keep feeding me the stuff—so that we can get the bad guys off the streets. Wouldn't you like to watch us do it?"

"How do you know I haven't already?"

"What?"

"How do you know I haven't been watching you? Just some passing civilian you didn't even notice, maybe, or one of the Piketon cops you took along to do the dangerous work."

"Cocksucker," Jacobs said again, although this time with a degree of admiration.

"Or maybe I'm one of your coworkers," Max said, "and I'm there with you all along, working in an adjacent office. How about that possibility?"

Jacobs said, "Hmm." He paused, then said thoughtfully, "No, I don't think so. You're right, of course. I can't be sure. But I sure would like to meet you. It's always just these phone calls. I never know when you're going to call—or if you are. I just have to wait. I should at least have a number where I can reach you."

"I like our romance just fine as it is," Max said. "It's been fun, Grady. I'll call again sometime."

"Hold on a minute, Max. I've spent a lot of time thinking about you, and I've arrived at a few conclusions. I'd like to hear your reaction to them. First of all, you're not involved in the crimes you tell me about. They're too varied in nature and too many different people are involved, people who have no connection to each other, so it's not as if you're ratting on some buddies in order to get a reward or keep from doing time yourself."

"I love this cop talk," Max said. "In a second, you'll say something about stuff going down and collars and perps."

"I probably would have if you hadn't said that," Jacobs admitted, laughing. "Anyway, what I conclude is that you somehow have a source of information of your own, or maybe a bunch of sources, so that you get all this good stuff. Then you pass it on to me because you really do want to see the bad guys behind bars, and you know that this is a good way to do it. I don't know, maybe you're some kind of private investigator or ex-cop with good sources. In any case, you've obviously got very noble instincts, but you have no way to use your information directly yourself."

"Not bad. Close enough."

"What I can't figure out," Jacobs continued, "is how you can have so many good sources without my having the same sources. I mean, Piketon isn't that big a city, so we'd probably know some of the same people, you and I. If they're willing to talk to you, they'd be willing to talk to me. Hmm. Unless you're extremely rich and can pay them a lot more than I can, given the budget I operate under."

"Whatever," Max said. "The details don't really matter, do they? What matters is that I keep giving you what you need."

"Oh, but they do matter. I see two problems with the arrangement we have now. The first one is your own safety. If your sources are passing info to you, then they can just as easily pass it in the other direction. By which I mean that *they'll* rat *you* out. Then you'll be in danger. The second problem is that so far, you've only given me what's basically small stuff, individual crimes. Each one is bad enough, and getting the perps—sorry, perpetrators—has done my career lots of good, obviously. But you're not making a dent in the real problems in the city. Organized crime, for instance, which do we have here, even though most people don't realize it. There's no coordination in what you're doing, you see. You're not using what you have as part of some kind of larger, organized effort to do some major good. Whereas, if you came in-house and worked directly with me and my staff—"

"Oops, sorry, gotta go," Max said. "There's a bunch of men at the door with Tommy guns, and I think they want to speak to me. Catch you later."

The disconnection clicked loudly in Jacobs' ear.

"Shit," Jacobs said. "I thought I had him, but I guess I scared him off."

Lynnette Salzmann, who had been sitting in her boss' office listening quietly to one side of the conversation, said, "I don't trust him."

"I know you don't. I'm skeptical, too, but his information's gold."

"So far. Maybe it won't continue to be. Maybe this Max guy is setting you up."

"Setting me up for what?"

"For a fall. For getting you out of office. For destroying your career."

"Oh, come on!"

"Seriously, Grady. You're the best there is. A lot of people are afraid of you and want you gone. Then there are your potential political opponents. They want to cut you down while they still can. You have a great future. I can see you in the White House, and so can they."

Grady laughed. "The White House! I'm not thinking that far ahead."

"I am. I see the path: DA, mayor, governor, senator, president."

"DA, sure. Mayor, maybe. That's it."

"You underestimate yourself."

"I don't think Karen would like Washington. She wants to raise our kids here. Her health couldn't handle the stress of campaigning, anyway."

Karen, Lynnette thought, her anger growing. The woman's a damned anchor. Why can't he see that? "She could stay here with the kids, and you could visit her. This would be the Western White House."

"You're really thinking ahead."

"I'm always looking out for you."

Thinking she had perhaps said too much, Lynnette rose. She had to plant seeds in Grady's mind and then give them time to germinate.

"I'd better get back to work," she said. "I wonder how many men named Max there are in the city. Maybe I can track this guy down."

Grady laughed. "That's a needle in a haystack. It's probably not even his real name. I don't think we'll ever know who he is."

Lynnette left, imagining a future very different from her

present.

As soon as the door closed behind her, Grady opened one of the drawers in his desk and took out an aspirin bottle. Sometimes, Lynnette gave him one hell of a headache.

Max had hung up because Jacobs had begun to make too much sense, although not in the way he had intended.

Since Max's sources were not aware that they were his sources, he was in no danger from them. Moreover, since he had no reason to believe that there was anyone else in the world who had the ability to read the thoughts of others, his sources would never find out about him as long as he was careful.

However, it had already occurred to Max that the crimes he had helped the district attorney's office solve were small ones. They were not small in terms of the individuals who suffered from them, certainly, but they were small in terms of making life safer for the average citizen. Max was not a publicized vigilante whose escapades frightened the criminal class and emboldened honest citizens to emulate him, resulting in a large drop in the crime rate. Nor could he see himself ever functioning that way, a real-life version of Charles Bronson in *Death Wish*. He had enjoyed that movie, but the idea of masquerading as a potential victim in order to draw violence to himself was a terrifying one.

But if word got out that the recent string of successes by the DA's office was no fluke, that those successes had been just the starting point, that major crime syndicates were targeted and were being broken up because of unerringly correct inside information constantly being fed to the DA's office, wouldn't that drive organized crime out of Piketon? Wouldn't that at least result in mutual distrust on the part of the members of the gangs Jacobs had just told him existed? Perhaps they would even start killing each other off. That would be a worthwhile outcome, Max thought, a beneficial use of his talent.

Then he could go back to picking up details about isolated crimes, as he had been doing already, but he could do it with a clearer conscience, clear of the ethical doubts Jacobs had just managed to implant in him.

So I have to make that happen, he thought. I have to find out where these supposed criminal bosses hang out and go to those places and try to pick up evidence that Jacobs can use in court. Great.

It was terrifying, but he knew he had to force himself to do it.

5

Max spent the next few days roaming the city.

He rode buses, transferring at random from one to another. He strolled along sidewalks. He sat in bars and restaurants and coffee shops, sipping cold beer or cooling coffee.

He had grown up in Piketon, but he found himself visiting neighborhoods he had never been in before. Some of them, such as North Hill, he had always heard were dangerous and mysterious places where Anglos were ill advised to go on foot. But when Max did finally venture into North Hill, no one paid attention to him. It was a shabby area of the city, with more boarded-up storefronts than in any other neighborhood, and the other pedestrians were preoccupied with their own lives and problems.

Fifteen years earlier, when Max was in high school, racial tensions had been higher in the city. Friends had told him horror stories of what happened to unnamed white boys caught alone on North Hill. Some of those stories might even have been true. Nowadays, the residents of North Hill had little time for anything but economic survival. The nation as a whole had gone through both good and bad times during those fifteen years, but for North Hill, the times had only been bad. Up there, reality was grim and stern.

He picked up none of the leads he was hoping for. He did overhear random thoughts about crimes, some small, some frightful, just as had been doing for many days now, but each of them was isolated. There was no hint of a connection to a crime syndicate.

He made a note of each of the serious crimes, though. He recorded whatever he could of names, dates, and places. Later, when Jacobs' needs were fulfilled and Piketon's mob had been destroyed, he would return to these unsettled matters and see what he could do to put more evil men behind bars.

Perps, he corrected himself. I'll make sure the perps go down, do time, get sent to the slammer, to the big house.

It was getting easier. He was picking up more all the time. He was hearing ever more trivial thoughts, even those not laden with powerful emotions. He wondered if that was the result of practice. Possibly it was a lingering effect of the shock of the thoughts he had overheard from Thompson and Hughes. Maybe his talent would fade again and be reduced to its original weak and unreliable state. He wasn't sure whether he welcomed that prospect or feared it.

There were moments when he felt as though his head had been broken open, exposing his brain, his self, the place where the essence of Max Iverson lived.

At other times, and most of the time, he could feel himself becoming more detached and analytical about his strange talent. Except for the very worst of the thoughts he picked up, the very bloodiest and most bestial of them, he reacted with little emotion. He was learning to examine the thoughts of others as they intruded into his mind, to look them over and decide objectively whether or not a particular person's memories were worth noting down for later investigation, and then to put it all aside.

It unsettled him to think of himself as unfeeling, but it was a relief to be unaffected. Each day during his quest, he found himself more able to concentrate his attention on tracking down the men Jacobs had asked him to look for.

But he couldn't find any of them.

At last he realized what the problem was. The kind of people Jacobs was after wouldn't be caught dead in the kinds of bars and restaurants where he had been spending his evenings. They would be living it up in the priciest places in town.

Max sighed and looked at the balance in his checkbook. Then he looked at the clothes in his closet. Then he sighed again. For such a noble cause, he would have to use the credit card he kept around for emergencies.

It was a chilly autumn evening, and the picturesque fire was flaming away in the central courtyard of the Trading Post. Max hadn't been there since the small party celebrating his father's retirement and his parents' move to Arizona. Nothing seemed to have changed.

Max had always liked the hokey ersatz Wild West atmosphere of the place. His parents had liked it, too, and they had often come here as a family, the three of them—Max, his father, and his stepmother.

In those days, though, his parents had always paid.

The food was as good as ever, but the price of dinner had gone way up. Normally, it would be far too rich for his current income. He suspected it would be too rich for his father's retirement income, especially given his stepmother's recent medical problems.

The feeling of being out of place faded quickly once Max entered the restaurant. Like the outside, the inside was unchanged, too. With his new clothes, purchased with plastic, Max looked like everyone else in the place, and he found himself slipping back easily into the mood of an earlier day, when he had been so at ease here.

He didn't recognize any of the staff. They were all too young to have been there in what he thought of as the old days. That was good. It meant that none of them would recognize him.

He was given a table near the wall, mostly window, that looked out over the city. From this height in the foothills, the view was magnificent. The lights of Piketon spread from the base of the hills eastward to the horizon. To the north and south, the shadowy bulk of hillsides cut them off. A waxing half moon was rising, hanging just above the eastern horizon, above the city lights.

The adobe walls radiated into the restaurant the heat they had absorbed from the sun during the day. Max took off his blazer and hung it on the back of his chair. He ordered one of the huge, powerful cocktails the restaurant specialized in and stared idly at the view. He listened to the hum of conversation, the clink of ice in glasses, of wine bottles against glass rims, of knives and forks against plates, savored the smell of the dishes at adjacent tables, and waited.

He relaxed deliberately, physically and mentally.

The images began.

Some were faint. Some were startlingly real and present.

At first, they were all tastes and smells and sounds—the sensory impressions of people at nearby tables.

I don't even need to spend money on a meal, he thought. I can just sit here and experience everyone else's.

For a moment, the lights of the city gave way to a woman's cleavage, framed in the V of a low-cut dress. Max scanned the tables near him casually. When he looked over his shoulder, he noticed a young couple seated behind him. The girl's back was toward him, but her dress could have been the one in the image he had caught. Her companion was staring at her in fascination.

How nice for him, Max thought, but he's broadcasting too strongly. It's interfering.

He began to pick up images of the young man's face—coming, he assumed, from the mind of the young woman. He felt sexual excitement. He couldn't even guess which of the two was radiating that. Perhaps both of them were. Between the two of them, they were making it impossible for him to receive anything from anyone else.

Then he relaxed and let himself enjoy their happiness and love and desire. It was a relief after the images of violence and death he had been steeping himself in.

His waiter reappeared, and Max ordered dinner.

By the time he was finished ordering, the young couple had left, off to work on the next stage of their date, taking their hot mutual desire with them. The milder emotions of the older patrons at other tables began to impinge on Max again.

Money was changing hands somewhere. Something to do with paying for dinner, Max guessed.

He tried to banish the image from his mind. But it persisted, as if there was too much emotion attached to it for it to go away. And the background, he realized, wasn't the restaurant. It was an office.

Max's waiter appeared, accompanied by an assistant. The assistant bore the tray with Max's dinner. The waiter's job seemed to be to supervise.

At the interruption, the pictures in Max's mind broke apart and drifted away. He tried to hold onto them but couldn't.

"Thank you," he said quickly, hoping he could somehow hurry the two men along. "Thanks, that's fine. That's okay, just like that, that's fine."

Finally, he was alone again. He cut his buffalo steak automatically and chewed a bite without tasting it. Meanwhile, he recreated in his mind the image of a roll of large-denomination bills, hoping that that would bring the original mental contact back into existence.

The picture he had recreated with his imagination solidified, changed, became a moving image seen through someone else's eyes. A hand took the roll of bills. The view rested on a heavy ring the hand wore, traveled up to the wrist, and rested again, this time on the gold band of a watch, then moved up the sleeve and to the face. It was a florid, self-satisfied face and one that Max was sure he knew, but he couldn't quite pin down the man's identity.

The face looked at him and said, "Thanks, Mr. Gall. I'll take care of Freiburg's case tonight."

The names meant nothing to Max, and he would have dismissed the entire matter if he had not suddenly recognized that beefy face with its mop of reddish-blond hair.

Jacobs would face a moral dilemma of his own this time. He might even refuse to use what Max had picked up.

Max turned his attention to his food. At the price he was paying for this evening, he decided he'd better get as much pleasure out of the meal as he could. And he'd better hope that Jacobs' reaction to his information would justify the expense.

He need not have worried.

One month later, Piketon District Attorney Henry Fredericks resigned in disgrace. He was accused of accepting a bribe from a local developer named Marcus Gall in return for getting charges dropped in an assault case against one of Gall's employees. According to the Piketon *Chronicle*, the employee, one Freddy Freiburg, was Gall's bodyguard, and Gall, also according to the *Chronicle*, was more Mafioso than developer.

"Is there a difference?" Max said into the telephone.

Jacobs laughed. "What a cynic! Actually, the guy makes a lot more money from his legitimate development projects than from his illegal activities. At least as far as we can tell."

"So he's not really the kind of big-time crook you were after, then?" Max felt disappointed—and inadequate, as though he had let Jacobs down.

"He's big enough," Jacobs said reassuringly. "Of course it would have been nice to get him, but being able to put his bodyguard away for five years will upset Gall, maybe put him off his game for a while. What was much more important was getting rid of Henry. We sure as hell don't need a crooked DA. I always knew he was a rotten apple, but there was never any proof."

"You continued to work for him."

Jacobs sighed. "Yes, I know. I did good work over here in spite of what Henry Fredericks was doing."

"And now you're acting DA, so you can do lots more good work, right?"

"Until the current term expires at the end of the year. There'll be quite a few people running for this office in November. In the meantime, I can do a lot more than when I was a deputy—even chief deputy. I need you more than ever, Max. This gives you an opportunity to do a lot more good."

"Grady..." Max hesitated. "Grady, it's not something I can depend on. You understand? The information I get and pass on to you, sometimes it comes my way, and sometimes it doesn't. I can't just go out and get it when it's needed, when you want it. I may never happen to get anything else you can use. By the way, now that you're the boss over there, if I do get something, who do I speak to about it?"

"Oh, me, of course. In fact, why don't you come in from the cold, Max?"

"Now you're using spy movie lingo."

"It applies to you, too. We've been operating this way, you phoning me occasionally, for almost a year now. If you came in here, into the office, I'd set you up with a desk and a telephone line of your own for your informants. They'd be able to call in their tips to you, and then you could just step across the hall into my office and tell me what you know. Your people would have just as much anonymity as they do now, and you'd be sure of reaching me right away. And you could help us out in other ways. For example, sometimes I have someone our people have brought charges against, and we almost have what we need, but not quite enough. Maybe you could activate your informants and get that last bit of data we need to put that guy where he belongs. Hell, I bet I could even put you on some kind of salary."

"Grady, Grady!" Max said. "What a silver tongue you have! You should consider politics."

"You mean, like run for DA? Or maybe even something higher?"

Max laughed into the receiver and hung up.

A cold breeze sprang up, a foretaste of winter. Max put his hands in the pockets of his windbreaker and hunched his shoulders.

Come in from the cold—yes, he'd like to do that literally. If nothing else, he wished he could make these phone calls from the warmth and comfort of his apartment.

He turned away from the payphone and starting walking down the street.

Walking around the city, listening with his mind, trying to

catch the secret thoughts of others—this was now his standard evening outing. He wished he were sitting in a warm office instead, not out here exposed to the weather and the repellent thoughts of passing strangers. He wished he were not filled with constant dread.

But he was stuck out in the cold. He would never be coming in from it.

The next day, the evening news carried the announcement that charges against Freddy Freiburg were being dropped. Acting District Attorney Grady Jacobs had decided that the evidence against Freiburg was insufficient to bring in a guilty verdict.

Jacobs appeared on the screen, staring into the camera.

"Our case against Mr. Freiburg was based on information we received from informants," Jacobs told the camera. "However, as the time for trial approached, our main informant made it clear that he was either unwilling or unable to come forward with the additional details we needed to go to trial. I'm personally convinced that Mr. Freiburg is a guilty man, just as I'm convinced that his employer, Marcus Gall, is guilty of a range of serious crimes. However, unless I have in my possession what I need to make a case, I have no intention of wasting the taxpayers' money with a trial that won't result in a guilty verdict."

Jacobs narrowed his eyes and assumed a determined look, a Defender of the People look, and said, "I hope that the informant I referred to is watching this news broadcast and will think long and hard about what his failure to cooperate with us is costing the people of this city. I can only hope that he will change his mind and do his civic duty before it's too late in the Freiburg case."

"You manipulative bastard," Max said to the screen.

He had always hated it when people tried to manipulate him. Too often, they succeeded, and then he hated himself for being manipulated.

The next item on the news dealt with the case against Henry Fredericks. That case was proceeding, despite the collapse of the case against Freiburg.

Big surprise, Max thought. Jacobs owes his present office to Fredericks' resignation. He's not going to drop the case against his former boss.

Fredericks deserved punishment, though. Max had seen the man's guilt through the eyes of Marcus Gall, and now he wanted to see him suffer for perverting the justice system.

And I voted for him, Max marveled. I was so sure he was honest and incorruptible. I guess he manipulated me! Said the right words, pushed my buttons. Jesus. Now I'm going to have to try to read every candidate's mind before every election.

Something else occurred to him, a realization that shook him.

If I was so wrong about Fredericks, how can I be sure about Jacobs? I've never been close enough to him to have a chance of reading his mind. If he *is* honest, then how about his underlings?

It was a disturbing thought.

Another one followed.

It seemed likely to him that sometime in the future, he would catch too few details of an incident of high-level corruption. Perhaps he would miss the names or official titles of those involved. Unknown to him, they might be people who worked in the DA's office. When he passed information to Jacobs' office, he would be alerting the criminals themselves.

Later in the newscast, the announcer mentioned a recent study of the American justice system that showed that perhaps as many as twenty percent of those convicted of crimes and sent to prison were actually innocent. "Presumably," the announcer said, "the same percentage applies to those who have been executed."

Max was stunned. He had never even thought of that possibility. Had innocent people been executed for murders that others had committed? He imagined the terror and despair of an innocent man watching the hypodermic go into his arm, watching the poison being injected into him—just another victim of a murderer who had himself escaped punishment.

I could prevent that, Max told himself. At least here in Piketon I could. If I could get close enough physically to the accused, maybe I could tell if they were really guilty.

If he were physically in the DA's office, he could check out Jacobs and all the rest of the staff for honesty. He could also make sure that no innocent man was ever executed in the state, or even sent to prison for something he hadn't done. And yes, he could help make sure that the truly guilty did not escape punishment for their crimes. That included Jacobs or anyone else on his staff who turned out to be corrupt. Max would see to it that they were punished, too.

Jacobs might be playing fast and loose with the justice system in order to manipulate Max into helping him, but he was right. It *was* Max's duty to join Jacobs' staff and work full time at seeing to it that the guilty were punished and the innocent saved.

He couldn't join up openly, under his own name. Not right away. First he had to determine if Jacobs and his staff were honest.

Max went to bed feeling that he had resolved his moral dilemma. Tomorrow, he would think of some way of getting a job inside the DA's office and beginning his check of everyone's thoughts.

He fell asleep quickly and slept soundly.

6

In the morning, the task he had set himself seemed less simple. With no professional education and no office skills, how was he to get a job in the DA's office?

He wasn't even sure where the office was.

The city's website gave him the address and displayed a map. The DA's office was in the huge gray stone office building that housed the other joint city and county agencies.

After breakfast, Max called up his workplace and left a message for his current boss saying he was ill and wouldn't be in until the next day. Then he put on his lined leather jacket and headed downtown.

It was cloudy, the temperature was in the low fifties, and a light mist filled the streets—an unusual sight in this normally arid city. As he walked toward the bus stop, Max felt occasional cold drops of rain on his face. He wondered if it would snow that night. Winter often came suddenly in Piketon.

The Number 14 bus headed south until it reached South Street, where it turned west. It was a forty-five minute trip to the downtown stop Max wanted.

Number 14 was a convenient bus for him. A lot of the places he needed to go—work, shopping, downtown for his rare recreation—lay along its route. The same must be true for many other people, for the bus was crowded at just about any time of day.

He often wished that he still had his car. Back then, he had taken River Drive whenever possible. That usually took him out of his way, but he loved the old road along the river, and the river itself, especially in the spring, when it was swollen with melting snow from the mountains. The rest of the year, the Pike was a narrow stream, little bigger than the creeks that flowed down from the mountains into it. But for a week or two in springtime, it filled its banks, roared over the rocks, and flung up spray. It became something wild and dangerous and alien, nature stretching down from the mountains into the city, reminding humans of its presence.

He got off the bus a few blocks before his stop so that he could walk through the downtown business district on his way to the City and County Building. He wanted the busy crowds for the illusion they gave him of having human company—but even more for the static buzz of their minds, a meaningless hum of jumbled phrases and incomplete thoughts. It was a comforting white noise that he could use to drown out individual threads and safeguard him from seeing the horror and evil he knew were there.

The city center was full of frowning, hurrying, overdressed men and women. This was Suitland, a strange place where Max could never belong.

I should have dressed for a job interview, he thought. But there is no interview, and I don't even know what kind of job I'm looking for.

Janitorial work! That's perfect. I'm probably qualified for that. I should have thought of that before.

Surely there were a lot of people working menial jobs in the City and County Building. They would be ubiquitous and invisible. He would be able to move around inside the huge building and eavesdrop on minds without anyone noticing.

But this probably isn't where I can apply for one of those jobs, he realized. The city surely contracts out janitorial work to some company, or maybe even a few companies, so I have to find out who they are and where their offices are. That's where I have to go to apply for a job here. I wasted my time coming here. Stupid! Now I have to go back home and start looking for the information online.

He hesitated, reluctant to accept how foolish he had been. While he stood undecided, he felt something pulling at him. It was the faintest of tugs: not physical, but almost like a distant, barely heard voice.

What was it? Where was it coming from? He couldn't answer either question. He stood still, eyes closed, trying to focus on the strange sensation. But the harder he concentrated on it, the more the tugging sensation lost definition and went out of focus. He tried relaxing, not thinking about it, the way you have to look to the side of a faint light rather than directly at it in order to see it.

It grew stronger. Now it felt almost physical, and he could almost hear the voice. He let it pull him. It drew him across a concrete plaza and through double glass doors. He walked through the lobby, eyes half closed, scarcely seeing the earnest, hurrying people around him, nor the uniformed armed guard at the desk in the lobby, who looked at him suspiciously for a moment and then lost interest.

He knew he had to go up. There was a bank of elevators ahead, with a suited, briefcase-carrying crowd gathered by the doors. Max grimaced and looked for a stairway sign. It was beyond the elevators. He opened the door below the sign and began climbing.

He hoped he wouldn't be climbing too many flights. The day before had been his leg day at the gym, and he thought his legs would give out quickly.

As he climbed, the weird tugging sensation grew stronger. It pulled him to the exit door only one flight up, for which he was thankful. He opened that door and was faced with a door to which was affixed a brass plate reading DISTRICT ATTORNEY.

Well, I'll be damned, he thought. Here I am after all. But what do I do now? Turn around and go home and think this through, that's what.

But he couldn't turn away. There was something beyond that door. He couldn't pin it down, couldn't make it take proper shape in his mind, couldn't give it definition. But it was there.

I'll just go inside the office and see if I can pick something up, he thought. I'll sit for a while in the waiting room, pretending to read a magazine, listening with my mind, and no one will even pay attention to me.

He turned the handle and pulled the door open. He found himself in a small room containing only a receptionist's desk—no couches, no chairs, and no magazines. Behind the desk sat a remarkably large uniformed guard. The guard and the desk blocked the entrance to a hallway beyond the desk. There were closed doors along the hallway and a window at the far end.

What now?

I'd better leave, he thought. I'll just take a minute to see if I can get anything in here.

He closed his eyes and focused.

The call he had felt had become more diffuse, less focused. It was still coming from here, but he couldn't tell more than that. It had no direction to it, and even as he concentrated on it, it disappeared into a background noise, the mental buzz of many intense minds in close quarters.

He felt on edge. He was trapped. He panted for breath.

He opened his eyes.

The guard was standing, looking Max up and down. His right hand rested on the gun holstered on his right side. Max felt the man's alertness and readiness to do violence. He saw himself in the guard's mind: a large, threatening figure behaving oddly, breathing hard, a danger.

"I'm here to see Grady Jacobs," Max said impulsively.

"You have an appointment?"

"No, but he'll see me. I have information for him."

He tried to project peacefulness, but the image of him in the guard's mind didn't change.

"Wait outside in the hallway."

Max smiled, still trying. "Sure."

He went back out to the hallway and leaned against the wall, trying to calm himself. He wondered what he was doing.

Busy people passed by. Most of them were young. Many were attractive. All were expensively dressed. They were mentally focused, their minds full of work details. He was invisible to them.

There might be advantages to working in a place like this, he thought. Eye candy. A good salary. Might as well cash in on this weird talent of mine.

Minutes passed. He began to wonder if anyone would be coming for him. Maybe if anyone did, it would be building security. Maybe he should go home.

The guard emerged. "He'll see you."

He stood holding the door open and gestured for Max to enter. "Down the hallway. Third door on the right. Knock."

Max smiled at the guard again. The image of him in the guard's mind didn't change.

Max knocked on the indicated door, and Grady Jacobs'

voice, familiar from television and the telephone, said, "Come in."

Jacobs was sitting behind his desk, facing the door.

Max entered, closed the door behind him, and stood staring at Jacobs, saying nothing.

The staring contest went on for a while.

Finally, Jacobs laughed and said, "Max, right? Somehow, when the guard described you, I just knew."

"Wow, that's creepy," Max said. "It's almost like you can read my mind."

"If I could do that, I wouldn't need you, would I? So?"

"It's cold outside."

"That it is. It's nice and warm in here. It's air conditioned in summer."

"I won't be here that much. I'll be out contacting people."

"They can call you here. I'll have an outside line installed for you. It'll go straight to your desk."

Max shook his head. "That won't work."

"So you want a paycheck, benefits, and the right to come and go as you please, no questions asked. Anything else?"

"A pony and free beer, but you can hold off on those for now."

"We actually have free beer on Friday afternoons. But no ponies."

"Okay, we'll skip the pony. And I'll help you with Freiburg if I can."

"Oh, you don't have to. We have enough to proceed against him."

"You manipulative bastard."

Jacobs laughed. In what he believed was the privacy of his thoughts, he gloated.

The job Max had on paper was meaningless. The paycheck was real and large. Max wondered how Jacobs had managed to get that through the city's Human Resources department and how he had done it so quickly. He also wondered why Human Resources departments were given that dehumanizing name, but he didn't wonder enough to ask. His attention was elsewhere.

The office was a bullpen—many desks crammed into a large open space, helter skelter, not aligned in any way. It gave the place a chaotic air, at least for Max.

The mental atmosphere was chaos, too. The mental pull he had followed was absent. Even so, he knew somehow that he was in the right place, that there was something here for him.

Someone from HR had given him a stack of reading material to familiarize himself with the organization. He assumed that was standard practice. It was all meaningless and irrelevant for him, but pretending to read it let him appear to be doing something while he focused on the people around him and tried to pick up their thoughts.

The hum and buzz from so many minds in close proximity made that impossible at first. In time, though, he learned to isolate individual streams of thought from the torrent.

The result was mind-numbing but reassuring. Everyone else in the office seemed to be serious, focused, and dedicated. There was no reason to fear giving Jacobs and his crew any information he uncovered. Max didn't detect dishonest thoughts connected with the job.

I guess I'm the only person who's here under false pretenses, he thought.

He chuckled at the irony.

The head of a woman at a nearby desk jerked up at the sound. She looked annoyed.

"Bad grammar in these documents," Max said. "That always makes me laugh."

She glared at him. "Keep it down."

She looked familiar, but he was sure he'd never met her before. The nameplate on her desk said Lynnette Salzmann. He couldn't read her name in her thoughts. Nor could he read anything else there. All he could detect from her was anger. It was like a loud, continuous noise. There were no words, no distinct thoughts, just a mixture of annoyance, resentment, anger, and distrust mixed with images of a big, beefy, ugly man.

It's me, he realized. That's how she sees me. She resents me. Maybe word's spread that I was put in a well-paid position I'm not qualified for.

For a moment, he had the feeling that the pull he had felt earlier had something to do with her. He tried again to detect her thoughts.

She was looking at papers on her desk, but her attention was focused on him, and the loud noise from her mind grew louder. It became uncomfortable. Max felt the need to get away from her.

The pull isn't coming from her, he thought. All that's coming from her is repulsion. Maybe it isn't as cold outside as it is in here.

He took his jacket from the back of his chair and headed for the exit.

Max wandered the streets of downtown Piketon, rifling through the minds of passersby.

The ease of doing so frightened him, made him feel like a voyeur. It was all in a good cause, he reminded himself. He wasn't eavesdropping for titillation. He was fighting crime.

I've helped bring murderers to justice, he reminded himself. I ended the career of a corrupt politician. Those are things to be proud of.

He ignored stray thoughts of small-scale thievery, memories of adultery, and similar misdeeds. He found them despicable, but if he devoted his time and energy to such matters, he'd have nothing left over for crimes that affected large numbers of people.

What could he do about these smaller matters, anyway? By himself, he could do nothing. He had to operate through Grady Jacobs and the DA's office, and he could imagine the result if he went to Jacobs with reports about what he had picked up on this walk.

So many nasty thoughts! Were most people evil? Or at least sleazy?

As the ease of picking up thoughts increased, and as he encountered more and more people while walking around, his opinion of the human race kept declining.

On a whim, he decided to do something about one of those small crimes.

He had passed a priest who was walking back to his church after spending an hour with a prostitute. He had paid for the time with money taken from the church's poor box.

To Max, all religions and their rules were bunk. However, this man had robbed from the poor. That was despicable. Then there was the man's hypocrisy, something Max had always abhorred.

Max turned around and followed the priest.

He loitered outside the church until the priest had entered. He followed the priest's progress by the images in his mind. The man walked to the confessional booth at the far end of the nave and entered one side of it. He sat down, pulled a phone from a pocket in his cassock, and began reading the news.

Max entered the church and walked down the center aisle. The priest heard his footsteps and looked up briefly from his reading.

First ripple of the daily tide, the priest thought. Some stupid little sin.

He laughed mentally at the contrast between the small, foolish sins that tormented his flock and what he did a couple of times a week.

Max entered the other side of the booth, sat down on the bench, and said, "Curse you, Father, for you have sinned."

"What?"

The phone fell to the wooden floor with a loud thump.

"It has been thirty minutes since your last transgression. I don't think that's what the church means when they tell you to put it in the poor box."

The priest jumped to his feet."Who are you?" His voice was hushed and strained.

"Stay where you are," Max said. "It's best you don't see my face. Think of me..." He sifted through the man's superstitious fears, catching the words that were uppermost. "I'm a messenger."

There was another thump. This time, Max could tell from his thoughts that it was the sound of the priest falling to his knees. He prayed loudly, weeping.

Max let him babble for a few minutes. Then he said, "You've been given a second chance. Use it wisely. There won't be a third."

Max left while the priest was still crying out that he would never sin again.

Perhaps he was sincere. Max had no intention of checking up on him to find out. He had done a small good deed, prevented the recurrence of a small crime, but the city contained thousands, perhaps millions, of such misdeeds. He couldn't remedy all of them. This had been satisfying, but he must move on.

As Max exited the church, the beefy, ugly image of himself came into his mind again, along with the anger he had sensed before.

He had intended to return to the office, but instead, he strolled aimlessly for a while, concentrating on that image. It weakened and strengthened but was always there.

It's her, he thought, Lynnette Salzmann, the woman from the office. She's following me.

Why? Was she hoping to gather dirt on him, something that would get him fired?

No, he thought. That would be silly. This is Grady's doing. He's hoping to find out who my sources are.

He walked back to the office, moving rapidly. The woman following him fell steadily farther behind. The ugly image of him in her mind faded with distance, but if anything, the anger grew.

Max entered the office and walked into Grady Jacobs' office without knocking.

"Your spy will tell you that I went to church."

"What?"

"Lynnette. Your spy."

"You went to church?"

"Confession. It's good for the soul. You should try it."

"I'm not Catholic," Jacobs said with a nervous laugh.

That's okay, Max thought. You just confessed anyway.

He could see it all in Jacobs' mind. Lynnette had been following Max on Jacobs' orders.

"I expected better of you," Max said. "I also expected better of your employees. Better technique, I mean. It shouldn't have been that easy for me to tell that I was being followed and who was doing it."

"I'm sorry. It won't happen again. Honest to God."

Max could see in Jacobs' mind that he meant it. He could also see that Jacobs was trying to think of other ways to accomplish the same goal.

"You'll never find out who my sources are," Max said. "If you keep trying, our deal's off."

Jacobs threw up his hands. "Okay! I won't do anything more. You're in charge."

Max paused. "Right. Now you're telling the truth."

He left Jacobs' office and returned to his desk.

Lynnette was back at hers, not looking at him, but thinking about him. The image in her mind had grown in stature but also in ugliness. There was a sinister aura around it now.

Jesus, Max thought. My life was so much simpler before. This place is already giving me a headache. I can't stay here.

Lynnette waited until Max had left and then went into Jacobs' office. "What's going on?" she asked.

"He knew you were following him."

"How? That's not possible."

Jacobs shrugged. "He knew. And he's pissed."

"Too bad. We both know there's something wrong about him, and I'm going to find out what it is."

"No, you're not. I promised him it wouldn't happen again."

"Grady—"

"Lynnette, stop. I'm ordering you to forget about him and focus on your cases. For now, we're going to have to trust him. I don't know why you have it in for him, anyway."

"Because I think he's a danger to you, to your career."

He had the feeling there was more behind her behavior, but he kept his suspicions to himself.

"Never mind about that," he said. "Here's something funny." He gestured at his computer monitor. "I was glancing through Max's HR file, and it turns out that he has the same birthday as you."

"December 5th?"

"Yes, and even the same year. You two are exactly the same age."

"That's an unpleasant coincidence."

Jacobs grinned. "I think we should throw you guys a joint office birthday party."

"You do that, and I'll tell your wife all your secrets."

"You don't know all my secrets."

"Don't bet on it. No joint birthday party."

"Hmm, well..."

"I mean it, Grady."

He threw up his hands. "Okay, okay."

She was pleased, as she left his office, that he knew her birthday. That must mean something.

7

Days passed with nothing of importance coming Max's way. He spent most his time walking around downtown, with occasional bus trips to suburban shopping centers.

He realized that he didn't know what he was doing, and Jacobs was getting openly impatient.

From time to time, just to feel that he was accomplishing something, Max fixed a small transgression, as he had done with the priest. Those actions contributed nothing to the assignment he had accepted from Jacobs, but they were satisfying.

He decided to pay the priest another visit to see if he had fallen into his old ways.

Once again, Max entered the confessional booth. The priest was on the other side of the screen, radiating terror.

Of me? Max wondered. No, of course not. He doesn't know I'm the same person who threatened him before.

He couldn't tell what the priest was afraid of. The intensity of his fear blotted out any details. Max's silence was making things worse.

"Don't be afraid, Father. I'm just checking up on you."

"You're...the messenger."

"That's right, and I see you've been a good boy. Keep it up. Calm down. There's nothing to be afraid of."

"I haven't done any of those things again!"

"I know. I can see everything."

"Can you protect me?" the priest said. "From them?"

Images formed. Thoughts solidified.

The priest had been told of terrible deeds. It wasn't just one man, but a group, coordinated in action, killing people who were on a list they had been given. The confessor had incautiously mentioned the first names of some of his associates.

"Protect you from the man who was just in here confessing to you about his crimes—and from his partners, you mean. And from..." Max concentrated. "From the man who gave them the list. You're afraid he'll have second thoughts about confessing to you. He'll think that even though you're a priest and you heard his confession, you'll go to the police."

"Yes! They'll kill me!"

"They know who you are, I suppose. But you don't know them. You can't see my face clearly, and you couldn't see theirs. You're no threat to them."

"He attends this church regularly. I knew who he was right away."

A name and a face surfaced in the priest's mind. It was an ordinary face, but in the priest's thoughts, it was imbued with deadly menace.

"He knew I recognized him. I'm sure of it. Will you help me?"

"It's not up to me," Max said. "That's a decision to be made by the higher power I answer to."

"Oh. Yes. Of course."

"I'll see what I can do," Max said.

What had he uncovered? He had thought crime on this scale only existed in much bigger cities, not here in his hometown.

He left. Behind him, the priest prayed earnestly to an imaginary higher power instead of to the one Max had in mind.

Outside the church, Max paused to mull over the information he had heard from the priest and lifted from the man's mind. He had to give all of it to Jacobs right away, although he wasn't sure how it would be received. It seemed a bit outlandish, extreme, over the top. How could it be true?

But I read minds, he thought, so I should be able to accept anything, no matter how extraordinary. Hell, I'm Mr. Extraordinary.

He could see the downtown highrises in the distance, their upper stories against the sky, above the smaller, less imposing buildings nearby. He hesitated, thinking he should find a bus stop and figure out the best route to get back to the office. Then he decided that walking would probably be quicker.

Better for my mind, too, he thought. Calm me down.

He set off, walking quickly.

A few blocks along, he saw a billboard advertising a local furniture store. A smiling woman stood next to an armchair.

Suddenly, Max stopped walking. He stood frozen in place, struck by a vision.

Pedestrians swerved to avoid walking into him. They glared at him. He was oblivious to their looks, their presence, their thoughts. The vision consumed him. It enveloped him. It had replaced reality. It *was* reality.

It was a nightmare that had haunted him all his life, visiting him at night but fading when he awoke, leaving only tendrils of itself in his mind, shoved to the back of his consciousness and forgotten. Now it was real and alive.

Brakes squealed. There was a terrible impact and the sound of tearing metal. He felt himself airborne for just a moment, and then he smashed into the solid surface of a road, bones breaking and agony filling him. A shrieking baby lay on the ground beside him. A man in uniform leaned over him. Suddenly he was standing in front of an armchair. A furious man was shouting at him. The man seemed familiar, but Max couldn't think who he was. The man lashed out. Max flew backwards and hit the armchair, which toppled over. Max tumbled over with it, landing hard on the floor. Abdominal cramps gripped him.

The vision evaporated, and the world around him returned. He became aware of the annoyed thoughts directed at him, and he started walking again.

What was that? he wondered.

The nightmare, scarcely remembered during waking hours before, stayed with him now. He walked rapidly, as though hoping to leave it behind him, as if it were attached to the church and would stay there. It stayed with him instead.

It makes no sense, he thought. It's dream logic, so it doesn't have to make sense. But I'm not asleep. It's more like a memory than a dream.

His father and stepmother had told him about the car crash that had taken his mother's life and how an EMT had managed to deliver him while his mother lay dying on the road. The EMT had tried to save her, too, but had failed.

That's where the nightmares came from, he told himself. What just happened is just my mind reconstructing what I was told. But what was that other part, the baby also lying on the road and screaming at me?

Dream logic, he told himself again. Things make sense in dreams that don't when you wake up. The sleeping brain is a crazy brain.

But I was wide awake! What's happening to me?

Jacobs. He had to get this information to Jacobs. Nightmares, even waking ones, couldn't be allowed to stand in the way. What the priest had told him and thought to him had to do with a real nightmare in real, waking, daylight life.

He hurried along.

Once again Max walked into Grady Jacobs' office without knocking.

Jacobs looked up from his computer monitor. "What's up?"

Max closed the office door and sat down in the chair facing the desk. "I've got some new info for you, a lot of it. It's about those dead mobsters you've been worrying about."

"How did you— Never mind. There are loose lips in this office."

Loose minds, Max thought.

Aloud, he said, "Some of it's been on the news. Three bodies." Those were the ones the local TV news had been filled with in recent days.

Jacobs relaxed. "Sure. Everyone knows about that. It's no secret."

Max scanned him quickly. "And the four others the police are also investigating, the ones the reporters don't know about yet."

"Shit," Jacobs said.

Max laughed.

Jacobs sat forward, pulled a yellow legal pad to him, and took a ballpoint pen from the holder on his desk. "Okay. Tell me."

The gangster who had confessed to the priest had spared no details. Perhaps he had thought that if he hoped to be forgiven for everything, he must hold nothing back. In his terror, the priest had added his own imaginings. The thoughts that had rushed out of him were a stew of the terrible real and the terrible imagined.

As he spoke to Jacobs, Max sorted through the mess carefully, trying to pick out what he thought was factual. That was still a lot, and Jacobs scribbled furiously while Max spoke.

Max scanned the jumble of thoughts and images pouring from Jacobs: criminal gangs, mob warfare, the gangs feeling untouchable and protected, city government corrupt and in the mob's pocket, the city in peril. Max almost wished he hadn't seen any of those thoughts. This was not the way he had always seen his hometown.

The last image was Jacobs as a literal knight in shining armor. Max grinned at the last one and almost laughed aloud. Fortunately, Jacobs' attention was focused on his note-taking.

Finally, Max stopped talking.

Jacobs read over the pages of handwriting. "This is amazing," he said. "Names, dates, places. The names were what I wanted, but the rest all fits with what we know."

He looked up suddenly. "A more suspicious guy than me would say that you're part of all of this and you're just trying to get in the clear."

Max tensed. He probed carefully. What he felt from Jacobs was caution rather than suspicion.

"And yet I keep trusting you," Jacobs said.

"I have a trustworthy face."

"You do, you know. That's a good thing to have, especially if you're not trustworthy."

"Good thing I am. Anyway, even if I were involved in these crimes, I'd be at the bottom, just small potatoes. You want to go high up the chain."

Jacobs nodded. "I do."

"So start with the names I gave you. Isn't that how it works? Turn the guys at the bottom. They rat on the ones above them. And so on, up the ladder."

"That's how it works in TV cop shows. It's harder in real life. The guys on the bottom know what will happen to them if they help us. Hey, maybe I should start with you, assuming you're a guy at the bottom."

"Bring out the thumbscrews. But I've already told you what I know without being tortured. Anyway, I'm not involved. I just hear things."

"It's amazing what you hear. All right. I'll see what we can do with this." Jacobs stared at the pages again. He shook his head doubtfully. "Search warrants. We may be able to skip the bottom rungs."

"Do you have enough for that? You complained before about me not giving you enough to act on."

"Can you get more?"

"That's all I have for now. I don't know if I'll ever get more. It's always unpredictable."

"Maybe it's a problem, then. Maybe this won't be enough."

"You can't just drop it!"

"I don't want to, but you can understand my problem."

My problem is that I ever got involved with you, Max thought. I should just leave, right now. Maybe even move to a different city.

And what about the priest? I said I'd look into getting him some kind of protection, but if I ask Grady for that, then he or the cops will talk to the priest, and the priest will tell them about the divine messenger who knew what he was thinking. They'll think he's nuts, and Grady will think I'm a gullible idiot. They'll probably dismiss everything I've given Grady. I can't risk that. I didn't actually promise him anything. I just said I'd see what I could do about protection, and that turns out to be nothing.

"So?" Jacobs said. "Can you get me more?"

Max thought again of the killings the priest had been forced to hear about, of the pleas for mercy, of the sadistic pleasure, of the horror of those deaths.

"Let me see what I can dig up."

8

Max decided to start with the man who had confessed to the priest. He knew the man's name and what he looked like. The priest had said he was a regular at the church, so it was reasonable to assume that he lived somewhere in the neighborhood.

Max spent a couple of days walking idly in the area, trying to cover the blocks around the church. It was an old neighborhood of modest houses and boarded-up stores. There were a bar, a restaurant, and a grade school. There were few people on the street during the day. Except for the bar and the restaurant, there was little reason for people to leave their houses after work.

Just in case, he ate a sandwich in the restaurant in the evening and then went to the bar for a beer.

It was a small place, well-lit, clean, and quiet. Max looked around and saw a few people at the bar and a few in booths, some alone, some not.

It all seemed very ordinary. He wasn't sure what he had expected. Something dark, grim, and dramatic, he supposed. Maybe something more like Glenn's Hideaway.

He sat at the bar and ordered a beer. He caught thoughts about minor crimes but not the more important thoughts he was after.

There had been many times when Max had cursed the existence of the strange talent he regarded as an affliction. Now he cursed its unreliability. He seemed unable to pick out a single mind and concentrate on it. The thoughts he was picking up were a background buzz, with nothing emerging strongly.

Some private eye I am, he thought. I'm not even a good private third eye.

He sipped his beer, eyes half closed as he concentrated on his surroundings.

He began to pick up more. There were thoughts that surprised him, or angered him, or revolted him, but there was nothing that would be of significance to Jacobs. More important, there was no sign of the man he was hunting.

Even though he thought he was sipping slowly, the beer was soon gone. He couldn't sit at the bar without drinking something, so he ordered another. That one also disappeared.

The thoughts were fading away into an incoherent jumble, mere noise.

Maybe it's the beer, he thought.

Maybe alcohol dulled his ability, just as it dulled the senses. He had never experimented with this.

His bladder was suddenly full.

He pushed himself off the barstool and headed for the dimly lit sign at the rear of the room that read RESTROOMS.

The men's room held two urinals and one stall. Max stood at one of the urinals and relieved himself.

The sinks were to his left. A mirror covered the wall above them. The door was farther to his left, beyond the sinks.

The door opened and someone came in. Incuriously, Max glanced to his left at the mirror as the man walked past the sinks.

The face was unmistakable. It was the man in the priest's memory.

Max gasped.

The man glared at him.

Murderous rage washed over Max. Images of blood, of bodies with horrible wounds. For a moment, the man paused behind Max, thinking of driving a knife into his back.

Terrified, Max held his breath, eyes closed, waiting for something to happen.

The man passed on and entered the stall, closing the door. The images and rage faded away.

Max breathed again.

Think, he told himself. Be calm. Wait and think.

Some of the terrible images matched the descriptions in the priest's memory. Max knew the man's face from that memory. He didn't need confirmation, but the images gave it to him anyway.

Max zipped up his pants and went to the sink. He took his time washing his hands. He was focusing on the man in the stall, hoping to catch more.

He could tell himself to be calm, but he wasn't. Part of him wanted to get as far away as possible. At the least, he didn't want to be there when the killer emerged from the stall.

For now, the man was thinking trivial thoughts, mostly about his bodily functions. This was not what Max wanted to use his mindreading ability for.

Finally the killer's thoughts turned to the list of people to be eliminated. There were a few on the list that the killer and his associates hadn't yet located. His rage mounted again as he speculated that they knew they were in danger and were hiding from him. He was outraged that they would dare to do so. He would make them suffer for it before he killed them. He indulged in fantasies about exactly how he would make them suffer.

Max leaned on the sink to support himself. His legs were shaking. In the mirror, his face looked white.

The man's thoughts turned to his own danger if he didn't track down the last few names and finish the job. He thought of his boss. There was the image of a tall, fat man, terrifying to the killer. A name floated through his mind: Al Freeman.

Now the killer was in a hurry to get back to work. He finished up, stood up, and pulled up his pants.

Max left the men's room and the bar quickly and made for home.

Al Freeman. It was a start. Google gave Max much more.

Max was back in his apartment. It was evening. The traffic noises outside were subsiding. This was the time of day when people relaxed after work, taking pleasure in knowing that they were free for a few hours and that bed awaited.

Max was tense, irrationally fearing that the man whose mind he had read had somehow read his in return. That was nonsense, but Max couldn't help fearing that killers were silently climbing the stairs to his apartment and that he wouldn't last the night.

All the more reason to get something to Grady first, he thought.

He tried to concentrate on searching the Web.

There were a few Al Freemans in Piketon, but there was only one whose image matched the one Max had seen in the killer's mind. This Al Freeman owned a company that had built many of the recent additions to the city's highways.

He was shown in a video attending a dressy event with other corporate chiefs and the mayor. He was smiling, shaking hands, chatting, laughing. He didn't look like a threat at all, but the menacing image of him in the killer's mind was now laid over the one on Max's laptop screen.

Freeman lived in Redland Hills. No surprise there. There wasn't a lot of money in Piketon and few great fortunes, but what there was accumulated in that wealthy suburb.

Max had been through there once, on a city bus that had made a very wrong turn. The bus had rumbled along wide, tree-lined streets while the increasingly upset driver tried to figure out how to get back on his route. There were few cars parked by the curb; those few were expensive luxury models. The houses and lawns had seemed immense to Max. A couple of times, a figure had emerged from one of the houses to stare at the bus. Later, Max heard that the driver had been fired immediately after that errant trip.

According to Google, Freeman's company's head office was in a downtown highrise, not far from the City and County Building.

On his way to work the next day, Max took a detour to that highrise. He rode the elevator to the thirtieth floor, all of which was occupied by Freeman's company.

The elevator opened directly into the reception area.

Now what? Max wondered.

He had counted on there being a hallway to loiter in while listening to minds. Instead, a glossily attractive young woman seated behind a desk that faced the elevator smiled broadly at him and said, "Can I help you?"

He saw himself in her mind: a reasonably attractive man, impressively big, which she liked, but wearing clothes that shouted that he was beneath her notice.

I guess I won't ask her for a date, Max thought.

Buying time, he looked around at the furniture, the

carpeting, the art on the walls. He wondered how much it had all cost.

Bull by the horns, he told himself.

"I was wondering if I could see Al Freeman."

The smile vanished. The image of him in her mind shrank.

"I'm afraid Mr. Freeman isn't in."

"Do you know when he will be?"

"No." *Go away!* her mind shouted.

You mean he's not in for people like me, Max thought.

Then he concentrated and realized that she meant that Freeman was never in. This was his company's headquarters, but he never appeared here.

"Oh, of course," Max said. "I should have remembered. He told me once that he always works from home. Thanks. I'll call him there."

Sure you will, she thought.

"I have his home number," Max said.

He left.

He was amused by her confusion, but he realized that he had made a mistake. Perhaps she would dismiss him as a crank, but she might think he was a danger, or possibly in fact a friend of Freeman's. In either of those cases, she would probably let her boss know about the strange visit.

They'll track me down, Max thought. I'll end up on that list of people to be eliminated.

This made matters more urgent. Now he had to get enough information to tie Freeman to the list and the murders and pass that information on to Jacobs.

How? he wondered.

He kept wondering as he walked the few blocks to his office.

Jacobs was in his office. The door was open.

Max walked in. "Your door was open, so I figured you were available."

"Last time, my door was closed and you opened it."

"Yeah, well."

"Do you have something?"

"Soon. I need a car."

Jacobs' eyebrows rose. "You don't have a car? I thought everyone had a car."

"You need to get out more. A lot of people don't have cars. Normally, I don't need a car, but I need one now."

"Why?"

"I have a new source, a really good one, but he lives in Redland Heights. I need to get out there to see him."

He watched Jacobs' mind weighing possible names, the wealthy and important who lived in Redland Heights. Al Freeman wasn't among them.

"That's interesting," Jacobs said. "Okay, I guess I could arrange that. Your driver's license up to date?"

"I don't have one."

"Jesus Christ! I can't let you use a city car. Maybe I could go with you."

"Oh, sure. That's a good way to scare off a source."

"When do you need to do this?"

"Right away. Maybe someone can drop me off there and pick me up a couple of hours later."

The image of Lynnette Salzmann's face surfaced in Jacobs' mind.

Of course, Max thought. The woman you assigned to spy on me. Who else would it be?

"I'll see if Lynnette's available," Jacobs said.

"I'm sure she is."

She was. Jacobs pretended to be surprised. So did Max.

Lynnette's car was a BMW. Max continued to be unsurprised.

During the first half of the long drive from the underground parking garage in the City and County Building out to Redland Heights, Lynnette said nothing. Max looked out the window and watched the suspicious, angry thoughts running through her head. She considered and abandoned various conversation openings designed to make Max say something she could use as a weapon against him.

Finally, Max said, "Why are you so hostile to me?"

Startled, she said, "I'm not—"

There was a long pause as she carefully formulated her answer. Max watched it take shape, admiring the way she polished it before uttering a word.

Did everyone in Jacobs' organization have this ability? he wondered. No wonder I don't fit in there.

"You think I'm an upstart, right?" Max said. "I shouldn't even be there. I'm nobody."

She forgot about her carefully polished response and spoke honestly. "I checked you out. You've been a dishwasher, a short order cook, and a janitor. I got through college and law school on scholarships and loans and part–time jobs. I earned my position. Who the hell are you? You're just a snitch who got lucky, and you've pulled the wool over Grady's eyes."

And you're in love with Jacobs, Max realized. She had kept that thought hidden, almost as if she knew someone might detect it, but it shone brightly when she said his first name.

"Have you ever met his wife?" Max asked.

An image suddenly dominated her mind. It was a woman, a sinister one. She was powerful, dangerous. Rather than walking, she lurched menacingly, aided by a huge stick, almost a small tree branch, that she held in one mighty hand. The woman was named Karen.

"Karen's her name, right?" Max said. "I hear she's nice."

Lynnette said nothing, just stared ahead, teeth clenched, hands gripping the wheel tightly, anger and bitterness radiating from her.

After a long silence, she said, "Address?"

"Lafarge Street."

"Number?"

He had no intention of giving her that. She might recognize Freeman's address. Max wasn't ready to reveal the man's name yet. At this point, he didn't have anything on Freeman. Maybe he never would.

"Drop me off in the 3,000 block. I'll walk. You keep driving around. Go up and down Lafarge. I'll signal you when I'm ready to be picked up."

"That's ridiculous."

"I don't want you scaring my man off. I may not get another chance."

She grunted.

There was another long silence.

They reached the intersection where the 3,000 block of Lafarge began. Lynnette pulled to the curb and stopped, still saying nothing.

Max said, "Just drive around. Don't do anything to draw attention to yourself."

He got out, and the car started to move as soon as he closed the door. It felt to him as though the car were filled with black, boiling rage.

It's not my problem, he told himself.

As Lynnette drove away, the weight of her hatred and anger lifted, and Max was able to pay attention to his surroundings. He strolled along the sidewalk, enjoying the shade from the giant trees, the green of the huge lawns, the beautiful houses, the peacefulness. He couldn't even detect any thoughts from the houses.

That's how calm it is here, he thought. The peacefulness is real. Even the thoughts behind those walls are calm and peaceful. I could enjoy living this way.

For the first time, it occurred to him that he probably could live this way. All he had to do was read the right minds at the right time, pick up the right information, and he'd be able to make a killing in the stock market, or perhaps even win high-stakes card games.

Both ideas repelled him. He had no idea how long his strange ability would stay with him, but while it did, he would use it for good, not mere gain, and certainly not for cheating people.

Freeman's house was three blocks farther along. Lynnette passed him twice before he got there, once on the other side of the road and once going in the same direction as he was. Each time, he was aware of her hatred before he saw the car.

He glanced at the car both times, feigning disinterest, the way a pedestrian might look incuriously at a passing car. If someone was watching from one of the houses, he hoped his act was convincing.

It's a good thing they can't read her mind, he thought.

Or can they?

Why did he keep thinking that he was the only person in the world with this ability? If there was one such person, weren't there bound to be others? If so, who were they? Where were they? What were they doing with their talent?

Focus! he told himself. You can't get distracted.

He walked past Freeman's house, keeping up his slow, steady pace.

I'm a casual passerby, he thought. Pay no attention to me.

What if he picked up nothing? His ability was always unpredictable. Why should it work now?

Would he have to find a way to get inside the house?

The thought terrified him.

I'll keep walking, he thought. Maybe something will happen.

Something did.

He was two houses past Freeman's house when an image pushed its way into his mind. A man was unlocking a desk drawer and taking a sheet of paper from it. The paper was surrounded by violent emotions.

Without realizing he was doing so, Max stopped walking.

The paper held the list of names, the same list Max had seen before. The man looking at it now was Freeman. Freeman took a black marker from a holder on the desk and drew a thick line through one of the names. With a great feeling of satisfaction, he locked the paper in the desk again.

The image faded away. Max started walking again.

He felt Lynnette's hatred growing stronger.

The car was on his side of the street, coming up behind him. This time, Max paused and turned to look at her. He nodded, then resumed walking.

Lynnette drove past and turned into the next cross street. Max continued at an unhurried pace and turned the same corner.

She was parked by the curb, waiting for him. He climbed in and closed the door.

"I was afraid my signal might be too subtle for you," he said.

"You think that was subtle? It was damned obvious. I hope no one was watching. Did you make contact?"

"Oh, yes. I've got what I need. We can go back to the office now."

Grady Jacobs wasn't happy.

"A sheet of paper in a desk drawer, and it has the names of some murder victims?"

"Past and future victims. The past victims have been crossed out. It's a slam dunk."

"Maybe on a TV cop show." Jacobs spoke dismissively, but his mind betrayed eagerness. "Your contact knows for sure it's there? And what's in it?"

"He's seen the list, and he saw it being locked in the desk."

"It's not much. What if the paper's been moved somewhere else? Or burned?"

"I guess there's no time to waste, then," Max said. "I've done my part. I'm going home. Don't throw this away."

Lynnette waited until she thought Max had left the building. Then she went into Jacobs' office. She put a pair of binoculars on the desk. "You can have these back."

"Could you see anything with them? What house did he go to?"

"I watched him from about three blocks away. He didn't go up to any house. He just walked down the block, very slowly. He stopped walking at one point, but then he started again."

"He didn't go into a house or meet with anyone?"

She shook her head. "I would have seen it."

"What kind of game is our boy playing?" Grady mused. "Maybe he's deeply involved himself and there is no contact, or maybe he's using some kind of communication equipment. Either way, he's not telling the truth."

"I'm telling you, he's just a con man. He got lucky a few times, or maybe he did know about some crimes. He was probably involved in those. Anyway, he used that information to con you into giving him a paycheck and a nice place to get out of the weather."

"No, there's more to it than that. I'm sure of it."

"Grady, I'm trying to protect you. If you pay any more attention to this jerk, you could end up destroying your career."

"You said he paused for a moment. What house was he in front of?"

"I couldn't tell. It was around the middle of the block."

Jacobs nodded. "That's consistent. He gave me the address where that sheet of paper supposedly is. 3045 Lafarge. You know who lives there?"

"No. Should I?"

"Albert Freeman."

"Still nothing."

"Big money. Big contributor to campaigns, including the mayor's. Supposedly, he made his money in the scrap business in Ohio and then moved out here. Now he concentrates on his investments—and on political influence."

"Nice work if you can get it," Lynnette said.

"I don't buy it. I've had a couple of people trying to find out where his money really comes from, but no luck. I think he's got his fingers in all kinds of business in Piketon, most of it illegal."

"And you think your friend Max Iverson just gave you the key to getting the guy."

"I do."

"Or maybe Iverson is working for Freeman, Freeman knows you're investigating him, and they're setting you up in order to destroy you. If you get a warrant and search his house, the house of this man with so much political influence, and there's nothing there, what happens to your job?"

"I'll go back to chasing ambulances."

"You've never chased ambulances."

"I'll start. This is worth the risk."

"Let me follow Iverson, Grady. I'll find out the truth."

"No. I promised him I wouldn't have him followed."

"And then you gave me binoculars to watch him with."

"That wasn't following," Jacobs said uncomfortably. "Watching when you're already there isn't following."

"Maintaining visual or physical proximity. That's the definition of following. That's what I did."

"You were in physical proximity because he asked you to drive him there and to hang around. You watched him because you were in a position to do so because of his request."

"Gee. Spoken like a lawyer. Maybe I'll just happen to be where he is from now on."

Jacobs shook his head. "I didn't break my word to him, but I sure did bend it. That makes me uncomfortable."

"Maybe there's another way to find out what he's up to that doesn't involve following him. I have an idea about that."

"No, Lynnette, leave it! I know Max isn't telling me everything, but he's not in bed with the bad guys. I can just feel it."

Lynnette snorted.

"Don't you get feelings about people?" he asked.

"Sure, and my feelings tell me he's scum and he's dangerous to you."

"Anyway," Jacobs said, "you're busy. I've overloaded you as it is. You don't have time to go chasing Max around the city."

"You're going to regret this, Grady."

"Then it's on my shoulders."

And mine, she thought. I'll be there to pull your fat out of the fire again. That wife of yours isn't going to do it for you.

She left, scowling, and Jacobs pulled the aspirin bottle from his desk drawer again.

9

Max's phone rang while he was on the bus headed home and wondering if Jacobs would act on the information he had given him.

I exposed myself to get it, Max thought. He'd better do something with it.

Either way, he felt he was done with all of this. Better to eke out a living doing low–level work. Safer.

The call was from his father. Max put the phone to his ear, trying to ignore the jumble of sounds and thoughts in the bus.

"Hi, Dad. What's up?"

"It's your mother. She's very ill. Can you come down here? I'll pay for your ticket."

Stepmother, Max thought.

"I can pay my own way," Max said. "What's wrong with her?"

He knew he should have said, "with Mom?" He had almost called her Aunt Mary instead. He didn't know why. He had never called her that, even though she was his aunt. He had always called her Mom until now.

"It's her heart. You know, it runs in her family. Her sister had the same problem. The autopsy found it after the crash."

Her sister, he thought. My mother.

The crash. The car crash in which his mother, pregnant with him, had died. He saw the EMT pulling the baby from the mangled body.

This was more than the faint memory of a nightmare. It was reality. It was what had happened. His father and stepmother had told him about it when they had thought he was old enough to hear it, and their story had become as strong and detailed and corrosive as a real and terrible memory, haunting his nights.

Except that on that day in the movie theater, when he had suddenly read a murderer's mind, it had changed from a pseudo-memory of a car crash to a real memory of an angry man, shouting, red-faced, striking out. At that moment, Max had become his mother, stumbling backwards, tripping over a chair, landing heavily on her back. Her head had struck the floor. He had felt the skull crack. Consciousness had faded. Then there were people shouting, blood, cutting, bright lights, terror filling him.

That couldn't be. Nothing like that had happened, not to his mother. Even if it had happened, it would be impossible for him to remember any of it. And yet it seemed so real. It washed over him now, pulling him into it.

It must be someone else's memory, he thought. Something I picked up from someone's mind. Some poor woman, not his mother.

"Max?" His father's voice pulled him back.

"Sorry, Dad. I think the signal was lost for a second. How serious is it?"

"We don't know yet. I'd like you to be here, just in case."

"Sure. Okay. I'll call you later this evening with my flight info."

The flight down was uneventful. It was quiet with a silence Max had not experienced for a while: a total absence of the thoughts of others. Even during a brief moment of turbulence, no one got upset—or at least not enough to broadcast their thoughts to Max. No one onboard was guilty of anything—or if so, they were at peace with their guilt.

Or maybe I'm losing my weird ability, he thought.

It had appeared suddenly, out of nowhere. Perhaps it had disappeared the same way.

My life will be simple again, he thought. Simple and safe.

He pulled an in-flight magazine from the pouch in the seat in front of him and leafed through it. It was mostly advertisements, but there were a few articles, one of which he found interesting. It dealt with the latest work in designing headsets that could interpret the wearer's brainwaves. Someday, the article speculated, small, lightweight versions of such headsets would let those wearing them transmit their thoughts over the internet. That would give people the ability to communicate directly with each other, mind to mind. It would be an electronic form of mindreading. The tone of the article was excited anticipation.

Careful what you wish for, Max thought. But people will be in control. Not like me. They won't share their thoughts if they don't want to. Horror won't force its way into people's minds. They'll probably just flood the net with trivialities. And porn. Inevitably, porn. It might not be so bad.

He returned the magazine to the pouch and leaned back, closing his eyes, concentrating.

Nothing.

The mental silence continued for the rest of the flight. After landing, Max became distracted by the business of pulling his small carryon from the overhead bin, waiting for the crowded plane to empty, and then finding the rental car desk.

He took the shuttle to the cheap rental car company's lot, far from the airport. The shuttle was crowded. Again, there was mental silence.

Weird, Max thought. Kind of nice, though. No blood, no horrors, just a normal world. But the blood and horror are part of the normal world. I just didn't know it before.

An early spring day in Phoenix was like a hot summer day in Piketon. Max threw his jacket in the back seat of the rental car. He wouldn't need it until he got back home.

The rental car had been sitting in the baking sunlight in the company's parking lot. Max turned the air conditioning up all the way and sat with the motor idling while he called his father to let him know he had arrived. There was no point in texting. His father had never figured out how to deal with texts.

The call went to voicemail. Max was surprised. He had emailed with the details of his flight, and his father had replied that they were looking forward to seeing him.

"It's me," he said. "I just picked up the rental. I should be there around 7:00 or a bit later, depending on traffic."

He put his cell phone on the passenger seat where he could grab it if they called back. He headed for I–10 and then west, into the blinding, setting sun.

He fiddled with the radio as he drove. He had been here only once before, five years earlier, when his father and stepmother had moved down from Piketon. Then, Max had found an oldies station he liked, but he couldn't find it again. Now it was all country and western and rightwing talk radio. It wasn't what he had expected. He had assumed the area had become more cosmopolitan since his previous visit, not more provincial.

He found an NPR station that was doing the news and

decided to stick with that. It became a relaxing background noise, voices talking, saying nothing of importance.

He focused on the scenery, such as it was. The ground was brown, the sky was blue, and the buildings all seemed to be pink stucco. Arizona suburbia: pink stucco, palm trees, and cacti. He wondered how his father and stepmother could stand it.

"When you get to feeling cold all the time," his father had told him five years earlier, "you'll start thinking about moving down here, too."

"I'll kill myself first," Max had said.

The word *Piketon* jerked his attention back to the radio.

"The arrest caps a long investigation, according to the Piketon District Attorney's office," the announcer said. "A number of politicians and influential business figures have been implicated. Freeman is believed to have been running a major extortion racket throughout the Mountain West. He is being charged with first-degree murder and conspiracy to commit murder in a number of cases."

The reporter moved on to the details of the day's activity on the stock market. Max was surprised that a local crime was being given national coverage. He imagined Grady Jacobs listening eagerly to the news and being disappointed that his name wasn't mentioned.

But it will be mentioned locally, Max thought. My boy's on the way up. He's going to want even more from me. This will just whet his appetite. I'll have to disappoint him. I can't tell him the truth, that I've lost the ability to read minds. I'll just say that all my sources have dried up.

He exited the freeway and made his way through winding suburban streets lined with pink stucco walls. Occasionally there was a splash of white stucco.

Stuck in the land of stucco, he thought.

The walls disappeared. He was now in a more modest neighborhood. These houses were set near the street, and he saw only rocks, no lawns. There were some scrawny trees looking more dead than alive.

Everything looked different from the way he remembered it.

Five years, one trip, he thought. It's easy to forget a place you don't like and have only been to once before.

Fortunately, the GPS wasn't confused. It directed him to the correct driveway. The modest house—pink stucco, of course—suddenly looked familiar.

There was a short, skinny, half-dead tree in front, to the right of the door. Max remembered his father planting a sapling there after moving in. "This will shade the whole front in the afternoon," he had said. "It'll take a few years."

A lot more years, Max thought. Or it will die soon, screaming, "I don't want to live here!" in its sad little tree brain.

Max parked on the right-hand side of the doublewide driveway.

Dad's car must be in the garage, he thought. Or they're out. Maybe they forgot when I was coming.

The sun was low, but the sunlight coming through the car windows was still baking. Max sat in the air conditioning for a minute before he turned the engine off, steeled himself, and stepped into the outdoor oven.

"I'd give up, too," he said to the tree.

He rang the doorbell. Nothing. He rang it again. Still nothing.

He called the house on his cell phone. He could hear the phone ringing inside, but there was no movement. He called his father's cell phone and once again heard a ringing from inside the house. He called his stepmother's phone. It went straight to voicemail.

He stood there, indecisive, wondering what to do.

He didn't have a key to the house. His father had wanted to give him one, thinking it would encourage him to visit, but Max had refused.

The sunlight felt like a physical pressure. He had to move. He remembered that there was a covered porch in the rear. He could try climbing the stucco wall to get to that shade.

He was about to do that when his father's car pulled into the driveway beside him. The car stopped, and his father jumped out and hugged Max enthusiastically.

"Sorry!" his father said. "It took forever. I left my phone in the house, and I didn't have your cell number with me."

His father looked as robust as ever, unchanged in five years. Max was relieved to see it.

"It's okay. How's Aunt Mary?"

"Mom."

"Mom."

The passenger door opened, and his stepmother was struggling to get out. The two men rushed to help her.

The change in Max's stepmother was shocking. She had lost weight and looked frail. Her hair had gone completely white.

She smiled happily up at Max as he held her arm. "It's so nice to see you again," she said. Her voice was scarcely more than a whisper.

"How are you...Mom?" He didn't know why he was suddenly having trouble calling her that. He hoped neither of them had noticed his hesitation.

"Oh, I'm fine. Nothing broken. It was just a silly accident."

"Let's get inside," his father said. "It's an oven out here."

One on each side, holding her arms, they helped Mary Iverson to the front door. She walked slowly, leaning heavily on them.

How could she have changed that much in five years? Max wondered.

When they were inside, in the coolness, with the door safely closed against the heat, Max said, "Dad said on the phone that it was your heart."

"I fainted. Your father panicked. He thought it was my heart. But I just fainted. I do that sometimes. They checked me over. I'm fine."

Max's father shook his head. "Your sister was like that, too. She didn't take proper care of herself, just like you."

"Oh, Tim."

They had always spoken openly and easily about Max's mother, Tim's first wife and sister of his second. It had never bothered Max. It had always seemed natural. For the first time, it no longer felt that way.

"I need a stiff drink," Tim Iverson said. "Maxy?"

Max was struck by a nasty boyhood memory. Some schoolmates had overheard his father calling him Maxy and had started mockingly calling him Maxipad. Afraid of the violence he knew they barely kept in check, he had forced himself to smile in response, to willingly be the butt of their jokes.

I'd kill them now, he thought.

"Sure, Dad" he said.

"I'll take one, too," Mary said.

"No, you won't," Tim said. "Doctor's orders."

She laughed. "More like your orders. I didn't hear him say that."

"He said it to me while the nurse was helping you get dressed."

"Sure he did." But she laughed again and acquiesced.

Max looked around. "Nothing's changed since I was here

before."

"We're happy with things as they are," Mary said. "Why change? I wish nothing would ever change."

Her husband, his back to them, busily pouring various liquids into glasses, grunted his agreement.

"Even that candlestick," Max said. "I'm surprised you still have that. You should throw it away."

"Oh, never," she said.

"Your mother's proud of it," Tim said.

"You made that for me in fifth grade," Mary said fondly. "Remember?"

"Shop class," Max said.

He had cut it from a metal pipe he had found in the classroom and welded it to a five-pound weight plate he had found behind the school gym, part of a pile of miscellaneous junk waiting to be hauled away. Then he had painted the result yellow, convinced that the result looked like brass. It should have been a quick, simple job, but he had taken his time with it, filled with love, delighted to be making something his mother could use. He had thought it beautiful, and she had assured him it was. Now he could see how ugly and silly it looked, and the memory of his childhood feelings made him uncomfortable.

That thing's like my life, he thought. Periods of hard work with nothing to show for it.

"It's lopsided," he said. "It's going to fall over. Don't ever have a lighted candle in it."

"Oh, Maxy, it's perfect," Mary said.

"It's got real heft to it, and the weld is solid," Tim said. "If I ever need a hammer and can't find one, I'll use your candlestick."

"You'd better not," Mary said.

Tim handed a glass to Max, the ice tinkling in it with the

motion.

Max looked at the brown liquid, sniffed, sipped, and asked, "What is this?"

"One of my new concoctions. I don't have a name for it yet. Mostly whisky, plus a few other things."

"Mostly whisky, plus a few other things," Max repeated. "That's the recipe for all your concoctions."

"If it ain't broke."

"I can feel it in my brain already."

"That's the whole idea. Let me know when you're ready for another."

"I think one will do the job."

They chatted and sipped their drinks. Against his better judgment, Max accepted a second one.

His father asked about work. Max was evasive.

"Move down here," his father said. "This place is booming. You could find work easily."

"You'd be near us," Mary said drowsily, smiling.

"You know we'd be happy to help you financially," Tim said. "You could move down here, take your time looking for a job, live here with us. Free room and board for as long as you want."

"It's okay, Dad. I don't need any financial help."

"You always say that," his father said disappointedly. "You never let us help you."

Max made a grunting sound he hoped would constitute an adequate answer and drank quietly and determinedly.

Suddenly, Mary said, "Oh! I was falling asleep in this chair. I'd better go up to bed. Tim, can you help me? Max, dear, get your things in from the car. Your room is ready for you. I'll see you in the morning. We can talk more then."

Max set the drink aside and went out to his car. He got his jacket and carryon and took them upstairs to what Mary insisted was his room, even though he had only stayed in it once before, and then only for a few days.

By the time he finished, he was sweating. The house had seemed cool at first, but no longer. He thought his father and stepmother were setting the thermostat higher than five years before.

He would just have to get used to it.

It's only a few days, he thought. I can make it.

When he went back downstairs to finish his drink, his father was there, pouring himself a third.

"Maxy?" Tim asked, holding up the whisky bottle.

Max shook his head. "Definitely stopping at two."

His father nodded. His earlier joviality had disappeared. He lowered his voice. "I'm really worried about her."

"But the doctor said she's okay, right?"

"Yes, he did. It's not that. She didn't just faint. She fell backwards over that armchair, the one she was sitting in just now. I was terrified. I know it's different. Your mother died in a car crash, but I couldn't help thinking about how it was when I lost her."

"Fell backwards over the chair," Max repeated, his eyes suddenly wide.

His father kept talking, but his words didn't register with Max. The nightmare had suddenly returned. This time, it was different. It was clear and sharp, in focus. It was real, a memory from the past, not a fantasy fabricated by his unconscious.

He was the woman, heavily pregnant, and he was also the baby inside her. He was his mother in the last moments of her life, in the moments before his premature birth. She was trying to protect herself against the fists of a red-faced man. The man was his father, different from the father he had known all his life—not just forty years younger, but drunk, violent, screaming in fury.

Max couldn't make out his father's words, but he knew his mother's thoughts. She had just accused her husband of sleeping with her sister, Mary.

Trapped within this nightmare from the past, Max could read his nightmare father's thoughts. The accusation was true, and so was the murderous rage.

A blow landed. The woman staggered back, fell backwards over a chair, hit her head, and felt something convulsing inside her as her consciousness died.

"Died from the impact, and I was born," Max said, speaking to the figures in his nightmare.

They were thin, tenuous, fading away.

"Well, yes. That's what I meant. That's why it terrified me. I rushed her to the hospital. I forgot all about your arrival."

"Rushed Aunt Mary to the hospital."

"Mom," his father corrected him automatically.

"Mom," Max repeated. "Mother."

During the few remaining days of his visit, Max could tell that Tim and Mary—he could only think of them now by their first names, not as Dad and Mom—were puzzled and hurt by his new coldness and distance. This was not the warm, loving son and stepson they had known all his life. He tried to pretend that he was still the same Max, but he failed.

He tried to read their thoughts, but nothing came to him.

He spent hours away from them, sipping coffee in coffee shops, wandering in malls, walking on busy sidewalks despite the dreadful heat.

He tried to pick up something. Among so many people, there must be powerful emotions. Someone must be broadcasting.

There was nothing. His mindreading was gone. After what he had learned about his violent birth, he didn't want it back.

And he was sure that he had learned it. He was sure that the vision, the solidified version of the old nightmare, was real. He knew beyond any doubt that Tim and Mary had had an affair, that Max's mother had found out and had confronted Tim, and that the violence he had witnessed in his nightmare had been the result. The story Tim had told his son—that his pregnant wife had suffered heart failure while driving, that she had crashed, suffering mortal injuries, and that an EMT had arrived on the scene in time to deliver the baby, Max, while his mother died—all of that had been an invention to cover up the truth.

Now he knew the truth. Could he prove it? Wouldn't there be records of domestic violence, of the injured woman giving birth before dying in her own house? And wouldn't there be a suspicious lack of a record of the supposed car crash?

He could dig up the real records and demonstrate the non-existence of the false one. He could confront Tim and Mary with the truth.

To what end? he asked himself.

It wouldn't bring his mother back. If there hadn't been legal cause to prosecute Tim at the time, then there still wouldn't be.

He didn't want to do any of it. He just wanted to get away from there as soon as possible and never come back. He wanted to cut off all contact with these two evil people. He would never see them again while they lived. He would not go to their funerals.

On the screen, a car drove slowly past. Sometime later, a man strolled along the sidewalk.

"Go back to that car. Now enlarge it. Damn it, I can't make out the driver."

"He's on the other side. It's a bad angle. And there's shade. Besides, it's just a car. What about the pedestrian?"

"He's just a pedestrian."

"People don't walk in that neighborhood. His clothes are wrong, too. Cheap looking."

"That's ridiculous. We'll keep watching."

The same car passed again, this time on the opposite side of the street.

"Freeze! Enlarge it. Now we can see him."

"Her. It's a woman. Oh, man. I know who she is. She works for Grady Jacobs."

"Damn. Maybe you were right about the pedestrian. Find out who he is. But that woman, the one driving the car. She's the key. I'll make a call up the line and see what they want us to do."

The flight back home was as uneventful as the one to Phoenix, and Max still couldn't pick up any thoughts. In the airport and on the airplane, he heard noises and voices, but he was hearing only with his ears.

It was still a relief in a way, but what did this mean for his future? The end of his job, of course. He had nothing more to offer Grady Jacobs.

Back to low-level jobs and barely scraping by, he thought. Until the robots take over those jobs. Then I'll be on the street. I guess I should have used my talent to make a killing in the stock market after all. Taking a few criminals off the streets! What the hell does that mean in the long run?

The plane touched down in Piketon barely in advance of a powerful spring snowstorm. Outside the main terminal building, a crowd was waiting for the slowly moving line of taxis. Max huddled inside his warm coat, glad he had taken it with him, while he waited his turn. A steady wind drove icy pellets of freezing rain into his face.

By the time the taxi reached his apartment building, the freezing rain had turned to big, wet flakes of snow. The streets were wet but not yet slippery. They would be by morning. Getting to work would be unpleasant. It would take forever to get downtown.

He could simply call up Jacobs and tell him he was quitting, but he felt an obligation to do that in person.

Jacobs was already there when Max arrived. Few other people were.

Jacobs motioned Max into his office and waved in the direction of the chair in front of his desk.

"How are your mom and dad?"

"They're okay," Max said. "It was a false alarm."

"That's good. You probably didn't hear about what happened here while you were away."

"About the arrests and all the great publicity? It was on the news down there."

"Really?" Jacobs grinned in delight. "Wow! That's great!"

"How long before you run for president?"

"Oh, you know, I'm going to do it in steps. Mayor. Governor. Senator. Then president. The usual sort of thing. But seriously, it was mostly your doing. You should get the credit."

"I don't want any. My sources—"

"Of course. You have to keep a low profile."

Max had been about to say that his sources had dried up and he didn't think he could be of any more help to the office.

"I meant to say that my sources—"

"It's okay. You don't have to say anything more. Anyway, I didn't call you in to talk about that. I've reserved a banquet hall at the Franklin for Saturday night. Celebratory dinner for the whole office. Bring a date. Dress up. It's going to be fun."

"That's an expensive place."

"You guys deserve it. Especially you. There'll be a place for you in the White House if I ever get there."

The White House, Max thought. If I could still read minds, what terrifying secrets would I read in that building?

"I was writing an email to the office with the details when I saw you," Jacobs said. "Go back to your desk and RSVP when you get it."

"Will do."

He would wait till Monday to hand in his resignation. He might as well get one really good meal out of this job before returning to his old lifestyle.

"Don't forget to bring a date," Jacobs said.

"Maybe I'll ask Lynnette."

They both laughed.

10

By Friday, the storm had passed, and the city was sunny and warm again. Max spent the day walking around downtown, partly for pleasure and partly to see if anything had changed, if he could once again read minds.

There was nothing. No thoughts intruded other than his own troubled ones. He was as he had been before his experience in the movie theater.

The memory of the horrors he had seen in the minds of others would stay with him for years, he knew, but it would fade eventually. He hoped so, anyway. It was comforting to know that there would be no new memories of the same type.

The memory of what he had discovered about his father and aunt would never leave him; he was sure of that.

He had decided to walk home, great though the distance was. He needed the exercise and the time to think about things.

Three-quarters of the way there, he started to feel that he should have taken the bus. The light was fading, and he was feeling hungry.

I could have been there already, he thought. I could have been relaxing with a meal and maybe a beer. Not very good food, a cheap beer, in my dingy apartment. Jesus, what have I made of my life? And after Monday, no more fat paycheck.

He was passing the Franklin Hotel. Why wait till Saturday? He would give it a try now. One last splurge. One last good meal.

The maître d' looked Max up and down disapprovingly and asked if he had a reservation.

Max looked into the dining room. It was half empty.

"Do I really need one this early?" Max asked.

Or do I just need dressy clothing, like the people you've already seated? he thought. Fuck it. I'll grab a burger somewhere.

He was aware of his growing anger but unaware that he was standing straighter, sticking his chest out. The maître d' stepped back. Max couldn't read the man's mind, but he could see the fear in his face.

Max laughed awkwardly. "Left my tux at the dry cleaners. Sorry. I'll know better when I'm here on Saturday night."

"Saturday night?"

"Grady Jacobs. I work for him. He's throwing a party for us here on Saturday."

"Ah, yes. Just a moment, sir. Let me check."

He made a show of perusing the seating chart on the lectern in front of him.

"How fortunate! We do have a table. Please follow me."

The prices on the menu gave Max pause.

I should have saved the money, he thought.

He wondered how much Saturday's party would cost Jacobs. Or would he charge it to his office?

Meaning I'll be paying for it with my taxes, Max thought.

He ordered a glass of wine. "Red. Dark red. Not too dark. Sweetish."

The waiter stared at him expressionlessly for a moment and then went away, returning a short while later with a glass half filled with dark red wine. It was not too dark. It was sweetish. It was just what Max wanted.

Damn, they're good, he thought.

He chose a dish almost at random, sure that it would be excellent.

After the waiter had left with his order, Max relaxed, sipped his wine, and looked around.

This is the life, he thought. Not that it will ever be mine.

His eye was caught by a couple being led to their table by the maître d'. He thought that most people would consider the man handsome, although there was a slickness about him that repelled Max. He thought the woman looked familiar, but he could see her only from behind and wasn't sure. She was talking animatedly to the man as they walked, occasionally touching his arm lightly. She was carrying a coat over the other arm. Her dress was a bit light and skimpy for the weather, but Max assumed she hadn't chosen it with weather in mind.

When they were seated at a table not far from his, Max could see her in profile and suddenly recognized her. It was Lynnette Salzmann, but a very different Lynnette from the woman in the office. This Lynnette talked too much instead of too little. She moved easily, even gracefully, instead of holding herself tightly, as though always ready to fend off an attack. The constant frown was gone and her mouth wasn't pursed angrily. She was smiling and laughing. She leaned forward toward her date.

What's the guy's secret? Max wondered. I should study his technique.

He tried not to stare, but couldn't help himself. When his food arrived, he ate it mechanically, scarcely tasting anything. He was studying Lynnette and her date, wishing he could read both their minds.

They were still engrossed in each other when Max finished

his meal. He wanted to keep watching, but the place was filling up, and he knew he had to pay and leave. He did so, wincing at the amount he was adding to his credit card, and left the building.

He stood on the sidewalk outside the Franklin, thinking how strange it was that someone could exhibit two such very different personalities under different circumstances. It was like his father and stepmother: loving and kind to him throughout his life, and yet they had betrayed and murdered his mother.

The memories came boiling up again—the red-faced, shouting man, the blow, falling backwards over the chair...

Max shivered. He felt chilled through. There was no traffic on the street, and no one else was on the sidewalk. The streetlights were bright, and yet he felt trapped in darkness. He was alone with the memories, unable to escape them.

Laughter pulled him out of it. Lynnette was leaving the hotel arm-in-arm with her date. She was laughing a bit too loudly, her head thrown back. Her light coat was open. Her dress had a low neckline. Max was astonished that she wasn't cold.

She staggered and giggled, clutching her date's arm with both hands to keep her balance.

Ah, Max thought, the warming effects of alcohol and pheromones.

He watched them walk away down the sidewalk. He shook his head.

Time to go home, he thought.

Lynnette's date glanced quickly from side to side, then turned aside into an alley, pulling Lynnette roughly with him.

What the hell? Max thought.

He hesitated. This wasn't his business. Maybe it was her idea. Maybe this was what she liked.

Rage filled him. Just as suddenly, it stopped, leaving him

shaken and bewildered.

Those weren't his own feelings. They had come from outside.

Someone else's mind! he thought. I can do it again. But who—?

Lynnette. The feeling of her anger was unique.

Is something wrong? he wondered. Should I do something?

He stood still, eyes closed, trying to sense her thoughts, but nothing came. His unpredictable, unreliable talent had deserted him again as quickly as it had returned.

Then it washed over him again. Confusion, this time. He was Lynnette, dizzy with drink, unable to see in the dark alley. She couldn't breathe. Confusion changed to terror. She was being pressing back against a brick wall. She couldn't escape. Hands tore at her clothes. She struggled ineffectually to push him away, the charming date who had changed into something terrifying.

Through it all, Max caught a glimpse of the man's thoughts, his pleasure at her fear.

Max ran down the sidewalk, toward the alley. He could still feel Lynnette's emotions, but nothing else. She drowned out all other minds.

The man released Lynnette and she slid limply down the wall to the ground. He walked down the alley to the sidewalk.

A figure appeared at the end of the alley, a large man, silhouetted against the lights of the street. "Hey!" he yelled. "Lynnette!"

The assailant muttered a curse and broke into a run. He hit the silhouetted man with his shoulder and kept running.

Max saw him coming too late to jump aside. The man's shoulder hit him in the chest and he staggered back, spun around trying to regain his balance, and fell on one knee on the concrete. Pain shot up his leg and the side of his body.

Gasping, Max pushed himself to his feet. He knew he couldn't pursue the running man now. He could barely stand. Instead, he focused on the receding back, trying to get the man's name.

For a moment, he almost he had it, but then Lynnette's mental shriek blared out again, and the man's thoughts were gone. Max watched as a car pulled up to the sidewalk at the end of the block, the man climbed in, and the car sped away.

Max turned and limped into the alley. His entire leg ached with each step, and he wondered how bad the damage was. But he was more worried about Lynnette. Her mental screaming made it impossible to think about much else.

She was a shadowy form at the base of the brick wall. He realized that she was sitting huddled on the dirty concrete of the alley. Her mental screaming subsided. He could feel her shutting herself away, retreating into herself.

He grabbed her arm and pulled her to her feet. He shouted, "Lynnette! Come on! You're in danger."

Focus on now, he thought, hoping he could force the thought into her mind. Don't pull away from the present.

Gripping her arm, he walked quickly from the alley.

She came with him, offering no resistance. He thought she was still in a daze. In truth, he was supporting himself on her as much as helping her walk.

Back on the lighted sidewalk, Max looked around warily. People were leaving the hotel, singly, in pairs, and in small groups. Cars were arriving to pick them up. He saw no one who aroused his suspicion. He sensed no hostile thoughts, but he wasn't sure if he could have sensed them. He didn't know if his mindreading talent was really back.

"Who was he?" he asked Lynnette.

"Who? What?"

"Your date. The man you were with. The man who tried to—"

Not that, he thought.

"The man you were with," he repeated.

She frowned, concentrating. He could feel the confusion in her mind beginning to clear slowly.

"Joe...something."

"Where do you know him from?"

"I don't know him. I was having a drink after work with a friend. She left, and then he came over, and we started talking. He seemed like a nice guy. He suggested dinner, and I said okay."

Jesus, Max thought, she's like Jekyll and Hyde.

He remembered the fragment he had caught from the man's thoughts. He hadn't really been trying to rape Lynnette. He had been trying to frighten her.

Why? Max wondered. Who is he and what is he up to?

"That's really all you know about him?"

"That's what I said!" Her mind was clear again and her tone was sharp. She was again the Lynnette he was familiar with. "I was wrong, okay? He's just another piece of shit. Just another man." She paused, then added grudgingly, "Thanks for helping me." Again she paused. Finally, she said, "Walk me to my car. Please."

Fortunately, she was parked in a lot behind the hotel. He wasn't sure how far he could walk.

As she unlocked the driver's-side door, he said, "Go home and lock your door."

"God, yes!"

He watched her drive away, annoyed that she hadn't asked him if he needed a lift home. He told himself he should excuse the lapse under the circumstances.

Would have been nice, though, he thought.

He wasn't sure he could walk as far as the nearest bus stop.

Joe tried to read the emotions of the driver in the glow of passing streetlights and failed. The old man's face was impassive.

Joe was annoyed. He didn't appreciate the silent treatment. I should teach this old fart a lesson, he thought. Weak old piece of shit.

The driver smiled.

Joe said, "I did what you told me."

The old man nodded. "You did well."

"But I didn't do anything."

"You scared her. You terrified her. That was enough."

"I don't understand." Joe's annoyance was growing again.

The driver glanced at him and then back at the road ahead. "Don't ask questions," he said. "You were told that before."

Joe shivered. He couldn't say why, but suddenly the frail old man seemed dangerous, and Joe didn't want to make him angry. "Sorry."

The old man nodded. "All right. Your work's not done. I have another task for you tonight."

He told Joe what the task was.

"You going to wait for me?"

"Good God, of course not. I don't even know how long it will take. In any case, I don't want to be anywhere nearby. When you're finished, walk home. Or call a friend to pick you up if it's too far. Don't take a bus or a taxi. Nothing that can be traced."

Joe nodded. "Got it. I've got pals who owe me favors."

"Of course you do."

I should call Lyft or Uber, Max thought. Or I could save the money and see how my knee does. Maybe I'll make it all the way.

He left the lot and began limping in the direction of his apartment. His knee improved as he walked.

Maybe the injury is minor after all, he thought. Maybe I should worry more about the weird thing that just happened, who the guy was and what he really wanted. And whether my mindreading is really back. Is that what it took to bring it back? Lynnette's mental yelling?

During the daytime, with normal traffic and waiting for lights to change before crossing streets, the walk would take about forty-five minutes. He hoped that at this time of day, it would be closer to half an hour.

He was soon away from the bright lights of downtown and walking along dimly lit streets. He walked as rapidly as he could, faster as the pain in his knee ebbed, feeling nervous, worried about who might be hiding in the shadows.

In a little more than half an hour, he was climbing the stairs in his apartment building. He had the door key in his hand and was finally feeling relaxed. In retrospect, he was amused by his earlier attack of nerves.

He unlocked the door, reached inside carefully, and switched on the overhead hallway light before entering. He felt silly, but the light comforted him.

He entered, shut the door behind him, and headed down the hallway towards the kitchen.

He felt the attack coming from behind.

He threw himself to the right. He hit the wall, knocking the breath out of himself. His injured knee gave way, and he slid halfway down the wall.

His attacker tripped over Max's extended leg and fell heavily.

As the man struggled to get to his feet, something rolled out of his grip. Max grabbed it, raised it, brought it down on the man's back.

The man collapsed on the floor. He gasped for breath and tried to rise.

The object Max held was about a foot long, with a wide, heavy head. The other end, where Max held it, felt good in his hand. He raised it and slammed it into the back of the man's head.

The attacker collapsed and didn't move.

I should keep hitting him, Max thought. Not like people in movies who hit the bad guy once and then run away, and then the bad guy gets up and comes after them. I should keep hitting the fucker until he never moves again.

But then the flood of thoughts from the injured man's brain hit him. It was as though the contents of the man's mind were emptying out, like water from a bathtub when the plug is pulled.

This was more like the contents of a sewer—images of violence that shocked Max despite what he had already seen in the minds of murderers, memories of inflicting fear and taking pleasure in his victims' terror. And worse.

Max recoiled. He didn't want to add this to the mental burden he already carried from the thoughts he had sensed. But then he caught images of himself. He saw a television monitor showing him walking past Al Freeman's house. He saw an image of Lynnette driving past Freeman's house. He saw her terrified face in the alley. With the assailant, he ran from the alley, shoved aside a man standing at the entrance, and jumped into a car that took him to safety. The driver of the car was an old man who gave the assailant Max's name and address and orders to eliminate him.

"That was you in the alley?" Max said.

The man said nothing.

Max grabbed his shoulder and shook him vigorously. "Answer me!"

The thoughts became more muddled, mixing memories from adulthood with those from childhood, some fantastical, dreamlike.

The thoughts were fading away.

"Stay alive," Max muttered.

He tried to pull the thoughts from the attacker's dying mind. He felt like a kind of vampire, unclean, a monster himself, but he couldn't stop. It was too important.

Max caught glimpses of a shadowy organization the man worked for. He had been following orders in the alley, deliberately terrifying Lynnette, and then he had been driven to Max's apartment and told to hide in wait for Max and kill him.

"How much did she tell you?" Max demanded. "Who drove you? Who gave you those orders?"

The dying mind struggled to respond, to present an image of the driver of the car that had taken him to Max's apartment, but the image wouldn't resolve. It remained shadowy and indistinct.

Then the thoughts faded almost to nothing. For a few seconds, there were odd little glimpses, like tiny sparks of light, death cries from the few brain cells that still survived. Then even those stopped.

What was real? Max wondered.

The man had been dying. Maybe what Max had seen was meaningless, like the strange, half-waking dreams he himself experienced when he was falling asleep at night.

Or perhaps some of it was real. Someone knew his name and address and the fact that he was a danger to...someone. Someone who wanted him dead.

How do they know about me? he wondered. How did they get that information?

He had hoped to get some names from the dying man, but he hadn't even extracted the man's own name.

It was time to call the police.

When the police arrived, Grady Jacobs was with them.

The uniformed men asked some questions, took notes, and left, taking the body and the weapon with them.

"That's it?" Max asked. "I expected to be arrested."

"Don't worry about it," Jacobs said. "You have friends in high places. I took care of that ahead of time."

"Well...thanks. Why are you here?"

"I was arranging to send someone here to protect you when your call came in. Lynnette told me what happened earlier."

"That body they just took away, it's the same guy who attacked her in the alley. I thought that was attempted date rape, but now I'm thinking maybe not."

"Definitely not. I think he was planning to beat some information out of her. There was a camera in Freeman's house aimed at the sidewalk in front of the place. They must have identified Lynnette from it. And of course they already know who you are. They're your pals, after all."

Max shook his head. "No pals of mine."

"Business associates, then. You feed us tips about them. That means you know them. And that means they know you. So now they've figured out that you're working with us, that you're our source, and they've decided to eliminate you."

"Makes sense," Max said.

Better to let Jacobs think that, Max thought. I can hardly say that I don't know them, that I just read their minds.

"You know them, so you know what kind of people they are," Jacobs said.

"Monsters."

"Yeah. They want you dead, and you're no use to me dead."

"Thanks, man."

"That's reality. I need to keep you alive."

Jacobs was talking about Max but thinking about Lynnette. He was under stress, and Max could read his thoughts easily.

I've warned her about her habit of picking up men in bars, Jacobs thought. So she finds it exciting. So what?

A surge of jealousy filled Jacobs' mind, obscuring his thoughts. It faded, and Max could read him again.

She was bound to pick up someone dangerous, Jacobs thought. It was inevitable. It's some weird effect of her past.

There were fleeting thoughts about Lynnette's parents being murdered on the day she was born, a life spent in a series of foster homes and state-run institutions, a messed-up kid who screamed instead of spoke.

She needs someone who'll protect her, Jacobs thought. Help her get over that. I could do that if I weren't married. Maybe Karen would agree to… No, she would never agree.

Jesus, Max thought. I thought *my* life was messed up.

"I don't think I have any more information to give you," Max said aloud. "Especially after this. My sources will all avoid me now for their own safety."

"If I cut you loose," Jacobs said, "you're a dead man. I'm going to put Lynnette in a safe house while I look into this. Join her there. It'll be much safer for you."

"Then I'll only have to worry about her murdering me."

"I'll order her not to."

Max suddenly had a vision of himself walking down a

street, mentally trolling for information, constantly straining to catch signs of a killer coming up behind him.

He shivered.

"Yeah. Okay."

11

The safe house was actually a second-floor apartment. It was shabby and cheaply furnished.

Low-rent crime stopping, Max thought. No wonder the bad guys are winning.

Yet it was better accommodation than anywhere else Max had lived since leaving home. That was a depressing realization.

Of far more importance was the fact that he was trapped there. He was cut off from the internet, from reading, and from any form of exercise, whether inside or outside. He missed lifting weights, and he missed walking the streets of the city. He had started doing that in order to pluck useful information from the minds of passersby, but he had come to enjoy those long walks for their own sake.

Now he was cut off from those thoughts, and that made him feel trapped in the prison of his own head.

He was not cut off from the thoughts of his guards, three brawny young men, but their thoughts consisted mostly of mental grumbling about the boredom and pointlessness of their assignment, coupled with an odd contempt for the two people they were guarding.

Worst of all, he was not cut off from the thoughts of Lynnette, the other person being guarded in the safe house. He wished he were. She was blasting them out at full volume whenever she was awake, and she didn't seem to need much sleep. It made sleep impossible for him. He couldn't shut her out, and so he spent most of his waking hours feeling groggy from lack of sleep, despite drinking far more coffee than he was used to.

Out loud, Lynnette complained about the coffee and the food, about not being allowed out of the house, and about Max being there.

The guards ignored her. They talked to each other or spent hours doing things on their cell phones. They gobbled aspirin and thought—and said to each other—that the guy was okay, they guessed, but the woman was a total bitch, and they wished they could shut her up, and her voice gave them a headache.

In her thoughts, she shouted her anger at Max and her resentment at being beholden to him. She knew he had rescued her in the alley, and she hated him for it. She wanted her rescuer to have been someone else. That thought mingled with images of Grady Jacobs, although the version of him in her mind was taller and better looking than the actual man.

Her constant anger, her hatred of Max, and the loudness of her thoughts often drowned out the thoughts of the guards, even though they were physically so close by.

If we're in danger from someone outside the house, Max thought, I won't be able to tell. I won't be able to hear them. She's making me blind.

That realization kept him on edge. He was constantly listening—with his ears, not his mind—for the sound of someone breaking in. He knew that was foolish. The guards, young, tough, and experienced, were more likely to hear such sounds than he was and were much more likely to know what to do about it.

It didn't help. He couldn't relax during the long hours when Lynnette was awake, complaining constantly and shouting with her mind.

This went on for three days. Max grew ever more exhausted. He could hardly eat. He grew increasingly hungry, but when he tried to force something down, he felt as though he might vomit. His head throbbed.

On the third night, Lynnette finally went to her bedroom and fell asleep around 2 a.m. The three guards who had just come on duty exchanged sarcastic jokes with the three they had relieved, who left the house with minds full of eagerness for home. Max collapsed on his bed and immediately fell into a deep sleep.

A few hours later, with his bedroom window glowing with the dawn, he awoke suddenly, sure he had heard a cry.

He lay in bed, straining his ears.

The house was silent.

The sound came again, but fainter, a fading cry of despair.

It wasn't a physical sound. It was a mental call.

Max rolled out of bed and walked quietly on bare feet into the short hallway connecting the bedrooms to the living room. He closed his bedroom door as quietly as he could. He paused, listening with his ears and his mind. He strained his eyes, waiting for the light to increase.

Nothing.

He moved slowly down the hallway. He made out a dark shape on the floor.

Max froze.

The shape separated into two. One rose, taking the form of a man in silhouette. The other remained a shadow on the floor.

Max understood. The cry he had heard was the dying mental scream of one of the guards. The standing man was his killer.

Now Max could sense the killer's thoughts.

First the woman, the killer was thinking.

The killer moved slowly, quietly, toward the door of Lynnette's bedroom.

He hadn't seen Max, motionless in the dark. Max stood unmoving, terrified, not knowing what to do.

Suddenly, he did know. In an instant, he absorbed the killer's bloodlust, knowledge, training, and muscle memory. His fear vanished.

The silhouette moved. Max moved faster. His fist slammed into the man's side, cracking ribs and driving the breath from him. As the man fell, Max yanked the pistol from his hand and shot him in the head.

Shouts erupted in the living room and lights came on. Lynnette's mind started screaming incoherently.

"It's me!" Max shouted. "It's me! Don't shoot!"

The two remaining guards, torn from their comfortable sleep on the couches in the living room, blinked at him and the two dead men in confusion.

Max put the gun down on the floor. His calmness astonished him.

Is this what it feels like to take lives as a matter of course? he wondered. Have I become like that man I just killed? Maybe it's not a bad thing.

"Good thing I was awake and knew what to do," he said to the guards. "You would have let both of us be killed."

"I'd better call this in," one of them muttered.

Lynnette opened her door. "Why are you naked?" she asked. "What's going on?"

"I just saved your life again," Max said. "I'm not naked. I'm wearing underpants. I didn't think I should take the extra time to get dressed."

I sound like a movie tough guy, he thought, marveling at himself.

Lynnette finally noticed the body in front of her door and the blood and brains on the floor. She gagged, stepped back into her room, and slammed the door.

One of the guards had his phone to his ear and was talking quietly.

The other said, "How did he get in? How did he know about this house?"

"He was told about it. He knew you two were asleep."

"How do you know that?"

"Guesswork."

But it wasn't. Max had gleaned that from the killer's mind. The man had been given the address, and he had waited outside until he received a phone call telling him that two of the guards were asleep and that the one who was still awake was inattentive.

How could that be? There was only one way that made sense. There must be other mindreaders in existence. That was why the assailant had deliberately terrified Lynnette in the alley, so that someone would be able to access her thoughts, her knowledge, Max's identity. There were mindreaders who worked for the people who wanted him and Lynnette dead, and her mental shouting had brought them to this place. A mindreader had waited for the mental signals of sleep from two of the guards and inattentiveness from the third, then had phoned the killer and told him to start moving.

The existence of other mindreaders wasn't a surprise. Max realized that he had been aware of it on some level, had known it must be so, but he hadn't wanted it to be true, and so he had refused to acknowledge the fact.

Thank God the killer wasn't a mindreader, Max thought. He would have been aware of me in the hallway. He would have known when I rushed him. But where's the mindreader who phoned him? Maybe waiting outside, close by. Maybe that person couldn't read me because I was asleep.

Can he read me now?

Max tried to keep his mind clear, to act without thought. He had no idea if that was working.

He went to his bedroom and threw on some clothes and shoes. Back in the living room, he picked up the gun he had put down earlier and headed for the front door.

He felt the guard's mental alarm even before the man spoke.

"Hey! You can't go out!"

"I can't stay here. Is someone coming?"

The other guard took his phone from his ear and said, "Mr. Jacobs is. I'm talking to him now."

"Tell him to stash Lynnette somewhere else. And give her a sedative."

"What?"

"Just tell him there's no safe place. Keep moving her around. Someone in Grady's office must be feeding information to the mob."

He was quite sure that wasn't the case. If the people who wanted him and Lynnette dead had a mindreader working for them, they would always be able to find her because of her mental loudness. They didn't need a mole in Grady Jacobs' office. But searching for a traitor in his office would keep Jacobs busy while Max searched for the mindreader.

Are you out there? he thought. Are you waiting for me?

Probably not, he decided.

The mindreader hadn't entered the house with the killer. That meant the mindreader wasn't a killer himself. He had probably fled when he realized things were going wrong. Perhaps his talent was as unreliable and unpredictable as Max's, and it had deserted him at the crucial moment.

I have to find him, Max thought. I have to stop him from reporting what happened.

Murder. That's what this means. I have to become just like them. I have to silence the mindreader before his employers kill me. I have to kill him first.

Or her. Or them. He couldn't assume there was only one.

This is crazy, he thought. I'm going up against professional killers working with people who can read my thoughts. I'm committing suicide. But if I don't do anything, I'm also committing suicide.

He opened the front door and looked down the flight of stairs.

Behind him, the guard said, "Don't go out there, man. They'll be waiting for you."

Max shook his head. "They don't know their man's dead. They'll be expecting him, not me."

He hoped that was true. He hoped that whoever was waiting outside couldn't read his mind and hadn't picked up the assassin's mental death cry, the way Max had heard that of the murdered guard.

Max didn't care. He couldn't take any more of this. He had to act.

He went down the stairs quickly, through the door at the bottom, and out into the early light.

The sidewalk was empty. A car was parked by the curb directly in front of him.

Max pointed the gun at the passenger window and bent down, trying to see inside. He saw an old man behind the wheel, shriveled and small, alarm on his face and filling his mind. He was the mindreader, and his thoughts were full of terror.

The old man thought, Killer! You're a killer! Oh, God!

He spun the wheel, screeched away from the curb, and raced away.

Max knew the car. It was the one that had been waiting outside the alley when Lynnette was assaulted. It was the car in which her attacker had escaped.

Max closed his eyes and focused on the mind in the car as the distance increased and the link faded away. Through the old man's terror, he caught a name: Felix Martinson. He was fleeing to Felix Martinson. In the man's mind, that name was associated with power and protection.

12

Max headed back inside. The two guards glanced at the gun in Max's hand and started to say something, but then stopped.

Max stared at them for a moment. They radiated fear—of him, to his astonishment. But then he felt the assassin's skills and cold-bloodedness in him, absorbed from the man as he died, felt that they sensed both, and he understood their fear.

One of the guards said hesitantly, "You should put that gun down, sir. It's a dangerous weapon."

"I know. That's why I'm holding it."

"I could make us all something to drink," the other guard said, affecting a bright, cheerful tone. "I think we could all use that. And then we can relax and talk. Maybe eat something, too, while we wait for Mr. Jacobs."

"He's on his way, is he?" Max asked.

"Yes, sir."

"And Lynnette?"

"Not a peep out of her. I think she's waiting for Mr. Jacobs."

"Her knight in shining armor," Max said.

The two men laughed uneasily.

"When Grady gets here, tell him I've gone out to try to get in touch with some of my contacts so I can find out how this happened. This safe house isn't very safe, so there's no point in my staying here."

"That's too dangerous," one of the men said. "Let me drive you home instead."

"No, and I don't need a driver. I can walk where I need to go."

"Sir, you should wait here," the other man said. "You're still safer here with us to protect you."

Max laughed. He picked up his jacket and the gun and left.

At the top of the stairs, he put on his jacket, zipped it up, and put the gun in the right-hand pocket. He walked down the stairs, out of the building, and turned right.

He had no idea where he was, but when he was outside before, he had glimpsed the bright lights and traffic of what seemed to be a busy street in that direction. He hoped that once there, he would be able to orient himself and find a bus stop. If there were people around, reading their minds should help him figure out where he was and how to get downtown.

What Max had told the guards about finding his contacts was nonsense, of course, but he hoped it would sound convincing to Grady Jacobs. In truth, he intended to go home, but he hoped that Jacobs would think he was elsewhere, somewhere unknown, and that should gain him some time.

The streets and sidewalks were busy with early morning traffic, and the city buses were running on their full schedules. In spite of that, because Max was traveling from one outlying part of the city to another, it took him over two hours of changing buses, waiting at bus stops, and walking to finally reach his apartment.

He paused outside, eyes closed, listening. He sensed nothing beyond the mental buzz of the city. There was no hint of danger waiting within.

Inside his apartment, he could see no sign of disturbance. He supposed that a professional could have been there and searched the place thoroughly without leaving a trace, but he was more concerned that someone might be waiting for him, and he made sure that no one was.

In any case, what would searching his apartment tell anyone?

They already know everything, Max thought. They lifted my name and address from Lynnette's mind. They know I'm the source of the tips being given to the police and Jacobs.

They could come after him at any time. They could be on their way at that moment. His only safety lay in getting to them first and hoping that his ability to read their minds would cancel out their ability to read his, giving neither side an advantage.

What a strange war this was! He didn't even know why it was a war. Why did these people care about him feeding tips to Grady Jacobs that resulted in criminals being locked up? What was the connection between the mindreaders and the criminals? The situation made no sense to him.

Could he block their ability to read his mind? That worked in the science fiction he had devoured all his life, but this was reality. How would he go about it? What mental gymnastics would he have to use? How would he know if it was working?

The hell with it, he thought.

He hung his jacket on the back of his desk chair, sat down in front of his computer, and searched for Felix Martinson. Google returned hundreds of thousands of hits.

"Shit," Max muttered.

He thought for a while and then entered the search string

+"felix martinson" +piketon +Arapahoe

Now there were fewer than a half-dozen hits, and they all referred to the same man. This Felix Martinson lived on a huge estate in the foothills, and judging by the two photographs Google found, was in his seventies.

The online sites linked to by the Google search results didn't offer much more information than that. The man's estate implied considerable wealth, so Max thought it odd that there wasn't more about him online.

Reclusive, socially isolated, but extremely wealthy, Max thought. Does that imply his money is inherited, or maybe that he gets it in illegal ways?

Did it matter? If this was the man behind the assassins who had been sent after him, then he was Max's target. Where his money came from didn't matter, except that it meant Martinson could afford lots of protection. His money would make it harder to get to him.

I have to get out of here, Max thought. By now, Grady might have guessed where I am. This is also where the bad guys will be looking for me. I'm in increasing danger every minute I stay here—or in any one place.

He wondered what his next step should be. He knew he had to get to Felix Martinson, and he knew where the man lived, but what good did that do? No doubt Martinson was heavily protected, surrounded by trained, armed men, and Max was one man, untrained, and armed with a pistol he had taken from someone else and didn't really know how to use.

But I do know! he realized.

He had absorbed that knowledge from the pistol owner's dying brain, and now that knowledge was embedded as firmly in his mind as it had been in the dead man's.

How had all that happened? He didn't know or care. What mattered was that the knowledge was his, and so was confidence in his ability to use the weapon.

I can kill, he thought. I know how, I've already done it, and I'll do it again if I have to.

Stunned, delighted, and unnerved at the same time, he stared at the laptop monitor, thinking about the path forward.

He relaxed for the first time in days. The hours of tension faded, and the lack of sleep exerted its power. His thoughts about what to do became strange imaginings of bloodshed and frenzied physical exertion. He dreamed he was walking through the grounds of Martinson's mansion, but it was a fantastical place, like nothing he had seen in life.

His eyes closed, his head sank forward, his chin rested on his chest, and he slept.

In his dream, he entered the unlocked front door of the mansion and made his way down a dark hallway. A door at the end of the hall opened into an office in which a man sat at a desk, his back to the door, silhouetted against the glowing screen of a computer. Max stopped in the hallway and raised his pistol, aiming at the back of the man's head. His finger tightened on the trigger.

Just before the crack of the pistol sounded, Max awoke and threw himself to the side, falling to the floor and rolling. The bullet smashed through his laptop screen.

Max lay silently on the floor, holding his breath. Unlike the setting of his dream, the sun shone through the window, and Max could see himself clearly through his assailant's eyes.

Fuck, the man thought. Is he faking it? Did I get him? I can't tell from here. They said to be careful, that he's dangerous.

He laughed aloud.

Bullshit, he thought. He's a pansy. This is almost too easy.

His mind showed him parking his car a block away and approaching Max's apartment building slowly and with infinite caution.

I took way more care than I needed to, he thought. This guy's nothing.

Max lay still. He weighed his options. If he moved, the man would shoot him. If he didn't move, the man would probably come closer and shoot him to make sure the job was done.

That's what I would do, Max thought.

The pistol he now thought of as his was on the desk, beside the ruined laptop. It was useless to him now.

I'm done for, he thought. There's nothing I can do. I'll be dead seconds from now. I should have locked the door behind me.

Someone pounded on the apartment door and rattled the handle.

Max caught confused, frightened thoughts from outside: Gunshot? Call the cops?

Startled, the killer turned toward the door. Max read his alarm and saw the door through his eyes.

Before the man could collect his thoughts and turn back, Max was on him, sweeping his feet from under him, breaking his right arm and removing his gun, flipping him onto his stomach, kneeling on him, locking his fingers around his throat.

He was surprised at how easy it was for him.

Max's first impulse was to choke his attacker to death as quickly and quietly as he could. The man outside the door was trying to dial 911 on his cell phone. He was terrified, and his hands were shaking, but Max was sure he'd manage to make the call soon. He had to finish this killing and get away before the police arrived.

But then he thought about his ability to gain lifesaving skills and knowledge from men like the one struggling underneath him. He loosened his grip a bit, just enough to keep the killer's life from ebbing too quickly.

Greedily, Max sucked knowledge from the man's brain as it faded away.

"You don't deserve to die quickly, you son of a bitch," he whispered in the man's ear, and he felt the dying mind react to his words with terror and horror.

At last it was over. Max searched the killer's pockets and found his keys. Max rose to his feet feeling only satisfaction and a new sense of competence. He also knew who had contracted with this killer. It wasn't Martinson. It was someone named Krakowski, who worked for Martinson.

I'll take care of the lower-level flunkies first, Max thought. I'll strip the monster of his protection before I go after him. And I'll get better at this with each kill.

He checked the mind of the man outside the apartment door. He read the man's name: Joey. Joey was still terrified, still trying to use his phone.

Poor Joey, Max thought.

He was partly sympathetic, partly contemptuously amused.

What a waste of space you are, Joey, he thought.

His desk chair was lying on its side. His jacket was partly draped over it, partly pinned under it. He pulled the chair back onto its castors, picked up the jacket, put it on, picked the gun up from the desk, and put it in the jacket's right pocket.

What about the second gun, the one belonging to the new would-be killer, the second man Max had killed?

One pistol will be enough, he thought. I can do a lot with one. This new one fired the bullet that ruined my laptop. Better leave it here at the scene of the crime.

What about ammunition?

He would have to think about that later. Right now, he needed to deal with Joey.

He zipped up his jacket, looked around quickly, and then went to the door and pulled it open.

Joey, a tall, cadaverously thin man, stared at him openmouthed.

"Hey, Joey," Max said. "How's it going? Need help?"

He took the phone from Joey's shaking hands and punched in 911, then handed the phone back.

"There you go. 'Bye, Joey."

Outside, in the bright sunlight and amidst the hurrying crowds, Max thought about the crosstown trip ahead of him. In the past, he would have had to take the bus downtown and then catch another bus headed out to his suburban destination. He would have had to change buses a couple of times along the way.

Fuck that bullshit, he thought. Now I have a car, and I know how to drive like an assassin.

It was an old car, fortunately, one that still used a key for the door and ignition. Max walked rapidly to where it was parked, unlocked it, and got in behind the wheel.

For just a moment, his newfound confidence deserted him. He stared at the dashboard in confusion and then in fear at the traffic roaring by.

I can't do this!

He closed his eyes, calmed his breathing, and concentrated on the killer's memory of driving here to kill him.

Trace it backwards, Max thought. Do the trip in reverse. It will be simple.

And fun.

He opened his eyes, smiled, started the car, and took off.

13

Grady Jacobs got to work early, as he often did. Lynnette was already at her desk, as she always was. He could almost believe she slept in the office. But that was in normal times, which these times were not.

"Why are you here?" he asked. "I told you to go away for a while."

"The police don't think there's any danger. No more safe house, no more guards."

"I disagree with them. That's why I said you should go out of town."

"That attack... I think the guy was a rapist who lost his nerve. I don't think there was anything more complicated to it than that."

"Isn't that bad enough? Anyway, what about the attack on Max? That was the same man."

"Oh, I think he was afraid Iverson could identify him, so he followed him home and tried to shut him up. Except Iverson got lucky."

"You make it sound so simple," Jacobs said.

"It *is* simple."

"Okay, but what about you? After what you went through, I think it would be a good idea for you to be away from all this. Do something entirely different. Spend time—"

"With my family?"

"Sorry." The family that had died violently when she was born. He cursed himself for reminding her of it. "You could, um, talk to someone. The city would pay."

"Shrinks never did me any good. They tried when I was in the foster system. Anyway, I've got a lot of work stacked up. I can't afford to take time off right now."

Jacobs stepped up to her desk and looked at her computer monitor. "Is that the Walton case?"

"It is."

"I thought Walton was wrapped up."

"Not quite. I was thinking we should drop it."

"What? Why? It's done. He confessed."

"Not in writing or on tape."

Grady pulled a chair over from Max's desk. He wondered where Max was. He felt a moment of uneasiness about his mysterious employee, but he tried to quell it and focus on Lynnette, something he normally had no trouble doing.

"I thought you were in the process of getting his written confession," he said.

"I thought so, too, but he's being slippery. I don't know if it's worth the time and resources to continue with it."

"He was able to track his wife's movements very accurately, and he threatened her. He's dangerous."

"He just fantasized about harming her. He never actually did anything. Come on, Grady, this is so minor compared to the other stuff we're involved in. We're taking on what you say is some kind of giant criminal enterprise, and we're already stretched thin. Do you really want to direct resources from that to sending some small-time fantasist away? This guy is nothing."

"No, you're wrong. He's everything. Putting mobsters

behind bars may grab headlines, but what Walton is doing is exactly the kind of crime we need to quash. You know the numbers. Women all over the city—the state—are being harassed and threatened in exactly this way. We have to be their shield."

Lynnette managed not to smile.

You mean you have to get the women's vote in the mayoral race, she thought.

A case like Walton's, if probably publicized, would do just that. But Lynnette's interest in Walton had little to do with helping Jacobs garner votes from female voters and very much to do with protecting him and his career from Max Iverson.

Let's see that wife of yours help you this way, she thought.

"Okay," she said. "I'll go see Walton and try again. I'll call him now and make sure he'll be there after his shift ends."

"He's still working as a janitor?"

"Cleaning toilets in an office park."

"Well, that seems somehow appropriate, doesn't it? Make it clear to him that he's going to prison, and the only question is for how long and where. Don't be soft. Be tough."

"I can do that."

"I know you can."

Jacobs headed for his office and the aspirin bottle in his desk. His headache had started unusually early this morning.

That evening, Lynnette drove to the small apartment Freddy Walton had been living in since his wife had kicked him out. She found a parking spot a block away and walked quickly, nervously along the poorly lit sidewalk. She passed a few other people—shadowy, unidentifiable figures in the near dark.

She entered the vestibule of Walton's apartment building with relief. The outer door didn't lock, and the space was lit by a single low-wattage bulb. Nonetheless, she felt less vulnerable here than outside in the dark.

It'll be even darker when I leave, she thought. Shit.

Pieces of paper taped to one wall listed the apartments and the names of their residents. One read WALTON 2C. There were no buttons set into the wall beside the little paper signs.

How the hell am I supposed to signal him to buzz me in? she wondered.

She tried the handle of the vestibule's inner door. It, too, was unlocked, and she went inside and began to climb the dark, narrow staircase to the second floor.

The stairs creaked ominously. The place stank of stale food, beer, and innumerable other smells she couldn't identify and didn't want to.

This is almost as bad as prison, she thought.

Walton opened the door of 2C as she approached it. He was a tall, powerfully built man, but he seemed to shrink when he saw her.

"How bad is it?" he asked, his voice quavering. "What's going to happen to me?"

Lynnette gestured. "Inside."

Inside the tiny apartment, the smell was even worse than in the stairwell. The place consisted of one room with a kitchenette at one end, a bed at the other, and a couch and small, round table in the middle. It was crammed with junk, and the floor was littered with food wrappers and pizza boxes. Some of the indistinguishable junk had been piled up as dividers between the spaces that functioned as kitchen, bedroom, and dining and living room, as though Walton was trying to pretend that he had interior walls.

"Christ, Freddy!" Lynnette said. "You've only been here for a few weeks. How did you get it so filthy?"

"It was this way when I moved in," Walton said defensively.

That could well be true, she thought.

"Okay," she said. "Never mind that. The news is bad."

"Shit." Trembling, Freddy sat down heavily on the couch, landing on an old pizza box but seemingly oblivious to that. "How bad?"

"You're going to jail."

Freddy moaned.

"For a really long time. Forever, in reality. You probably won't live to complete your sentence."

He moaned again. "Maybe I'll just kill myself. No one cares about me, anyway."

"Don't do that." Not while I need your help, she thought.

"Yeah? Why not?"

"Because it would make your ex-wife happy."

He jumped to his feet. "That bitch!"

Lynnette took a step back. "You don't want her to be happy, right?"

"I'll show her! I won't kill myself!" He deflated suddenly and collapsed onto the couch again. "But I can't go to jail."

"Maybe there's a way out."

Freddy was all ears.

"I know that you had some way of tracking your ex. We never could figure out how. We couldn't find trackers on her car or in any of her belongings. I want to know how you did it."

"That's all? I just have to tell you how I tracked that bitch, and you'll keep me out of jail?"

"That's the first step. What happens next depends on what you tell me."

"Why do you want to know how I tracked her?" Freddy asked suspiciously.

Lynnette hesitated. She didn't want to tell this creep anything, but she knew she had no choice. "I need to follow someone closely, but this is all deep undercover work, so I can't do it through my job."

Suddenly, Freddy became self-confident. He chuckled. "It's personal, isn't it? It's nothing to do with your work. What is it? Ex-boyfriend? Something like that?"

"It's not— *Goddamn it!*" she shouted.

Freddy winced. He swayed on his feet. "I need an aspirin." He headed for the kitchen, opened a door Lynnette hadn't noticed before, and disappeared behind it. She assumed that was his bathroom.

While he was absent in the bathroom, Lynnette tried to calm down. She couldn't afford anger. She needed him.

When Freddy returned, she said, "The details don't matter. Help me, and maybe you'll stay out of jail."

"You didn't say maybe before."

She snarled. "Don't play games with me."

Freddy winced again. He sat back down on the couch, trembling and white. "Okay. Yeah. The tracking."

"I'm guessing you used Apple AirTags, or something like that."

He smirked. "Nope. You watch too much TV. You can detect those things. Our secret is that we're low tech."

"'Our'?"

"Uh, yeah." He licked his lips. "Some friends. I don't wanna—"

"I don't care about your goddamned friends!"

Walton shrank back into the couch.

Lynnette calmed herself again. "I'm not after your friends. I'm not even after you. I'm here because I need to track someone, and I don't want him or anyone else to know that I'm doing it. Play ball with me, and I'll make sure you don't get prosecuted. So, Freddy, tell me. *How did you do it?"*

"Don't yell," Freddy whined.

"Jesus Christ."

"Okay! Okay! I have a network, a group of friends. We all have the same problem. We want to keep track of...um...people in our lives."

"Wives and girlfriends?"

"And kids. And sometimes other people."

He does belong in jail, she thought. And his friends, too. I'll do something about that later, after I've taken care of Iverson and have no more need for this creep. If I can show Grady what Iverson really is, he won't care what happens to Freddy.

"Continue," she said.

"We're scattered all over the city. We just use our phones. We send each other photos and names and addresses of people we're tracking. Then we just keep our eyes open. We communicate. We keep in touch with each other. Text messages, usually. We can follow anyone that way," he said proudly.

"That's it? That's all there is to it? Christ, I thought you must be some kind of genius."

"I am! It's low tech, it's undetectable, and it works."

"The Pervert Tracking Network," she said with a sneer. "That's all it is."

He hid his anger, knowing he couldn't afford to antagonize her.

"So if I give you a man's picture, his name, and his address," Lynnette said, "your Pervert Tracking Network will be able to tell me everywhere he goes. Right?"

"Well, maybe not everywhere, just everywhere one of us happens to see him."

"Oh, it will be everywhere. Otherwise, you'll go to jail, and so will all your pervert friends."

Freddy blustered about his rights and his lawyer, but he

quickly ran out of steam under Lynnette's cold glare. He knew how vulnerable he was, what she and the DA's office could do to him. Besides, his head felt as though it was about to explode, and he just wanted to get away from her and into the open air.

Lynnette sent Max Iverson's photo, name, and address to Freddy's phone, and while she watched his every move, he sent the information to every phone in the Pervert Tracking Network.

He was beginning to think of it by that name himself.

14

"Sir, we haven't heard from the man we sent to Iverson's apartment. He hasn't checked in, and his phone goes to voice mail."

The speaker was young and powerfully built. He had killed men with his bare hands, but he quailed in front of the old man sitting in an armchair in front of him.

"I could go over there myself," he offered.

The old man waved dismissively. "Pointless. Iverson no doubt killed him, and he'll kill you."

"Mr. Martinson, sir, I can handle that—"

"No, you can't."

"Sir..." He fell silent under the old man's glare.

"You're a fool. You have no idea what's going on here. There's more to Iverson than you know—more than I realized, for that matter. We need a different approach. Are the others waiting?"

The younger man nodded. "They're in the dining room, sir."

"Good." He pushed himself to his feet and stood for a moment, breathing. "Go find something useful to do."

"Yes, sir." The younger man left quickly, feeling that he had escaped danger and wondering, as he always did, how that frail little old man was able to frighten him so.

Martinson left the room and walked down the hallway to the dining room. A few other old men sat around the large table, staring dully into space. When Martinson entered, they struggled to rise to their feet.

"Don't get up," Martinson said.

Relieved, they sank back into their chairs.

Martinson watched them with a mixture of pity and contempt. What losers they are, he thought. He remembered them as they had been at the beginning and was angry at how they had all changed.

They've gone to wrack and ruin, he thought. Even Johnny. He was my right-hand man! And what a man he was in those days. Up for anything. Look at him now. He panicked at the safe house. Hell, look at all of them. They're close to worthless.

He was shielding, of course. He hadn't been unshielded with these men for decades. They might see themselves as his partners, but he knew they were his underlings. Surely even without being able to read his mind they could tell how he viewed them. He could easily read the resentment and subservience in their faces and postures. He thought it best to maintain the pretense of politeness. Perhaps he would eventually think of a way to dispense with them and run matters by himself. They were of little help nowadays.

When the time's right, he told himself.

He took the empty chair at the head of the table.

"As you know," he said, "Max Iverson is a problem."

They nodded solemnly.

"I'm not sure you realize how great a problem."

One of the men held up his hand.

Martinson nodded at him. "Johnny."

"We'll just keep throwing men at him. Sooner or later, one of them will do the job."

The others nodded.

Their minds are going the way of their bodies, Martinson thought. They're more hindrance than help. Their time is coming soon.

"If only it were that simple," he said. "The man can handle himself."

"But how? We looked into his background. He doesn't have any kind of training or experience, not like the men we can send against him."

"Haven't you figured it out yet?" Martinson said sharply, annoyed by their slow-wittedness. "He's getting his skills directly from them, from our men. He's pulling it from their minds. On top of that, he knows what they're going to do before they do it."

They looked confused. They shook their heads. One of them said, "Oh, come on, Felix. That's ridiculous."

Martinson glared at him.

There was an uncomfortable silence. Finally, the other man said, "Sir, I don't understand."

"He's reading their minds. He can do what we can do, only better."

They stared at him blankly.

Martinson cursed them mentally. "Think back forty years. That experiment of ours."

"Which failed," Johnny said.

"So we thought," Martinson said. "I've had some of our people look into Iverson's background. I've pinpointed it." He tried to remind them of a specific incident in that old experiment of theirs, but he could tell they didn't remember it—even though they pretended they did so as not to anger him.

God, what a bunch of yucks, he thought.

"Never mind," he said aloud. "I remember, and that's all

that matters."

"If you're right," Johnny said, "then we'll have to work together against him. We'll have to unshield together." He licked his lips nervously and looked around at the others, who all looked distressed.

Martinson laughed internally at the thought of this gang of geezers going up against Max Iverson. "I don't think that would do much good. Based on what's happened, I think his talent must be very strong. I assume that, like ours, it draws its strength from the field. So instead of trying to overwhelm him with numbers, which would probably be futile, we have to get him far away from the base point and us. Then we'll be able to take him out in the usual way."

"How are we going to do that?"

"Oh, I think I know how."

15

Max drove confidently through the heavy city traffic. He squinted in the bright sunlight. Sunglasses, he thought, as he unknowingly passed an optometrist's office. I really should take more care to protect against cataracts.

He thought about the two assassins he had killed. Neither had been a mindreader. If either of them had been, he would be dead.

What did that mean? It was clear that there were others who could read minds and that they were his enemies and were trying to kill him. Why weren't they coming after him themselves? Why were they sending men who, no matter how competent they were at killing, were blind compared to Max?

He supposed that didn't really matter, but he was curious.

The car made an odd sound and lurched before resuming its smooth motion.

The son of a bitch couldn't even take proper care of his own car, Max thought. Probably too busy killing people to bother. Loser.

He arrived at the strip mall where the dead loser's car trip had begun. He parked in the half-empty parking lot and swept his eyes across the row of storefronts. Laundromat, Chinese restaurant, insurance broker, and so on—no different from what he would find in many other rundown, dying strip malls all over the city.

Max sat in the car and opened his mind. He picked up some interesting information about the laundromat and Chinese restaurant businesses, but that was all.

What the fuck? he thought. This is bullshit.

Then he realized that he should also be absorbing information about the insurance business, but he wasn't. The insurance broker's office wasn't what it proclaimed itself to be. It was a front.

The brokerage had the name Krakowski on its window. Max focused his attention on it.

He caught a shred of a dream. Felix Martinson, looking much younger and more powerful than the photos of him Max had found online, was bending down toward the dreamer and smiling. Martinson said something about a reward. The dreamer squirmed in delight, like a dog being petted. The man's pleasure was almost sexual. It put Max on edge.

The dreamer was Carl Krakowski, the owner of the brokerage, and he was dreaming that he was being rewarded for having Max killed.

You son of a bitch! Max thought. Stay asleep. Keep dreaming.

Max got out of the car. He put his hand in the pocket with the gun, touching it lightly, ready to take it out when he needed it. He started walking swiftly, angrily toward the insurance office, ready to kill.

He paused.

What if Krakowski is also a mindreader? he thought.

Then he'll know I'm coming. I can't tell if he's alone. I can't tell much about him. His dream is interfering. I don't know what's real and what's part of his dream.

Better hope he stays asleep. Where is he? Must be in a room at the back, out of sight of possible customers. If there *are* any customers. He won't have any if the storefront is just a front.

In that case, he's bound to have protection. Human guards, electronic gadgets. I'd be able to sense human guards, and I don't. Gadgets are the danger. I can't sense those.

Max walked more slowly now, more cautiously. He reached the glass front door of the office and stopped. He stood still, focusing his attention, trying to feel the presence of danger.

Instead, Krakowski's dream continued, but now it had devolved into strange scenes that made no sense and bizarre fragments of sentences.

How can I be picking this up? Max wondered. There are no strong emotions, and I'm too far away. I always have to be close to the person.

Perhaps Krakowski's delight at being rewarded by Martinson in his dream was sufficiently extreme. But Max had read those thoughts from across the parking lot, and he could still read the man's thoughts, even though they now contained no strong emotions of any kind.

He wondered if his ability to read minds was increasing.

Does it get stronger the more I do it? he wondered. Is this the long-term result of Lynnette's mental scream? Will my ability keep growing? Will I eventually be able to hear the whole world's thoughts?

This is pointless, he told himself. Why am I wasting time on speculation? Get on with it!

Through the big front window, he could see a small room containing a single desk. There was a door behind the desk. No one was in the room. Would a bell sound if he pushed the door open?

He hesitated again.

Oh, fuck this, he thought.

He drew the pistol from his pocket, held it ready in his right hand, and pushed the door open with his left.

A bell sounded somewhere in the back.

Max burst into motion, racing past the empty desk, banging open the door behind it.

The room beyond the door was dark and small. Light flooded in from the open door. The room contained a cot and a small table. Krakowski lay on the cot, startled awake. His mind was full of confusion and fear. He struggled to sit up.

Max slapped him hard, and Krakowski fell back, whimpering, covering his face with his hands. Max knelt on his chest and pressed the muzzle of his gun against Krakowski's forehead.

"Take your hands away!" Max barked. "Look at me!"

Krakowski whimpered again.

"Look at me!"

Hesitantly, he moved his hands. "I can't breathe."

"Tough shit." Max could see his own face through the man's eyes—a frightening face.

Max said, "You know who I am?"

Krakowski squeaked out a yes. Max had already seen the answer in his mind. There was more information there, but Max couldn't read it through the man's fear.

"Your man is dead," Max said. "I killed him."

Krakowski stared at him in confusion and disbelief.

"It was easy. You should be more careful who you hire. Now I'm going to kill you."

Krakowski moaned. "Please! I was just following orders!"

Max laughed. "Do you know how old that line is? Whose orders?"

"I—I can't tell you," Krakowski said as the answer filled his mind.

"I bet it was Felix Martinson. I bet he sent you my picture and name and where I live."

"How did you—?"

So the underlings really don't know about this mindreading thing, Max thought. Best to keep it that way.

"You'd be surprised how much I know."

He asked Krakowski more questions—not because he was interested in the man's replies, most of which were lies, but to make him think the truth.

Krakowski was under orders to kill Max, but he didn't know why. He was never told why he should send his men to rough up or kill someone. He really was just following orders. Those orders came from Martinson. Krakowski knew that much but no more. He had learned early on not to ask questions or object to the orders. It was safest to do what he was told, and it was lucrative, too. He was comfortable with the arrangement.

"You go there, to his home," Max said, "and he gives you instructions in person."

The image that arose in Krakowski's mind was of the same old man Max had found via Google search, but shrouded in an aura of power and threat. Martinson's home was a mansion, at least in Krakowski's mind, a mansion in the foothills, on a huge property.

Krakowski said, "Mr. Martinson doesn't trust telephone calls. He's afraid—"

"That the lines are tapped," Max finished for him.

Krakowski stared up at him openmouthed, his fear growing.

This guy knows everything! he thought. How's that possible?

"If Martinson doesn't trust the phone, how does he know

when you've done what he told you to?" Max asked.

He read the answer in Krakowski's mind, but the man didn't want to say it aloud.

"You could send someone to him with the message," Max said in a musing tone, as if he were trying to figure it out. "But I bet you'd go there yourself just so you could visit the center of power. Right?"

Max paused, savoring the man's fear, then said, "Yeah, that's it. I can see it in your eyes."

"Please don't kill me!" Krakowski said, gasping for breath. "I can help you! I can go to Martinson and tell him you're dead. Then you'll be free. You can go far away and be safe."

Max sneered. "Right. And all I have to do is trust you. But I like part of your plan. I won't kill you. We'll go to Martinson together."

Terror filled Krakowski's mind. "No, please! He'll kill me if I take you there!"

"I'll kill you here if you don't. That's your choice. Take me to him, and you have a chance of surviving. Get me to Martinson without warning him, and as soon as he's dead, I'll let you go."

Krakowski's terror faded, and the canny man who had successfully managed a stable of thugs and killers for years reemerged. Max watched his thoughts in amusement as Krakowski feigned fear while coolly weighing his options. Finally, Krakowski decided that his best chance was to take Max to Martinson and then immediately turn on him, claiming to his boss that he had lured Max there so that he could be destroyed.

"Okay," Krakowski said, his voice trembling. "You'll protect me from him, right? Otherwise, when he sees me with you, he'll think I've changed sides, and then I'm a dead man."

"You're putting a lot of faith in me," Max said. "How do you know I'll be able to protect you?"

It was like poking a stick into a nest of ants, Max thought, watching the thoughts scurrying through the man's brain.

"You got this far in spite of everything we threw at you," Krakowski said. "I think you can do it."

Max felt a grudging admiration.

I could never be this cool and analytical in such a situation, he thought. I guess that's why he's a criminal boss and I'm not.

"We'll take your car," he said to Krakowski. "You'll drive."

And I'll be watching you, looking for the first mental hint of the inevitable double cross.

They drove for some time, north out of the city and into the countryside. It was the wrong direction. Martinson's house—or mansion—was west of town. Max monitored Krakowski's thoughts to see if he actually intended to drive to Martinson's home and not somewhere else. Those thoughts revealed that Krakowski did intend to end up at the mansion, but he was taking a roundabout route to give himself more time to think.

"It must be really far," Max said. "This is taking a long time."

I was right, Krakowski thought. He doesn't know where it is. I can go anywhere. I'll just keep going till I lose that car tailing me. This guy won't know. He'll run out of patience eventually and just give up. I'll say I'm lost, or that I can't remember how to get there because I'm so scared.

Max twisted around and looked out the back window. He had been aware of the driver behind them ever since they'd left the city. He couldn't identify the driver, but the image of Lynnette Salzmann's face kept showing up in the driver's mind.

The woman is getting annoying, Max thought.

Aloud, he said, "Is someone following us?"

"I think so. I'm...trying to lose them."

"It's not working. For a while, there, I thought you were just driving out into the country to confuse me. I was thinking about shooting you, dumping your body out here, and taking your car."

Krakowski swallowed hard. "You're right. It's not working. I'll turn around. But what if the guy behind us follows us all the way to Mr. Martinson's home?"

"I'd say that's Mr. Martinson's problem, not ours. So where does he live?"

"Out in the foothills. West of town."

"Suburbia?"

"Sort of. I guess it's becoming suburbs. But his house is really old. I think it was there long before the suburbs, back when it was just farms and small towns out there. It's a huge place. He's got acres of land around it, with trees and a high wall around the place. You can't see any of it from the outside. The place is really something." His mind filled with images of Martinson's estate. The images were tinged with bitterness.

"Sounds like Martinson's got lots of money."

"Oh, yeah," Krakowski said.

"He pays you well, though, doesn't he? I bet you have a nice place of your own."

"Nothing like his."

The bitterness increased. I do the dirty work, Krakowski thought, and Martinson gets the dough, the fucker. I do all the dangerous work. I should be getting a lot more.

Status envy in the criminal underworld, Max thought, intrigued despite the situation. Maybe all human organizations are basically the same.

"Maybe he should be paying you more," Max said.

"No shit."

"Once he's out of the way, maybe you can become the big boss and get the big bucks."

He's right! Krakowski thought. Maybe I'd better help this guy for real.

His mind filled with images of himself as lord of the manor—the manor that currently belonged to Martinson. Beautiful women suddenly materialized to cater to him.

"Yeah," he said softly.

"It's a good thing you're a man of simple tastes," Max said. "Is the tail still with us?"

Krakowski glanced in the rearview mirror. "Yeah, he is."

Max closed his eyes and focused. For a brief moment, he glimpsed the rear end of Krakowski's car and picked up the image of his own face in the eyes of the driver of the car behind them.

He knew no more about the driver than before. There was a connection to Lynnette Salzmann, but what was it? Was this something to worry about?

They had entered the western suburbs.

"Lose him," Max said.

"I'm not really trained for that kind of driving," Krakowski said nervously.

"I don't think he is, either. Turn off your lights. Turn corners randomly. Use your imagination."

Krakowski obeyed—tentatively at first, but with growing confidence and even enjoyment. His enthusiasm grew to the point that his speeding down the dimly lit streets began to make Max nervous.

The thoughts from the car behind grew startled, alarmed, angry, and finally faded away.

"He's gone," Max said. "Turn on your headlights again."

"Are you sure? Maybe I should keep doing this for a while."

"No! Drive normally. Slow down. Stop screeching around corners."

To Max's relief, Krakowski obeyed.

He was also lost. He was trying to act calm, but his thoughts told Max that the preceding bout of wild driving and random turning of corners had taken them to an area Krakowski didn't recognize.

Max tried to keep his anger from showing. "How much longer?" he asked.

"Oh, not much. We're getting close."

"Five minutes? Ten?"

"Yeah. About that."

Idiot, Max thought.

He was tempted to shove the man out of the car and take over, but that wouldn't help. He had even less idea where they were than Krakowski did. He forced himself to stay calm and watch the panicked thoughts scurrying through Krakowski's mind. Sooner or later, Max hoped, the man would recognize something in their surroundings and orient himself.

It took quite a while, but it finally happened. The street signs at an intersection rang a bell in Krakowski's mind, and he cheered up considerably. "Not long now," he said.

Max didn't reply. He had caught strong mental emanations of anger, along with an image of an ugly version of himself that he knew all too well. The follower they had lost had been replaced by Lynnette herself.

She's a damned bloodhound, he thought. Doesn't she ever give up?

Krakowski braked suddenly.

Red lights were flashing ahead of them, and a bell was ringing. A railroad crossing arm was slowly lowering in front of them. Fear of being hit by an oncoming train filled Krakowski's mind.

"Step on it!" Max yelled.

Krakowski gripped the steering wheel and pressed his foot even harder on the brake.

"Can't," he said. "Blocked."

"God damn you! You could have made it."

"You said to drive more carefully." Fear of the train warred in his mind with fear of Max.

"I didn't mean—" Max took a deep breath. "Well, it's too late now. Who knows how long we'll be stuck here?"

He watched through Lynnette's eyes as she crept closer to his car, imagining herself invisible to him.

He could have laughed at that, but he had the beginnings of a headache.

Not surprising, he thought, considering everything that's been going on and what's ahead of me. Why is she checking the license plate? That doesn't matter. She's telling herself that I'm in this car. We'll see what she does with that information.

The train passed, and the gate arm lifted.

"Get moving," Max growled.

Krakowski stamped on the accelerator, and the car lurched forward, bumping wildly across the tracks.

"But try not to kill us," Max added.

About fifteen minutes later, they turned into a long, wide, curving concrete driveway lined with tall old trees.

Lynnette had been staying far back, far enough to make her thoughts faint, but not far enough that Max couldn't detect her. He thought she had stopped when Krakowski had turned into the driveway, but he couldn't be sure.

Probably won't follow us in, Max thought. Wise decision. I'll have to do something about her sooner or later, but what?

He was tired of her obsession with him.

Childish bitch, he thought.

The image of the baby lying on its back in the road beside

him as his mother died giving birth to him suddenly filled his mind. It was the old, terrible nightmare image. For just a moment, it drove Lynnette's mental presence away. Even Krakowski's thoughts became faint.

Dangerous, Max told himself. Get control of yourself. Stay in control.

The image faded, and the thoughts of the two others returned.

The trees fell away and the driveway straightened, revealing a huge, sprawling, three-story stone house.

Max whistled. "I can smell the money."

"Yeah. There's a shitload of it."

Krakowski stopped the car with the house a short distance away.

"How do you want to do this?" he asked. "They know we're here by now. There should have been armed men coming to check us out already. I wonder where they are."

"Maybe one of them is up on that roof with a sniper rifle aimed at the middle of your forehead."

Krakowski jumped and turned white.

"But probably not, since they know you."

Max was puzzled, though. He could read Krakowski's memories of previous visits to this place, when heavily armed men had indeed shown up to stop the car and inspect it carefully for hidden weapons or explosives. Martinson was normally well protected, but today he wasn't. Why not?

"Drive up close to the front door," Max said. "We'll get out and knock. Something's bound to happen sooner or later."

Krakowski drove forward slowly, his fear increasing.

"Jesus Christ!" Max said. "Step on it!"

The car lurched forward and then screeched to a halt in front of the concrete steps leading up to the big, ornate wooden door.

"Come on." Max jumped from the car, bounded up the steps, and pounded on the door.

The banging echoed within as though the house were empty, and Max was fairly certain it was. He had been straining his senses from the moment they passed through the wide-open entry gates. He had detected no human minds other than his own, Krakowski's, and Lynnette's.

Perhaps people were there, but for some reason, he couldn't detect them. Perhaps they were mindreaders who could keep him from reading their minds. But if that were the case, he would surely have been killed or taken captive by now.

He tried the doorknob. It turned smoothly, and the door opened.

"Is this normal?" he asked Krakowski.

The other man shook his head. "It's always locked." He pointed at the wall above them, where a surveillance camera was mounted, aimed at them. "You don't get in unless they like what they see."

"Then I guess they like what they see. Or they've gone. You've been abandoned."

Senses straining, Max stepped forward into the foyer. Darkness lay beyond. Max fumbled at the wall beside the door, searching for a light switch and not finding one.

Suddenly, overhead lights came on, bathing the foyer in brightness.

Both men froze.

Finally, his voice strained, Krakowski said, "It does that. I think it's motion sensors."

Still, Max could catch no hint of minds other than theirs and Lynnette's, and he could tell that hers was distant.

He looked around at the paneling, the landscapes on the

walls, the furniture, and said, "I like this place. You'll be happy living here."

Krakowski panicked again. "Don't say that aloud!"

Max laughed. "Too late."

I bet you've been feeling envy and resentment every time you come here, he thought. Martinson surely read those thoughts, and he's only letting you live because you're useful to him.

"Where does he usually meet with you?" Max asked.

"There's an office up ahead," Krakowski said, pointing.

"Lead the way."

Krakowski crept forward.

"Faster!" Max barked.

Shivering, scarcely able to walk, Krakowski made his way across the foyer to a closed door at the far end. He put his hand on the doorknob and hesitated.

"I can't just— I've always been shown in before."

"God Almighty," Max muttered. He pushed Krakowski aside and opened the door.

Lights came on as he stepped inside.

"Motion sensors," Krakowski repeated, sounding uncertain.

The office beyond was huge and as expensively appointed as the foyer. A giant desk of some heavy, dark wood occupied the center of the room.

As Max had expected, the room was uninhabited to his sight and to his probing mind.

"That's a big desk for a big bad guy," he said, but he wondered what to do next. He was in the supervillain's lair, but there was no supervillain.

Anticlimactic, he thought.

Krakowski stepped around him and went up to the desk. "There's an envelope on the desk. That's weird."

"All of this is weird. What's in it?"

Krakowski picked up a letter opener from the desk. Max tensed reflexively, but there was no hint in Krakowski's mind that he planned an attack.

Krakowski opened the envelope and drew out a folded sheet. "I shouldn't be doing this," he said. "This is Mr. Martinson's—"

Max growled and snatched the paper from his hand. He unfolded it and read the words hand printed on it:

Max Iverson, call your parents.

Max froze in astonishment. He couldn't think, and for a moment, even the background buzz of Krakowski's busy thoughts disappeared.

Mechanically, he pulled his phone from his pocket. The signal was weak, but he punched in his father and stepmother's number anyway.

His father answered almost immediately. "Max! What's going on? What have you done? There are men here with guns. They said you—"

There were some muffled sounds. His father cried out in pain. Then a new voice came over the line, one Max didn't recognize.

"Hi there, Junior Iverson. You better get down here ASAP."

"Who the fuck is this? What do you want?"

"We want you. You have...um, let's say twenty-four hours. After that, we'll kill them."

Anger swept over Max. "Those are my parents. Mine. You tell Martinson that if—"

"Twenty-four hours, Junior. Then they're dead."

The line went dead.

"They're mine," Max repeated. "That fucker."

"What's going on?" Krakowski said.

Max glanced at his watch. "Shit. I've got to get to the airport. Your car. Give me the keys."

"But— Okay." Krakowski handed his keys over. "Or I can drive. I'll drop you off at the airport."

"You're staying here."

Max stalked from the house, filled with outrage.

I'll show that bastard, he thought. You don't fuck around with something that's mine.

He opened the car door and climbed in behind the steering wheel.

Krakowski was right behind him. "Don't leave me here! I don't know what they'll do to me when they get back."

"Get away from the car," Max said through gritted teeth. He slammed the door, locked it, and turned the ignition key.

Krakowski was yanking at the door handle.

Max put the car in gear, turned the wheel, and stepped on the gas.

Krakowski was knocked off his feet. One leg went under the car. Max couldn't hear the bones crunching, but he could hear Krakowski's mental scream of agony.

"Idiot," Max muttered.

He sped away.

16

Lynnette shrieked into her phone, "You lost him? How?"

"It wasn't me," Freddy whined. "It was one of my guys."

She pulled over to the curb. "What happened?"

"Your man was somewhere in the western suburbs. It's getting dark, and there aren't a lot of streetlights out there. My guy...got scared and turned back. He couldn't help it. I'm sorry."

"You're going to jail."

Lynnette ignored Freddy's pleas and blubbering while she wondered what to do next.

"Give me the exact location where he last saw him."

Freddy did so.

She stared at her phone and felt sick. The quickest route to the location Freddy had given her would take her past the house where she was born and her parents had died. She had avoided that entire part of the city all her life.

But I'm near there, she thought. Maybe I can find Iverson myself.

She had to do it.

"Car," she said. "Make, model, year, color, license plate."

"Huh?"

"You must have all of that if your perverts were able to follow him."

"Oh. Right. Yeah. I'll text that to you."

She read the text and started moving again.

Freddy was probably waiting to talk with her again, hoping to change her mind about jail.

Go to hell, she thought.

She drove west. It was twilight, and Freddy was right about the streetlights.

The streets were empty. She drove aimlessly, angrier by the minute, losing hope steadily. How could she find Iverson? How could she get the goods on him by driving aimlessly?

A double flash of red ahead. Brake lights!

She sped up. Her headlights were turned off, and she resisted the instinctive impulse to turn them on.

As she drew closer, she could see that the car ahead of her had its lights on, but the tail lights were dim. She got as close as she thought wise, just in case it was Iverson in the car. As far as she could tell in the fading light, the car matched Freddy's description. She couldn't read the license plate, so she wasn't sure.

How close should she get?

The car she was following stopped at a railroad crossing to let a train past.

Christ, Lynnette thought, we could be stuck here forever. Some of these damned trains are infinitely long.

She took the opportunity to creep closer. She trusted she was effectively invisible to the other driver thanks to the dim light and her own car's dark color.

He'll only know I'm here if he's looking for me, she thought. And why would he do that?

The license plate matched.

Iverson! she thought. Who needs the Pervert Tracking Network? I've got you now, you bastard. Now I'll find out what you're up to.

Thankfully, the train was not a long one, and it was moving fast. It took only a few minutes to rumble by. There was a light dangling from the side of the caboose at the end of the train. It flashed past, but as it did, she caught the silhouette of two people in the car in front of her.

An accomplice, she thought. A criminal accomplice! This could be even better than I'd hoped.

She let Iverson's car cross the tracks and pull some distance ahead before she started moving again.

The car ahead of her drove fast. Once more, she was tempted to turn on her headlights, but she controlled herself. She stayed as far behind Iverson as she dared. She didn't want to lose him, but given how he had somehow known before when she was following him, she was also afraid to get too close. What she had done at the railroad tracks had been out of necessity. That no longer applied.

There was a working streetlight up ahead, a bright one. She slowed still more, thinking she'd catch up to him again after he was well beyond the light. Instead, his brake lights came on, he turned right, and his tail lights disappeared.

She cursed and turned on her headlights. In their light and that of the streetlight, she could see a high brick wall to her right. There was a break in the wall ahead, opposite the streetlight. That was no doubt where Iverson had turned off.

This doesn't look like new suburbia, she thought. Where are we?

She passed the opening in the wall, pulled over to the curb, and parked.

What was this place? What to do now? She couldn't very well follow Iverson inside. Her car would be too obvious. Should she wait here for him to leave and then keep following him?

I could go inside on foot, she thought. Just a short distance, enough to get some idea of what's going on.

She wanted to go inside. She was drawn to the place in a way she couldn't put her finger on.

Ridiculous, she told herself, trying to shake off the feeling. I'll wait here a bit longer and then decide what to do.

She waited for a long time, her frustration growing. She had always hated being controlled by others. Now here she was, letting Iverson, a man she despised, dictate her course of action.

The hell with it, she thought. I'll drive in after him and find out what's going on in there.

She was about start her engine when Iverson's car rocketed out of the driveway, turned left on the road, tires squealing, and then shot away. Its dim taillights dwindled quickly.

I'll lose him! Lynnette thought.

She started her car, put it in gear, and was about to make a U turn and step on the gas, when she stepped on the brake instead.

Why follow Iverson? The Pervert Tracking Network would pick him up. She wanted to know what was in the place he had just come from. What was there that had drawn him and that he was now fleeing? There must be something incriminating in there, something she could use against him, something that would make Grady forget that she had disobeyed his order not to follow Iverson, something that would finally turn Grady against the man.

She took her foot off the brake, made the U turn, and then turned into the driveway. She drove slowly, not sure what she was looking for. In her headlights, the shadowy trees lining the drive made the place strange, confusing, and forbidding.

She drove down the long driveway until she saw the huge house at the end of it. She stopped her car and stared at the building in amazement. How could a place like this exist out here? She felt as if she had suddenly stepped onto the surface of another world.

Her headlights caught movement ahead of her on the ground in front of the house. Something lay there.

A guard dog? she wondered.

She checked to make sure all her windows were rolled up.

Whatever it was, it was staying where it was, not approaching her. She stared at the object, trying to make it out.

Suddenly it became clear. It was a man, and he was injured.

Iverson's doing, she thought. Maybe that's what he was running from.

She turned her engine off and got out of the car slowly and cautiously. Just as slowly and cautiously, she approached the injured man. She stopped, fumbled for her cell phone, and activated the flashlight. She swept the beam over the ground and the man.

His eyes were half closed, and he was muttering words she couldn't make out. His right leg was bent at a thirty-degree angle halfway down the shin. Red-white splintered bone stuck out, and blood covered the ground beneath him.

"Oh, my God!" Lynnette said. "Sir, are you all right?" She realized immediately what an absurd question that was. "What happened to you?"

"Iverson," he said.

"Max Iverson did this to you? That piece of shit!"

The man on the ground moaned.

"How did he do it?" she asked.

This could be it, she thought, what I need on that bastard.

"My car."

"Your car? What? Never mind. I'll go to the house for help."

He became more alert at that. "No! Stay away from there!

It's dangerous."

"But you need help."

"No one's there. Martinson's gone."

"Martinson?"

"He's not home. He tried to kill Iverson. Iverson tried to kill him."

"Why?"

"Iverson fights bad guys."

The alertness faded, and his speech became rambling fragments of sentences—mostly meaningless, but there was enough there for Lynnette to gather that this man had accompanied Max Iverson here to stop Martinson from doing something evil.

"You're not making any sense," she insisted.

His mind's gone because of the pain and the loss of blood, she thought. I've got to get help for him. He might be a useful witness.

She checked her phone. There were no bars.

"Martinson," the man said. "Controls everything."

"Who's Martinson?"

"Felix Martinson. Mr. Martinson. My boss. Big boss. Big, big, big. Biggest. Top man. He'll kill Iverson. You too."

"Yeah, okay."

The name Martinson meant something to her, but she couldn't say what. I'll look him up later, she thought.

"Scary man. Pain. Pain, pain, scary, scary…"

He's out of his mind, she thought.

She said, "There's no signal here. I'll take you to a hospital. Let's get you in my car. Stand up."

He muttered something.

"Come on, stand up! You're too big for me to carry you."

He said nothing.

"For Christ's sake," Lynnette muttered. "All right. Let's see." She bent and put her arms under his armpits. "Now!" she said, and heaved with all her might.

He came halfway to his feet. Then he screamed and collapsed. He lay unmoving, moaning faintly.

"God damn it," Lynnette muttered.

The man on the ground stopped moaning.

What now? There was no way she could drag him to her car and pull him into it without his cooperation.

She checked her phone again. Still no signal.

Maybe I *should* try the house, she thought. Maybe someone is there, and it's not dangerous. This guy's crazy with pain. His mind isn't working properly.

But she couldn't bring herself to approach the place. There was something about the house that frightened her. She couldn't say what, and she cursed her own irrationality. But there it was, and she couldn't overcome it.

"All right," she said. "Stay here. Don't move."

The unconscious man obeyed her.

"I'll drive till I get a signal, and then I'll call for help."

She felt silly talking to him, but it made her feel a bit less guilty about leaving him.

I should have his name and address, she thought. Just in case it's something I can use against Iverson.

She searched his pockets until she found his wallet. She shone her flashlight on his driver's license and committed his name and address to her ever-reliable memory.

"I'll be back as soon as I can," she said.

She went back to her car and drove slowly down the now-dark driveway. The trees on either side had become looming threats in the glow from her headlights, and she breathed a sigh of relief when she reached the light cast by the streetlight across from the driveway's exit.

She turned right, parked at the curb, and checked her phone again. There was a signal, but it was very weak.

She drove a few hundred feet and stopped again. The signal was a bit stronger. She hoped it would be good enough.

As she was about to punch 911 into her phone, lights flashed in her rearview mirror. She twisted around and saw a line of headlights. Illuminated by the streetlight, a convoy of black SUVs turned right into the driveway behind her.

She wondered if that was the mysterious Martinson returning to his house. She decided that the wisest course of action for her would be to leave right now.

What about the injured man? she asked herself. Oh, Martinson will take care of him.

So she hoped.

She drove off feeling guilty, but with each mile, her feelings of guilt decreased and her curiosity about Martinson grew. By the time she reached her destination, guilt had disappeared entirely and Felix Martinson obsessed her.

Lynnette had intended to go home and relax, but the name "Felix Martinson" nagged at her too much. Instead, she drove downtown, to the City and County Building, parked, and used her keycard to enter the locked building.

She showed her badge to the lobby guard, who gave it a cursory glance, and then she took the elevator to the floor her office was on.

Here she wasn't limited to Google or other such search engines. In this office, she had access to a literal world of criminal databases.

She sat at her desk, logged on, and began.

Lights showed in some of the windows of the office building across the street—other wage slaves working too late, just as she was. She didn't see any of that. She saw only her computer screen.

She found little mention of Martinson in the databases she searched. He had been flagged as suspicious by some agencies, but they had nothing solid on him.

Some criminal mastermind! she thought. Maybe Krakowski was hallucinating. Or maybe he was simply lying to me. But why would he have done that? What would have been in it for him? Was he even capable of lying, in his condition? Maybe I should search for him instead of Martinson.

She entered Krakowski's name into the search screen. The results were slightly more interesting. The man was suspected of involvement in contract killings, but again, nothing could be pinned on him. It was all suspicion and conjecture, although less insubstantial than in Martinson's case.

Yet it was enough to cause Lynnette to think that Krakowski had not invented the things he had said to her.

But in that case, she thought, Iverson isn't working for the other side. He's a good guy.

Her emotions rebelled. She had to find evidence of Max Iverson's guilt.

She returned to Felix Martinson.

Years earlier, a search warrant had been executed on a property of his. An informant had told the police that evidence of a crime was to be found there. But the search had turned up nothing. The police were convinced that Martinson had known they were coming and had had the evidence removed.

He must have had an informant in the police department, Lynnette thought. Someone like Max Iverson!

Like Iverson, perhaps, but not Iverson. She knew his

complete history, and a boring history it was. He had never been near the Piketon police department. He was innocent—at least of this.

She sighed and continued searching.

Now she wanted to find out about Martinson's business interests rather than any possible criminal activities. Without deliberately looking for it, she hit upon something.

There were deaths and disappearances associated with Martinson. Some were people he had competed with in business. Others were acquaintances, some of those of long standing. The number of such cases had focused investigatorial attention on him, but to no end. Nothing could be found implicating him in those deaths and disappearances.

Lynnette's anger grew.

I bet I could have found something, she thought. Incompetent fools.

The names in those cases of death and disappearance struck a bell. Where had she seen them before? Why, in her search for Krakowski!

She repeated her earlier searches on "Carl Krakowski." Yes, there they were: the same names. Her memory was as dependable as always. She had often wished she could forget the past, at least selectively, but at this moment, she was glad that her mind gripped facts and memories and refused to let them go.

Men employed by Krakowski's company, an insurance brokerage, had been suspects in a number of those deaths and a few of the disappearances. Once again, nothing had come of the initial investigations. As with Martinson, suspicions had been raised and then apparently filed away and forgotten.

Krakowski said he works for Martinson, Lynnette thought. Now I know what his job is: He kills people for his boss.

Why hadn't others seen this connection? It was so obvious to her. It didn't require a memory like hers. Simple database searches should have revealed it.

Maybe they did see it, she thought. Maybe Martinson has made himself immune. Blackmail? Extortion? Does he have damaging information on people? Or is it just that he has lots of money? Corruption is everywhere.

How she hated those people—the rich who bought others, and those who were willing to be bought. She wanted to see them rooted out, and she knew just the man to do it: Grady Jacobs.

Grady needs more power, she thought. I'm going to help him get it. He can make fun of what he calls my girl detective act all he wants. He'll change his tune when he's DA. Or attorney general. Or governor. President someday. I'll be the one who gets him there. He'll see how much he needs me and only me.

She dwelt happily for a moment in that imagined future. Then the image of Karen Jacobs intruded, and happiness gave way to fury.

But right now, Martinson was her target, not Karen Jacobs. Her anger focused on Martinson, the corrupter.

She needed something solid on Martinson, something she could give to Jacobs. But how to get it? She had reached the limit of what she could get from databases. Now she had to get more from the man himself.

He can't corrupt me, she thought. He can't blackmail or extort me. I've never done anything he can use against me. I'll go back there and confront him. I'll force the truth out of him.

The small remaining voice of reason in her head warned her that that was not a good idea, but she ignored it.

What about Iverson? she thought. Is he innocent after all?

She was suddenly sure of it.

He's on our side. Krakowski even told me that. Should I contact him? Ask him to help?

No. That was too much. She still detested Iverson because... She couldn't say why. She just knew that she couldn't stand the man.

The window of her office was gray with the light of dawn. The building across the road was dark. The obsessed workers there had gone home hours earlier.

She would go home, wash up, and then drive to Martinson's estate. But first, just in case something went wrong, and in obedience to the faint whispering of that dying voice of reason, she would write an email to Grady Jacobs telling him what she knew and what she planned. She would include everything, including her new conviction that Max Iverson was trustworthy.

She wouldn't send it right away. She would set it to send later. How much later?

Twenty-four hours, she thought. Tomorrow morning.

That would give her all the time she needed. With any luck, she would be back at her computer before that time elapsed, and then she should be in a position to add much more solid information to the email.

Enough to get Grady into the governor's mansion, she thought. And after that, the White House. And I'll be there with him.

17

All the way to the airport, Max worried about the availability of flights to Phoenix. He realized that he should have taken the time while at Martinson's house to use his phone to check for the next flight.

It was hard to concentrate on such practical thoughts. His senses seemed heightened, his mindreading abilities more powerful than ever. It was too much. Was someone still following him? He couldn't tell. He couldn't think. The collective mind of the city flooded into him, distracting him, angering him.

He gripped the steering wheel and shouted, "Shut up!"

He wondered if he should pull over and check for flights on his phone instead of driving. Then outrage overcame him again. He could think only of getting to his parents' home and killing Martinson and whatever men he had with him.

And I'll do it, too, he thought. I know I can. That fucker doesn't know what I'm capable of.

He parked as close to the terminal as he could. He hesitated. What about his gun? He couldn't get it through security.

Doesn't matter, he thought. I won't need it. Bare hands are better.

He thought of the ways he would kill Martinson and his

men with his bare hands, and he smiled in anticipatory pleasure.

He put the gun in the glove compartment.

He thought of leaving the car unlocked and with the keys in the ignition. Krakowski deserved that. But then he realized that he would need the car again when he returned, so he locked the car doors and dropped the keys into his pocket as he walked toward the terminal.

He was in luck. There was a flight leaving in an hour, with plenty of seats available.

Sitting on the plane waiting for takeoff, Max indulged in murderous fantasies about exactly what he would do to the men holding his parents captive.

Or I could just let those guys do whatever they want, he thought. I don't owe Mom and— Tim and Mary. I don't owe those two anything. They murdered my mother, and they lied to me my whole life.

Anger at the two old people filled him. He was about to undo his seatbelt and leave the plane when it began to move.

He settled back, resigned.

Oh well, he thought, if I don't show up, that won't stop Martinson. He'll just have them both killed and then come after me again. I have to put a stop to this once and for all.

Max became aware of intense discomfort in his groin. He heard a baby crying. He twisted in his seat, trying to locate the source of the sound.

A few rows back, a young mother sitting in an aisle seat leaned into view and then back out of view again. She was rocking her baby, trying to soothe it back into sleep.

Christ, lady, Max thought, what the hell is wrong with you? Change the kid's diaper. I can feel the poop from all the way over here.

He shifted uncomfortably in his seat.

A couple across the aisle were arguing in what they thought were low enough voices that their fellow passengers wouldn't be able to hear them. Max could hear every word in their thoughts. He could feel their growing anger with each other, their increasing hatred.

This is a nightmare, he thought. I have to find a way to keep these thoughts out of my head when I don't want to hear them.

The plane began moving, gathering speed, its engines roaring. The baby with the soiled diaper cried louder. As the plane lifted off and started to climb, the cries became screams. Max heard other passengers thinking that they hoped the kid wasn't going to scream all the way to Phoenix.

The higher the plane climbed, the fainter those thoughts became. He could still hear the baby crying, but now he was hearing it only with his ears, and he was no longer aware of the infant's physical sensations.

Just as on his previous flight to Phoenix, his ability to read minds was fading as the plane rose and drew farther away from Piketon.

As mental quiet descended, Max felt calmer. His anger faded. He wondered exactly what danger his father and stepmother were in and whether he could do anything about it. Perhaps getting this flight had been a mistake. Such impulsiveness was not characteristic of him. It was as if he had been possessed by the souls of the violent thugs he had killed, and now, as the plane rose and his access to the thoughts of others faded, those souls inside him were fading, too.

The previous time, the mental deafness had lasted during the flight, during his time in Phoenix, and during the flight back. Normality had only returned after he had been home in Piketon for a few days.

And even then, he thought, it took Lynnette's mental

scream to do the trick.

What about this time? Would his mindreading return on its own, or was it gone forever? He had no idea, but he couldn't worry about that now. He had to make this trip. He didn't know what would happen when he got there. He could only hope that the deadly skills he had absorbed from his victims were still there, still deeply ingrained in him.

The baby had stopped crying. The couple across the aisle were sitting in stony silence. No thoughts intruded from anyone on the plane. The engines droned steadily. The last few hours caught up with Max, and he fell asleep.

He dreamed he was talking to his mother. She looked like a younger version of her sister, his stepmother, but far more beautiful. She was the woman he knew only from photographs, the young wife whose photos his father still kept on the mantel in the living room.

She looked angry. "Why are you going down there to help them?" she demanded. "Risking your life for them? They murdered me. You owe them nothing. Leave them to their fate."

"It's me the bad guys really want," dream Max said. "They'll come after me whether I go to Phoenix or not. I have to put an end to this. Anyway, I'm the only one with the right to punish Dad and...your sister."

His mother glared at him.

He felt guilty and was trying to formulate a better answer when a voice intruded.

"We are beginning our descent into Phoenix Sky Harbor Airport."

Max awoke, feeling groggy. He listened, not quite comprehending as the voice told him to please make sure his seat was in the full upright position and to be careful because luggage in the overhead compartments could have shifted.

He had no luggage with him. As soon as he was in the terminal, he went outside and caught the shuttle bus to the car rental center.

All the while, he was trying to plan ahead. He strained to hear thoughts, but he failed. He felt blind. He was unarmed.

Back home, that had not been a problem. He had taken guns from his enemies without difficulty. This was an entirely different situation. Should he buy a gun before he headed for his father's house? He imagined that would be easy in Phoenix, but he didn't know that for sure, and he had no idea how to go about doing it. It was something he had never thought about doing before. The knowledge of how to buy a gun in Phoenix was probably in many of the minds he passed in the terminal, but that knowledge was now inaccessible to him.

He was frustrated and increasingly frightened. What if the men holding his parents were mindreaders? He would be helpless against them.

He paused in mid-stride. Maybe his mother was right. Maybe he should give up and catch the next flight home.

He rebelled at the thought. His anger returned. He gritted his teeth.

Can't back out now, he thought.

Before long, he was once again headed west on I-10 in a car that had been baking in the sun. It was night, but the car was still hot, and the air outside felt like an oven. This time, the air conditioning was barely functional. He didn't bother with the radio. He was too worried about what would happen next to look for music or fret about his physical discomfort. There was a good chance he'd soon be cold and dead.

He drove through the same suburbia again, pink stucco glowing in his headlights, and eventually came to the small stucco house, its porch light showing the nearly dead tree in front of it. The driveway was empty. A strange car, a new Chevrolet Malibu, was parked in front of the house. Max parked behind it, turned off the headlights and engine, and sat in the car for a while, trying to calm his breathing.

He closed his eyes and focused.

Nothing. He was still mentally blind.

He sighed in resignation, got out of the car, and walked toward the front door. Everything looked normal. He wasn't sure how he had expected it to look. Different, somehow.

The door opened as he approached it.

A man stood in the doorway, illuminated by the porch light. The man was tall and heavily muscled. Big though Max was, he felt small in comparison.

The waiting man smiled in a smug, contemptuous way that immediately filled Max with rage. "Junior. You made it."

"Let them go."

The man nodded. "We will. We'll keep our side of the agreement. I'll even give you a chance to say a tearful farewell to them."

"Where's Martinson? I want to talk to him."

"Oh, he's not here. He's staying far away from you. He doesn't want to talk to you."

"You said 'we.'"

"I meant me. I'm the only one here."

"Just one man for this job?"

The man snorted. "Look at me. Look at you. Yeah, just one man."

Max's fear faded away. He could feel the continued, reassuring presence of the violence he had absorbed.

"Overconfidence is weakness," Max said.

"You get that from a Kung Fu movie?"

But proper confidence is strength, Max thought. I'm going

to cut off your balls and make you eat them.

There was no response from the other man, no annoyance, no amusement.

Max thought it again, trying to do so more emphatically this time, trying to make his thoughts more powerful.

I'm going to cut off your balls and make you eat them.

Still no response.

Not a mindreader, Max thought. He can't read my mind any more than I can read his.

"Move aside so I can go to my parents," Max said.

The man stepped back inside the house, out of the way. "Make it quick."

"Mom? Dad?"

Max had used those names without thinking, but when he walked into the living room and saw his father and stepmother sitting tied to chairs, gagged, looking terrified, he was glad he had.

Max turned around and glared at the thug, who had closed the front door and come up behind him.

"Untie them," Max said. "Now."

"You don't give me orders, you piece of shit."

"I'm going to cut off your balls and make you eat them."

The other man's mouth opened in surprise, and then he burst out laughing. "I'm going to kill you slowly, Junior."

Max shrank back, feigning fear.

The thug smirked and moved forward, relaxed, filled with confidence. He didn't see the punch coming. Max's fist smashed into his throat. He stumbled backwards, struggling to breathe. He fell to one knee.

Max picked up his fifth-grade candlestick. He swung it up and brought it down with all his strength on the thug's head.

He could feel the crack through his arm as the man

collapsed on the floor.

Max moved his hand from side to side, feeling the satisfying weight of the candlestick.

Solid, he thought. Dad's right about the heft and the weld.

The man lying at his feet moved slightly and moaned.

Solid, unlike your skull, Max thought.

He bent forward and smashed the sharp edge of the candlestick's base onto the man's skull. The man stopped moving, but Max kept hitting him until his skull was misshapen and Max was sure he was dead.

Max dropped the candlestick beside the corpse and straightened. He turned to his parents, who had been watching wide–eyed.

"Don't worry," Max said. "I didn't really mean that stuff about his balls."

He untied them.

"Are you all right?" he asked. "Other than being scared, I mean. Did he hurt you?"

His father shook his head. He stood up slowly and then helped his wife to stand.

She looked even frailer than the last time Max had seen her. His father, robust when Max had visited before, seemed old and weak.

They're close to death, Max thought.

Sadness and a sense of impending loss warred with the anger he had felt toward both of them since his last visit.

They murdered my mother! he reminded himself.

But he couldn't muster the same outrage as before. How could he weigh the terrible thing they had done against the years of nurturing love they had given him?

Later, he told himself. Think about that later.

"I was too scared to do anything," his father said. "I just

followed his orders." He looked ashamed.

"That's okay," Max said. "These people are killers. You did the right thing. Is your car in the garage?"

"Sure. Of course."

"How about his?" He kicked the corpse.

His father shuddered. "I don't know. I guess he must have parked somewhere on the street."

"Did someone drop him off?"

"I don't know."

If someone did drop him off, Max thought, they'll probably be coming back. Maybe the car in front of the house is his. Let's hope so.

"We're not far from the desert, the way I remember," he said.

"That was five years ago, when I took you out there. The desert's farther away now. There are more houses."

"How far would I have to drive to get to someplace where there are no paved roads and no traffic?"

His father looked bewildered.

Max repeated the question.

"Oh. Um, maybe ten miles. Fifteen."

"Okay. I'm going to put this garbage—" he kicked the corpse again "—in your trunk. But first..."

He searched the dead man's clothing. The blood and brains soaking into the rug bothered him, but not enough to stop him. In one pants pocket, he found a cell phone and a car key fob with the Chevrolet logo on it. In the other pocket, he found a pistol.

Overconfident son of a bitch, he thought. He didn't even bother showing the gun. He was so sure that he was menacing enough without it that we would do what he wanted. He was right about them, just not about me.

"That's good," he said, straightening. He slipped the keys

and phone into his pocket. He held the pistol in his hand. "Okay. Let's hope that's his car in front of the house. I'll be driving it. I'll follow you. You'll drive to the place without roads or traffic you were thinking of, and we'll get rid of him there."

"Shouldn't you put that down?" his father said, pointing to the gun. "It could be loaded."

"It is."

"It's dangerous! You could hurt yourself!"

"It *is* dangerous, and I know how to use it."

"How do you know how to use a gun?"

"I was taught by the best." By the dying brains of killers I killed, Max thought.

His father stared at him, speechless.

"Shouldn't we call the police?" Mary said.

"I don't know if we can trust them. It's best if we do this quietly and not draw police attention to you."

"But he knew about you," his father said. "He came here to get you. He phoned you. I heard him threatening you."

Max nodded. "Yes. And when we're done here, I'm going to eliminate the threat."

"I think you should go to the police."

"Don't worry about it. I know how to take care of this. If you contact the police, you'll be putting yourselves in danger."

"But—" His father at Max and looked away quickly, frightened. "Okay, son. Whatever you say."

"Paper towels?"

"What?"

"Where are the paper towels? Still in the kitchen?"

"Oh. Yes."

Max went into the kitchen, tore off a lot of paper towels, and returned. He wiped the candlestick carefully, hoping he was getting all the human remnants off it. Fortunately, its surface was smooth.

Good thing I didn't have the skill to make it fancier when I was a kid, he thought.

He dropped the wet wad of paper towels on the carpet next to the corpse and took the candlestick back into the kitchen. He put it in the sink and washed it carefully and repeatedly with dish soap and water. What was left on the candlestick of the dead thug disappeared down the drain.

Will that be enough? he wondered. What if the police suspect the man was murdered here, and they search the house thoroughly? Will they find his DNA in spite of my cleaning? I should have tried to learn more about police investigative techniques when I was in Jacobs' office. Then I wouldn't have to depend on what I've seen on TV cop shows.

He'd have to hope for the best. On the bright side, thanks to what they had seen him using the candlestick for, maybe his parents would finally get rid of the damned thing.

He left the candlestick on the counter beside the sink and returned to the living room.

"What's happened?" Mary asked. "What are you involved in?"

"Nothing illegal. Don't worry. I'm working with the police."

"You're an undercover policeman?" his father asked in astonishment.

"Not exactly. Well, something like that."

He wished he could read their minds, could know the right words to take away their fear and make them cooperative. Suddenly, his patience deserted him.

"Christ, Dad. Just do what I say, okay?"

"Okay! Okay. Sure. Of course."

Max rolled up the rug with the corpse in it and heaved the gruesome bundle onto his shoulder. In death, the man was surprisingly light, even insubstantial, compared to his heavy, intimidating presence in life.

He could see no blood or brains on the wooden floor. "That's good," he said. "You'll need a new rug. This one's going to the desert."

He took the wrapped body into the garage and dumped it in the trunk of his father's car. Then he went back into the house and checked the floor again for blood and brains. It looked clean.

"Dad, let's go outside and make sure the man's keys work on that car parked outside. You'll drive it out to the desert, and I'll follow you in your car."

"Now?"

"Yes, now. Well, no. Not in the dark. We'll do it in the morning. I'm sure you both need a good night's sleep to recover."

He wondered how well they would sleep. He wondered how well he would.

Hesitantly, his father said, "I don't like driving strange cars. Couldn't we do it the other way around?"

"No. In case we're stopped, I want you in the clear."

Even as he said that, Max realized that if they were stopped, they'd both be in trouble, no matter who was driving which car. He'd have to cross that bridge if he came to it.

"I don't know what you mean," his father said.

"Never mind. We're doing it the way I said. Don't argue with me."

In the morning, Max went outside and pressed the button on the dead man's key fob that had an image of an open padlock. To his relief, there was a click from the car parked in front of the house.

They ate breakfast, during which the three of them made

strained conversation, trying to pretend that all was normal and there wasn't a body in the trunk of the car in the garage. Then the two men set out.

Max followed his father through miles of winding suburban streets that petered out into a narrow road. That, in turn, became a dirt track in the desert.

He wondered how soon this arid wasteland would be swallowed by Phoenix. What would it become? Strip malls? Office buildings? Housing developments? How many more sad little saplings would be condemned to suffer and die out here?

What would happen when a construction crew or surveyors discovered the dead man with a crushed skull wrapped in a rug? Or would someone see smoke from the car and report it to the police long before developers started working there?

It won't matter, Max thought, as long as they can't connect him to us.

The dirt track ended. After a few minutes, Max blew his horn, signaling his father to stop. If they went much farther, he feared his father's car would get stuck.

They switched positions, and Max drove the Malibu for a hundred feet or so. The wheels sank into loose sand, and the car stopped moving. He switched off the engine and got out, leaving the door open. He retrieved the body wrapped in the rug from the trunk of his father's car and heaved it into the Malibu's front seat.

"Back your car up a bit," he told his father. "I want you farther away."

"Why?"

"You'll see."

Did burning cars blow up the way they did in movies, or did they just burn? He wasn't sure, but he didn't want to take any chances. Strangely, none of the memories he had absorbed from violent men answered the question. That surprised him.

Max followed his father's car on foot as the older man backed up slowly. After a while, Max held up his hand, and his father stopped. Max thought he was far enough away to be safe.

Where was the gas tank in a Malibu? He wasn't sure. Somewhere underneath, he supposed. He was facing the rear of the car. He aimed the dead man's gun at the center of the rear bumper and fired. He waited. Nothing happened. He put two more holes in the car, to the left and the right of the first one. Again, nothing happened.

This wasn't how he had imagined it. He didn't know what to do next.

Then he heard the trickling of a liquid and smelled gasoline.

Now what? he wondered. The ground beneath the car is loose sand. I should have parked it over rocks. They would have struck a spark when hit by bullets. Well, shit. Nothing ventured, nothing gained.

He fired at the trunk again, shot after shot, until he had emptied the magazine. With the last shot, he saw sparks. There was a satisfying *whoomp*. Flames shot up from under the car. The vehicle was quickly enveloped.

Max walked as close to the car as the heat allowed and threw the empty gun into the open driver–side door.

"Come on, Dad. Let's get out of here before the cops show up."

"I thought you said you were working with them."

"Not the local ones. Anyway, I'm undercover."

Tim didn't talk again until they were almost home. "What did you just do?" he asked Max.

"I gave the local police a nicely wrapped present. Odds are that guy is someone they know, and they'll be happy to see him out of action. They'll assume he was killed by other people like him."

"But what about the people who sent him?"

"They want me, not you. And I told you: I'm going to put a stop to this."

Tim moved, shifted away from him. Max could tell that he knew his son was capable of doing what he said, and it frightened him.

"I shouldn't have left her alone," Tim said suddenly. "What if more of them showed up? Damn it! Why did I leave her?"

"We had to take care of the body."

"You could have done that by yourself. You didn't need me. I didn't want anything to do with it."

They pulled into the driveway of his parents' house, and Max thought, Thank God we're here.

"Thank God we're here," his father said.

He parked in the driveway, pushed open the door, and walked as quickly as he could, almost running, to the front door.

It opened as he approached, and Mary threw herself at him. Her arms went around his neck, and she pressed against him, sobbing.

"I've been so frightened!" she said.

"Shh. It's okay," Tim said, changing from a frightened man to his wife's protector. "Come inside. It's too hot for you out here."

Max followed them, closing the door behind him. He stood there, relishing the relative coolness and watching his father fussing over Mary.

He suddenly felt far less confident about their safety. What did he really know about the thinking process of killers like the one he had just set alight? A day earlier, he would have known how they thought as thoroughly as if he were one of them—

which he was, in a way, because of what he had absorbed from the minds of such men in Piketon. But that mindreading ability had left him, and the knowledge he had taken from those minds was suddenly draining away.

He felt the beginnings of panic.

I can't go back to the way I was, he thought. I have to keep being like them so that I can fight them. If I forget what I learned, I'll be a sitting duck.

He didn't have to read their minds to know how distressed his father and stepmother were, and he felt concerned for them. If not the love he had once felt, before the revelation of the part they had played in his mother's death, it was at least sympathy for two frightened old people who had been drawn into something terrible and terrifying.

"Dad, how about one of your concoctions?"

"What?"

"Your latest drink invention. I think it would help all of us. You too, Mom."

"Maybe you're right," Tim said. "It would be good for us."

Mary said, "I shouldn't.... Oh, all right. I'll have one, too. Make mine mostly water."

The alcohol seemed to help them. Tim sat beside his wife on the couch. He still looked worried, but no longer seemed about to lose control. Mary set her half-finished drink down on an end table, leaned back, closed her eyes, and soon dozed off.

Max sipped his drink, hoping for an effect but feeling none. His nerves were jangling, and he felt as though he were deaf and blind. The house could be surrounded by killers and he would have no awareness of them, no warning.

He stood still, closed his eyes, and strained to pick up thoughts, but there was only silence.

What was the plan? he wondered. The guy was supposed to

kill me and report to Martinson when it was done. Then he would probably have killed Tim and Mary, too.

His cell phone, Max thought.

He had forgotten about it until now.

That's my old mental carelessness, he thought. I had become focused and organized, but that's going away, too. Jesus! I don't want to go back to being the old Max Iverson.

The phone! he reminded himself. Stop wandering mentally. The guy's phone. He was probably supposed to call Martinson, so the number's probably in there.

The phone was still in his pocket. He drew it out.

It's probably locked, he thought. The bastard.

It wasn't locked.

Jesus Christ, he thought angrily, what an overconfident son of a bitch!

He searched the contact list, but couldn't find Martinson.

Well, shit, he thought. I guess it makes sense that the number's not there. Maybe he had it memorized. I would have been able to get it from his mind if I could still…

The cell phone rang.

Mary jerked awake. She and Tim stared at Max, open-mouthed, frozen.

Max swiped up and held the phone to his ear. "Hello?" He hoped his voice sounded calm.

There was a pause, then a weak voice, that of an old man, asked, "Who is this?"

"Not who you were expecting. He's out in the desert, working on his tan."

"Iverson?"

"Martinson?"

The old man sighed heavily. "I should have realized you'd be too powerful, even away from the base point."

"The base point?"

"I'll explain it to you later."

"Oh?" Max said. "Are we meeting for cocktails?"

"That's exactly what I had in mind. We've been pursuing the wrong tactics with you. Instead of treating you as the enemy, we should have seen you as one of us. We need new blood."

"I have no idea what you're talking about. You sent people to kill me. You terrorized my parents. I think I should just track you down and kill you."

"I hope I can change your mind."

"How?"

"Come back to Piketon and come see me at my home. I believe you know where it is. We'll talk over drinks, and then we'll have dinner. I have an excellent cook."

"Sounds cozy. But why would I trust you?"

"You'll know immediately if I'm planning to betray you."

But I won't know, Max thought. I won't know what you're thinking, and you'll realize that as soon as I'm close enough for you to read my mind.

He looked at his parents, huddled together and confused.

Perhaps this is the only way to really protect them, he thought. Just go to Martinson's mansion and get it over with. When he sees that I can no longer read minds and I'm no longer a threat, what then? He won't just let me go. I know enough to be dangerous. I could tell Grady what I know. Martinson won't want to risk that. He'll have me killed.

"And my parents?" Max asked.

"Tell them to put their minds at ease. I apologize for what was done to them. I'll put out word that they're to be left entirely alone. I'll also take care of the matter of the man who's working on his tan in the desert."

"All right. I'll do it. I'll be there in a day or two."

"Excellent. I look forward to meeting you in person."

"Right."

Max disconnected.

His parents were staring at him in confusion.

"It's all right," he told them. "You're safe now. Hold on."

He took out his own phone and checked for available flights back to Piketon. There was one leaving at 3:00 that afternoon. He could easily make that. He started to make the reservation, but then he glanced at his father and stepmother and changed his mind. Instead, he reserved a seat on a flight leaving early the following morning.

"I need to get up early tomorrow for my flight home," he said, "so I'm going to make an early evening of it. I think the two of you should do the same. You both look exhausted."

"You're right, dear," Mary said. "I almost feel as if I could go to bed right now and sleep forever."

There was an awkward pause after she said that.

"Let's just spend some family time together for the rest of the day," Max said.

They sat around the dining room table, trying to make conversation. Mary seemed to be half asleep and not entirely aware of what was happening or being said. Tim's mind was elsewhere—in the desert, Max felt sure, with the burning car and body. Max's own mind was preoccupied with thinking about what would happen to him the next day. He was not providing them with whatever emotional comfort he had imagined he would be able to. He felt guilty for that, and even guiltier at the knowledge that this was the last time they would see him alive. He had to try to leave them with happy memories of him.

"Mom and Dad, I want to thank you both for the love you've given me all my life."

You murdered my mother, he thought, but you loved me.

Mary brightened and became more alert. "Oh, darling, what a sweet thing to say! You were such a wonderful little boy that it was easy to love you. What happened to Sheila, that broke my heart. I always felt that you were her last gift to both of us, and I've loved you both for yourself and for my sister."

She pulled a Kleenex from the box on the table and dabbed her eyes. "Oh, my. I didn't mean to talk about that. I know how sad it must make you and your father, but you know, I miss her so much. My wonderful sister! I can't tell you how much I wish she could have watched you grow up. If only she could have been here to give you a mother's love."

Tim took her hand. "You gave that to Max in her place, my dear."

"Yes, that's right," Max said. He said it because he thought it was the right thing to say in the circumstances, and yet he realized that he meant it.

Mary drifted into reminiscences of the past, of Max's childhood and adolescence and her upbringing with her sister. It was clear to Max that she did still miss and love her sister. He couldn't reconcile that with what he was sure she and his father had done to Sheila Iverson.

He tried to tell himself that it was too late to matter—that there would never be justice, that he would soon be past caring, that it was better they remembered him as their loving son than as their accuser. He failed, but he said nothing. He just listened.

They ate a light lunch, played cards, and watched television. They were all trying to pretend it was a normal day during a normal visit. Mary kept drifting off into sleep and then jerking awake. Tim always seemed to have a drink in his hand. Max found himself longing for night, for sleep, for the transition to the next morning and his own departure.

Tim urged drinks on his son, but Max didn't want to drink.

He wanted his head clear. Yet he found himself accepting the drinks his father pressed on him. The alcohol seemed to affect him more than it did his father, despite their ages.

He has a pretty serious drinking problem, Max thought. Why did I never notice that before? I should have been aware of it years ago. I should have said something to him years ago.

He told himself it wasn't his concern. Nothing was, now that nothing but death awaited him. Even so, he worried about both of them.

He couldn't sort out his own tangled emotions.

Tomorrow will sort them out for me, he thought. Everything will be resolved tomorrow.

Finally, it was evening.

Mary rose from the couch. "I'm going to bed. I'm utterly exhausted. Tim, are you coming?"

"I'll be along. I think I need another drink."

"Oh. Well, make it a small one. You know how it disturbs your sleep. Please don't be late." She headed for the stairs.

She hesitated at the foot of them and turned to her husband.

"I'll help you up," he said quickly. To his son, he said, "I'll be back as soon as your mother is comfortable. Why don't you fix us both a drink? Scotch for me." He leaned close to Max and whispered, "Lots of Scotch."

Max watched them climb the stairs slowly and painfully. He went to the small bar and poured a small glass of Scotch for himself and an only slightly larger one for his father. Then he put two cubes of ice in his glass and three in his father's to make the glass appear to have more Scotch in it than it did.

By the time his father returned, Max realized to his surprise that he had finished his drink. He didn't remember drinking it. He hesitated, then poured himself a second one, also small.

"You didn't have to wait for me," his father said.

"I didn't. I guess I'm more shaken up by what happened than I realized."

"Of course you are!"

But he wasn't. He had said that to pacify his father, to make him think that his son hadn't changed.

It's just more violence, more death, Max thought. I've gotten so used to it. It comes so easily to me now.

They drank together for a while in awkward silence.

Then Max said, "I notice you don't have any pictures of Mom around. You did before."

"Of course I do," his father said in a puzzled tone. "There, on the mantel, pictures of our wedding, vacation trips, pictures with you."

"That's not what I meant. I didn't mean you and Aunt Mary."

"Aunt— Oh. Yes. I see. You meant Sheila, your other mother."

"Right. My *other* mother. You used to have pictures of her on the mantel. There was one I particularly liked, from when she was in college. She was very beautiful."

"Yes, she was." Tim drained his drink and poured himself another, much larger than the one Max had poured for him. "That was a wonderful photo." He sighed. "But it was too painful having those around. My wife, Mary's sister." He shook his head. "It hurt too much. It hurt both of us. So I removed them."

"Where are they? I'd like to have them."

"I burned them."

"You— Shit."

"I'm sorry. I didn't think you'd want them. You never even knew her. Mary's the only mother you've ever known."

Max finished his drink and decided that that was definitely enough alcohol. He could feel violence growling inside him and feared stoking it.

"Speaking of Sheila," his father said, "by coincidence, I got a postcard recently from the EMT who was first on the scene of the accident. He was the one who delivered you and tried to save Sheila's life. He's dying of cancer, and he wanted to reach out at the end and see how we're all doing. He got my address somehow."

You're really building up this hoax to try to cover up your crime, aren't you? Max thought. Did you sense that I've been seeing through you?

"Have you spoken to him?" Max asked. "Did he give you his phone number?"

Tim shook his head. "Just the address of the hospice. I was going to write to him, but I couldn't bring myself to. It's such a terrible memory."

Yeah, I bet it is, Max thought. "Maybe Aunt— Mom should write to him."

"Oh, she doesn't know about the postcard. I haven't told her. I don't think she could stand the reminder the way her health is now. Please don't say anything about it to her."

"So why did you tell me?"

"He's in hospice in Piketon. Jimmy Franks. That's his name. I was thinking that maybe you could go see him when you get back. I'll give you the address."

"Sure."

I'll go to the hospice to see the nonexistent EMT, he thought. They'll say they don't have anyone with that name. You'll say he must have died already and they probably don't keep records of dead patients, or something like that. Couldn't you have made up a more convincing fake name? Why are you bothering with this charade?

Aloud, he said, "Give me the postcard, and I'll go there."

"Oh, I don't have it. I copied down the address and then shredded the postcard. I didn't want to take the chance of Mary seeing it. I hope I got the address right. His handwriting was very shaky, hard to read."

So when I get there, Max thought, it will turn out to be something else entirely, not a hospice. Or maybe there isn't even any such address. God, I wish I could read your mind!

"Okay. Write down the address for me."

"It's in my phone. I'll text it to you tomorrow." He smiled self-consciously. "I've finally learned to do that. Just very slowly."

"Sure, okay," Max said, knowing that his father would never text him the supposed address. He would count on Max forgetting about it.

18

Max awoke with a start at 3 a.m. His heart was pounding, and his nerves were jangling.

He lay in bed straining to hear. Had a sound awakened him? Was there a stranger in the house, come to kill all of them?

All was silent. He tried to relax, but his heart refused to slow down. His muscles were tense. He couldn't calm himself.

Finally, he understood what was happening. He had experienced this before, at a time in the past when he had drunk alcohol habitually and to excess. Three o'clock in the morning is the drinker's hour, the time when the alcohol metabolites in the blood destroy sleep and awaken the drinker to self-loathing.

Max lay helplessly awake, reliving the previous day and fearing the day ahead.

He didn't know how long it took, but eventually his body calmed and relaxed, and he fell asleep again.

Seemingly only minutes later, the alarm on his phone woke him.

He was as quiet as possible as he showered and then got himself a bowl of cereal in the kitchen.

Not quiet enough, apparently. His parents came into the kitchen while he was eating. They were dressed in their nightclothes and robes and looked sleepy. His father tried to affect heartiness but with little success. He looked dreadful.

"Are you sure you have to leave?" Mary asked. "Couldn't you stay for a few more days?"

"I have an appointment. It's urgent. I can't miss it." His own words struck him as funny in a macabre way, but he kept a straight face.

"That's a shame," his father said. "When will you be able to come see us again?"

"It's hard to say." In fact, it was easy to say. Never. He could hardly tell them that, though. They'd find out eventually.

They fell into an awkward silence. Mary sat at the kitchen table, half-dozing. Tim stood in the kitchen, staring blankly into space. Max finished his cereal hurriedly, rinsed out the bowl, and put it in the sink.

"Are you all packed?" his father said suddenly.

"Nothing to pack. No luggage. Not even a toothbrush. I had to get here as fast as I could."

His father looked puzzled. "Why did you have to—? Oh. Yes, of course. Are you sure everything's going to be okay?"

"I'm sure. I guess I'm ready to go now."

"This early?" Mary said. "The traffic will be terrible."

"It's an early flight, and the traffic is why I have to allow extra time."

But not that much extra time. Not really. He welcomed the excuse to get away and avoid long conversations or lengthy farewells, in which he would have to fake emotions he knew he couldn't feel. And yet, when he left, he hugged them both and tried to reassure them. He told himself it was part of his own act, his attempt to convince them that they had fooled him about the past, but he recognized in himself a real desire to comfort them. They deserved it after what he had caused them to endure. As it was, he thought they feared him, and he wondered if he should have left the previous day.

Driving east into the blinding morning sun, he felt headachy and half asleep. He was angry at himself for having done this to himself by drinking so much. It wasn't logical, but he wanted to meet death with a clear head. He didn't want to waste a single remaining second of life in fuzzy-mindedness.

At the airport, he returned the rental car, checked in, and went to wait for his flight to board with a feeling of dreamy detachment. His thoughts were fragmented.

Coherent thought returned as he sat at the gate waiting for the call to board.

I'm forty-one years old, and I'm about to die, he thought. I've accomplished nothing other than help take down some criminals. I've read a lot of novels. I've lifted a lot of weights. I've bussed a lot of tables. I've worked the counter in some convenience stores. That's it. Soon I'll vanish, and no one will care or even remember me. Maybe my father and stepmother will, but I don't think they're long for this world, either, given the way they both look.

You've read minds and killed people, he reminded himself.

Yeah, I guess that's something.

Boarding began.

The stress of the previous day's events and the short night caught up with Max. The droning of the airplane's engines vibrating through him put him to sleep. He slumped to one side, his head resting against the window, and he dozed. His dreams were strange, fragmentary, and violent.

A baby was crying. It wasn't a dream, but real.

Max came groggily awake and looked around, seeking the source of the crying. The sound was strange and alarming.

The plane was less than half full. Max had the row of seats to himself. He slid out of the row and into the aisle and stood looking around.

He saw a young father in an aisle seat a couple of rows down, holding an infant and looking concerned. The baby seemed to be asleep, but it was stirring and making faces.

Max heard the crying again. Then the baby opened its eyes, smiled at its father, and the crying stopped.

It was dreaming, Max realized. I heard its dream. Its thoughts!

Annoyance intruded into his thoughts. He saw himself standing in the aisle—a large, oafish version of himself.

Sit down, you jerk, someone thought.

"Sir! Please return to your seat."

A flight attendant was standing the aisle behind him, looking exasperated.

"Sir, we're on our landing approach. Please sit down and fasten your seatbelt."

"Sorry. I was asleep. I didn't hear the announcement. I'll sit down. I will also return my seat back and tray table to their full upright positions."

She scowled and hurried away.

Being able to read minds should make me better at making jokes, Max thought. I guess nothing will.

I can read minds again. It's here, this place, Piketon. I can read minds here, but not when I'm away from here.

Maybe I won't die after all.

While the plane was taxiing to the gate, Max pulled his phone out and turned it on.

He had one text message waiting. It was from his father, and it contained the address for the hospice where Jimmy Franks was ending his days.

I'll be damned, Max thought. He did send the address. Okay, I'll go through with the charade. I'll do it today. Tomorrow I could be dead, and then I won't get the chance to expose this bullshit.

Thoughts intruded ever more strongly as he exited the plane and walked along the jet bridge to the terminal. Passengers, crew, airport personnel near and far—a tumult, a cacophony, a tsunami of mental noise.

His ability to read minds had returned with a vengeance.

He staggered and leaned against the jet bridge wall, hearing the thoughts of concern and annoyance from the other passengers.

"I'm all right," he said, answering the question no one had asked aloud.

He pushed himself erect and continued, doing his best to walk normally.

Only a few hours away from here, and I've already forgotten how to control this, he thought. Weird. But it's stronger than it was before. That's even weirder.

He focused as he walked. By the time he reached his car in the airport parking lot, he was able to reduce the roar of other people's thoughts so that it was a background hum, annoying but not disabling.

He opened the text message from his father again, selected the address, and waited for Google Maps to pop up.

Okay, he thought, I see how to get there.

And yet he was reluctant to start driving. Half of him was eager to prove that his father had invented the EMT named Jimmy Franks, while the other half wanted not to prove it, not to verify that his father had killed his mother.

Finally, he started the car, put it in gear, left the airport, and drove to the address his father had sent him.

The address turned out to be that of a rambling, one-story building surrounded by a small lawn. The building was one of many such in a part of town that had once been at the forefront of the city's growth and prosperity. Those days were long past, and now the area's appeal was that the rents were low. The buildings were therefore attractive to small, struggling businesses.

In this case, the business was indeed a hospice.

The sign in front said BEAUTIFUL MEMORIES HOSPICE CARE, which Max thought unintentionally morbid. A big cross was attached to the wall above the front door. A small sign said PARKING IN REAR.

He drove to the rear of the building. Trash was piled there, next to a row of overflowing dumpsters, and there were cracks in the parking lot. Max parked, turned off the car, closed his eyes, and listened.

Despair, loneliness, and addled thoughts. Not all the patients were mindless, but they were all near the end. He felt their sadness and resignation. A few cursed their reality, but even they could not deny the inevitability and nearness of death. He sensed administrators desperately juggling meager funds from the state and federal governments, and exhausted staff waiting for patients to die.

Max concentrated harder and caught the name Jimmy Franks.

His eyes flew open. Startled, he lost his connection to the minds within the building.

Jimmy Franks was real!

The building's rear door was unlocked. Beyond it was a guard desk with a book for visitors to sign in. No one was there.

Max ignored the book and walked down the hallway beyond, focusing. He tried to detect the thoughts of the man he was seeking, but there were no such thoughts. This was puzzling, and it also meant he didn't know where in the building he should go.

Then he caught the name Jimmy Franks again, in thoughts that were the byproduct of a conversation.

"Pretty close to the end. Have you contacted next of kin?"

"He doesn't have any."

"Poor Jimmy. Okay. Keep checking. Call me when it's time."

Now Max knew from their minds where Jimmy Franks' room was and how to get there. He also knew why he had been unable to detect Franks' thoughts directly.

If he's dead or dying, Max thought, his mind already gone, what's the point of this? I guess I can verify that he exists, that Dad wasn't inventing him, but I won't learn anything beyond that. I still won't know the truth, not for sure.

But he had to do this.

He walked quickly and purposefully, nodding briskly to the staff members he passed. I know where I'm going, his attitude said. I belong here.

The doors he passed were all partly open. The hallway smelled faintly of urine and feces. Max shut it out. Nothing mattered as much to him now as getting to Jimmy Franks while the man still lived.

Once, he sensed the thoughts of a guard coming in his direction along an intersecting corridor. The man's mind was alert, looking particularly for people who shouldn't be there.

Max stepped into the nearest room and hid behind the door, waiting for the guard to pass. He heard a sound behind him. A woman lay in a bed, passively looking at him. Max couldn't tell her age, only that she was old and frail. The mind was almost empty, the only thoughts vague and jumbled, a series of faint impressions and memories drifting through a mind that was almost gone. There was another bed in the room. The occupant of that one was asleep. That mind was even emptier, empty even of dreams.

The guard passed by and turned a corner, still looking unsuccessfully for someone on whom to exercise his authority. Max stepped back into the hallway and continued.

When he reached Franks' room, the hallway was empty. The room number sign beside the door had two slots for patient names. One slot read Jimmy Franks, and the other was empty. Max stepped into the room and pushed the door almost shut behind him.

There were two beds in the room, one of them empty. The man who lay in the other, on his back, silent, breathing shallowly, might once have been tall and robust. Now his body was a shadow of what it had been, and his mind was even less than a shadow.

Max stood by the bed and tried as hard as he could, but he sensed nothing. Jimmy Franks was there physically and still breathing, but his essence, his mind, all that had made him who he had once been, was gone.

Max sighed in disappointment.

What's the truth, Jimmy? he thought. You can't tell me. I'll never know.

Could he reach into the mind and retrieve memories from it, even if the intelligence that had once lived there no longer existed? He had been a receiver of thoughts until now. He had never actively dug them out. Was it even possible?

Nothing that's happened to me since I went into that movie house should be possible, Max thought. Might as well try.

He stood at the foot of the bed, his hands gripping the bedrail. He squinted, stared at the sleeping man's forehead, his own brow furrowed, as though his glare could penetrate the man's skull.

Nothing.

"Shit!" Max said. He thumped the bedrail with his closed fist.

Jimmy Franks moaned and stirred. His eyes opened slowly. He mumbled incoherently. His mind was fleetingly awake.

"Jimmy!" Max said.

Jimmy mumbled, "Who…?"

"You sent a postcard to Tim Iverson, my father. Do you remember a car crash and my mother, Sheila Iverson?"

Jimmy frowned. He tried to concentrate, but his thoughts kept sliding away into randomness.

Max groaned in frustration.

"Car crash," Jimmy said. "The baby. Saved the baby. Not the mother."

"So it really happened," Max said in wonder.

Suddenly, the memory was vivid in the old man's mind. Max was reliving it through Jimmy's eyes, the eyes of a vigorous man, running as fast as he could toward a mangled wreck of a car.

On the ground beside the car, a woman was in labor. Blood was everywhere. She moaned and writhed in pain. Applying all of his skill, training, and experience, Jimmy tried to save both mother and child. He yelled for help, but it was slow in coming. There were other victims inside another crushed car and lying in the roadway. The other EMTs were busy there.

He had to make a choice. The baby had a chance. Jimmy concentrated his efforts on the child.

The delivery was short and violent. Jimmy held a newborn boy in his arms. The mother opened her eyes. He couldn't tell if she was seeing anything or could comprehend what she saw.

"He'll be okay," he said, trying to reassure her, but she

didn't respond. He knew she never would again.

The dead woman's face was the one in the photographs Max had seen on the mantel while growing up. She resembled her younger sister, Mary, but even in death she was more beautiful than Mary had ever been.

The scene faded. The memory drifted away in tatters and gave way to disconnected images, which in turn faded away. Max could feel nothing where Jimmy Franks had been.

Then he felt the minds of people coming his way. Some device attached to Jimmy had signaled them, he supposed. They weren't hurrying. There was no sense of urgency. They had been through this numerous times in this sad building. Nonetheless, they were coming to Jimmy's room, and Max thought he had best not be there when they arrived.

He made his way from the building, choosing the safest route, the one where he would encounter the fewest people.

Outside, he sat in his car, gripping the steering wheel, his eyes closed, breathing rapidly.

What was real? He couldn't doubt that Jimmy's dying memory was real. As a child, Max had imagined his mother's final moments and his own birth from what his father and stepmother had told him. It was a scene that had haunted his dreams. Now he had seen almost the same scene through the eyes of Jimmy Franks, but imbued with gritty, terrible detail that the scene in his imagination had lacked. It felt real because it *was* real. It had to be.

Then what of the other, competing death scene, the seeming memory of his mother being struck by his father, falling backwards over a chair, and dying as a result as she gave birth? That had seemed just as real, but it couldn't be.

He yearned for seclusion, for his thoughts only while he tried to resolve this terrible conundrum. He didn't want to know what anyone else was thinking. He wanted to retreat within his head.

He drove home in a daze.

Despite his wish, he was subliminally aware that the shock of seeing Jimmy Franks' dying memory had increased his own mindreading ability. From time to time during the drive, he glimpsed his own face in the minds of pedestrians and other drivers. They seemed to be looking at his image on their phones.

Were those glimpses real? He could no longer be sure that anything he remembered or sensed was real.

He paused outside the door of his apartment, keys in his hand. Was there a body inside, that of the man who had tried to kill him? His neighbor Joey had been in the process of calling the police when Max left. Why was there no tape on the door?

Are the police looking for me? he wondered.

He closed his eyes and concentrated, filtering through the buzz of overlapping streams of thought. When he tried, like this, he could hear the thoughts of the entire building and of adjacent buildings. He had no idea how far he could read thoughts now. He only knew the mental flood was confusing, overwhelming, almost maddening.

He kept trying, shutting down individual thought streams one by one until he found the one he was looking for: Joey.

The man was watching television. Max waited and listened, hoping some chance association with what he was watching would cause a relevant memory to drift through Joey's mind. But Joey's mind was like a mirror, reflecting the dialog on the screen. He thought of nothing else, and the vapid sitcom he was watching was not likely to ever feature the police and the sound of shots from behind a closed door.

Max clenched his jaw in anger. "Idiot," he muttered.

This was taking too long.

He didn't know which apartment was Joey's, and he couldn't even pick that information out of the man's empty mind. He could hear Joey's thoughts, but he couldn't locate them without something additional from the man, some reference he could use. All he was getting was the sitcom's unfunny lines and frenetic canned laughter.

He walked down the hallway in one direction, hoping the signal would get stronger. It got weaker.

He walked back in the other direction, past his own door, and kept going. The signal got stronger. He stood in front of the door where it seemed strongest. He was about to knock when he realized that he couldn't hear Joey's television with his ears, only with his mind.

Not this door, he thought. Maybe not this floor?

He went to the stairs at the end of the hallway and down one flight. The signal was stronger here, and now he could faintly hear the increasingly annoying recorded crowd laughter.

Using his ears more than his mind, he found the right apartment door and knocked.

There was no response. Angrily, he knocked again, and then again, harder each time, pounding on the door furiously, so that it shook on its hinges.

At last he felt the sound break through Joey's concentration, and he could tell that the man was coming to the door.

It opened, and Joey was there, staring at Max in confusion. The images from the television screen faded in his mind, replaced by growing fear. He stepped back nervously. His fear of Max was blotting out everything else. Max could get nothing from his mind.

Max forced himself to smile. He tried to look relaxed and friendly. "Hey, Joey. I wanted to make sure you were okay."

"I'm...okay."

"Good, good! When I stopped by here to pick up some stuff on the way to the airport, I know I made a lot of noise inside my apartment. I apologize for that. I didn't mean to scare anyone. I knocked a few things over because I was in such a hurry. You know how that is."

Joe relaxed just a bit. His mind drifted to the scene outside Max's apartment door. He remembered his own fear at that time and began to tense up again.

Max cursed inwardly. "I'm glad you called the police. It's good to be sure about things. Better safe than sorry, right?"

"Yeah! That's what my dad always used to say."

"A wise man. Sounds like a good dad."

"Yeah, he was."

"Right. So the police came and checked everything out, did they?"

The memory of the event drifted through Joey's mind. Max watched the police arrive at the door of his apartment, accompanied by a man recognizable as a distorted version of Grady Jacobs. Jacobs thanked Joey and told him he could leave, but Joey hung around, fascinated. Joey watched in surprise the ease with which the police unlocked the apartment door, and he wondered if they could do that to his door as well. He watched as a dead man was removed from the apartment on a gurney. After spending some time inside the apartment, Jacobs emerged, thanked Joey again, and left, while the door was locked as quickly and easily as it had been unlocked.

"There was a dead man," Joey said, frightened again.

"No, that wasn't a dead man. I guess it must have looked like that. It's a boxing dummy. You know, those things you practice punching and kicking on. I'm trying to get into martial arts for self-protection."

Joey looked confused.

"I, um," Max said, "it didn't work. I didn't like using it, so I contributed it to the police gym."

"That's good!" Joey said.

"It's my good deed for the month. Okay, Joey. I have to go now. Thanks for being such a good neighbor."

Still wearing his forced smile, Max walked away.

That was exhausting, he thought. What about Grady? Should I be worried about him now? Can I reach him mentally? Can I reach that far, find his mind and tap into it? How much effort would that take?

He was too drained, too exhausted, to even try. He wanted only to sleep in his own bed.

He unlocked the door and stepped inside. All was neat and clean—more so than normal. There was no sign of the struggle or the death. The one sign that did remain was his mangled laptop computer, in pieces on the table and floor.

You could at least have replaced it, Grady, Max thought.

Max realized that he hadn't checked his email since he had last done so on the now–ruined laptop. For years, now, other than messages from his father, his email had consisted primarily of junk mail, so normally he would have felt no urgency to see what was there. Now he wondered if Grady was trying to reach him.

Probably not, Max thought. He could have texted or called me. I could use my phone to check email, but all I want now is to sleep. What could there be that's important? Everything will be resolved tomorrow.

What about Grady? He must be wondering where I am. I'll give him a call in the morning. Or maybe I won't. That won't matter for much longer, either. Tomorrow, I'll go over to Martinson's estate. In spite of his promise, I know he wants to have me killed. He'll probably succeed. Then nothing will matter to me. Mom and Dad will be safe, and the rest of the world can go to hell.

He went into the bedroom and lay down on the bed fully clothed. He was asleep almost instantly.

Two hours later, he awoke from a strange dream to find that it was not a dream. He could see his own face in a stranger's mind. Not far away, a man was looking at a photograph of Max on his phone.

Max lay awake, trying to drive the cloudiness from his brain. This was real! This was danger! He had to do something.

The man put the phone in his pocket and thought of other things, and the connection faded and broke.

Max lay awake for a time, trying to concentrate, trying to find the watching mind again to gauge the man's intentions. But he couldn't. There was nothing there.

Exhaustion took over, and he fell asleep again.

19

In the morning, Max ate a large and leisurely breakfast, watched the local news and saw nothing of interest, checked email via his phone and found only the usual collection of junk, and tried to prepare himself to die.

He shaved, showered, and dressed, all with extra care, thinking it important to do so on so important a day, although he could not have explained why he thought so.

Should I call Martinson and tell him I'm on my way? Max wondered. No, he'll know as soon as I'm in range. And his range is no doubt much greater than mine.

I'm going to die today. Why don't I feel anything?

All he felt was numbness.

It was a bright, sunny day. The air was warm but not hot. He drove with the car windows open, enjoying the soft breeze. It was a good day to be alive.

On the way, Max was once again aware of people watching him pass, comparing his face to a photograph they held or an image on their cell phones. He tried to reach out, to catch their thoughts, but he passed them too quickly, and they faded away with increasing distance.

Weird, he thought. I'll have to deal with it later.

He knew that he had often thought that when confronting a

difficulty, and he also knew that this time, there probably wouldn't be a later.

He drove through the gates of Martinson's estate and stopped at the beginning of the driveway. He sat, foot pressed on the brake pedal, hands on the steering wheel, eyes closed, suddenly frightened.

I'm going to die here!

He breathed slowly, trying to calm his pounding heart and regain his earlier feeling of detachment.

Thoughts crept into his mind like burrowing worms.

They were Martinson's thoughts.

Max stopped breathing. Time crawled. He waited for an attack.

Nothing happened.

Max breathed again.

Martinson was afraid. He was thinking of Max, wondering how close he was.

I can hear him, Max thought, but he can't hear me. I'm stronger than he is!

Max concentrated. He could hear no other minds. Surely, if anyone else were there, part of an ambush, their emotions would be heightened. If he could hear Martinson, he would be able to hear them. Martinson must be alone.

Nervous and restless, Martinson went into another room, where an array of monitors covered one wall. They were connected to cameras at various points outside the buildings. One of them showed Max's car at the end of the driveway.

Martinson gasped, and suddenly Max could no longer sense him mentally.

In that last split second before his mind disappeared, Martinson deployed a mental trick that shielded his thoughts.

So that's how it's done, Max thought. That's how he can

make his mind undetectable to me. Now I know how to do it, too!

And he did it immediately.

Feeling far more confident, Max took his foot off the brake pedal and drove the rest of the way, stopping in front of the steps leading up to the front door.

As he had before, he walked up the steps and opened the door. As before, the foyer was empty.

Max slammed the door shut behind him. The sound echoed in the huge space.

An old man entered hurriedly, alarm on his face. It was Martinson. "I couldn't detect you!" he said.

"And you never will again," Max said. "I know how to shield my mind."

"How did you—?"

"From you. I saw how you did it."

There was a long pause while Martinson struggled to control his emotions. Finally, he said, "Perhaps this is better. We'll use our physical voices, like everyone else. I was right about you. You have enormous potential. You just need guidance."

Max laughed. "Yours?"

"Of course."

"You tried to kill me and my parents, and now you want to guide me."

"That was a mistake. I've already said that. I want you to join us."

"Us? There's no one else here."

"I'll explain. Come this way."

Martinson led the way into a large formal dining room. The long table had two place settings.

"I know I promised you a fine meal, but I didn't know when

you planned to be here, and I thought it best to dismiss the staff in advance. We'll have to eat cold food that was prepared ahead of time. I hope you don't mind."

This is like a weird parody of genteel politeness, Max thought. Maybe being a mindreader for a long time has made him mentally unbalanced. Maybe it will do the same to me, if I survive this meeting and live long enough.

"Please," Martinson said. "Sit."

Max did so, and Martinson disappeared into another room. He returned carrying a tray holding two platters of food. He moved slowly, balancing his load carefully.

Max shoved his chair back and rose to help him.

"No, no," Martinson said. "You're a guest. I can't have you helping to serve the food. I'm already embarrassed enough that I have to serve you myself."

He put the tray down on the table with relief, placed one platter before each of them, and took his chair.

After we eat, Max wondered, will we retire to another room for brandy and cigars?

They ate for a while in silence.

Eventually, Max said, "Honestly, this might be the best meal I've ever eaten."

Martinson smiled happily. "I'm so glad. I told you my cook was excellent. I promised you a drink. We can have that whenever you're ready. Brandy in the library, if that's all right."

Christ, Max thought. This is weirder than being able to read minds. "I've never had brandy," he said.

"Really? Oh, you're in for quite an experience. I have the best, of course."

"Of course."

"And all of this," Martinson gestured around him, "can be yours, too. Just join us."

"Now we're finally getting to it. The food was great. I'm sure the brandy will be, too. But that's not why I'm here."

Martinson nodded. "Of course not. I have a lot to tell you—a lot of history, especially mine."

There was brandy, but fortunately for Max, there were no cigars.

They sat in deep, comfortable leather armchairs and sipped their brandy. Max assumed it was very good brandy, but he hated the taste of it. He was quite sure that, live or die, this was the last brandy he would ever drink.

Max gestured at the floor-to-ceiling shelves filled with books that lined the room. "You've read all of these?"

Martinson laughed. "Hardly any of them. They're mostly decorative." He paused, then said, "I grew up poor. I always dreamed of having a house like this, and now I do. You can, too."

I'm more comfortable in my dingy little apartment, Max thought. "And all I have to do is join you, whatever that means."

Martinson nodded. "As I said, I grew up poor. Not too far from here, as it happens. Back then, this whole area was small farms and little towns. It was a miserable place. Poverty, alcoholism, violence... I was an only child. My mother miscarried with what would have been my younger brother or sister, and somehow it made her sterile. Oh, that was a common story here. Piketon was a very small city in those days, and the outer edge of it was many miles away from here. It's grown a lot since then."

"I guess so."

"Yes. Well, there was some sort of government research center here, out in the middle of nowhere. I think it was run by the Department of Defense. It's long gone. I was able to buy the land where it stood and build this house right on the same spot."

"That's interesting, but—"

"But what does it have to do with why you're here?" Martinson leaned forward. "It's the crux of the whole thing, um... May I call you Max?"

"Sure."

"And you can call me Felix."

So now we're best buds, Max thought. But I'll keep you in front of me. "Please continue, Felix."

"Growing up, I had a small circle of close friends. They were all from around here, all poor kids like me...." His voice faded as he stared into the past.

He grunted and continued. "There was no future for any of us. We were destined to end up working as unskilled labor, probably on farms, or maybe we'd join the Army. However, when we were teenagers, we all suddenly started reading minds. At first, it was just glimpses. You know how that works. We caught what someone was thinking when they were overcome by strong emotions. Right?"

Max nodded. "Right."

"The first time it happened, it scared you, didn't it?"

There was no point in denying it. "It freaked me out."

Martinson smiled. "As you say. It freaked you out. Yes, that's a good way of putting it. If it had been only me, I would have thought I was going crazy, but my pals were experiencing the same thing."

"A bunch of you, all the same age, all at the same time?"

"Basically, yes. It was hard to discuss it, even with my best friends, but we finally opened up to each other, and we quickly realized that we had something wonderful. We had all been planning to drop out of school as soon as we turned sixteen, but suddenly, high school became very easy." He chuckled. "We could read the minds of the teachers, know what they were planning to ask in class the next day, what questions they were going to put on tests and the answers to those questions. We could read the minds of the best students, too. Our grades shot up, and we all got college scholarships."

"What about the strong emotions part? You could read a teacher's mind and know the answers to tests, but what if the teacher was feeling calm?"

Martinson waved his hand dismissively. "We figured out ways to rile up the grownups when we needed to. That's always been easy for teenagers. And our mindreading abilities became stronger as we used them." He looked at Max questioningly.

"Same here," Max said.

Except when I left town, he thought, and my ability to read minds disappeared. I'm not going to let you know about that.

"What happened next?" Max asked. "You all went off to college, got top grades, had lucrative careers, and lived happily ever after?"

Martinson stared at him as if pondering his next words.

Wondering how much to tell me, Max thought. I guess we're not really best buds after all.

After a while, Martinson continued. "That happened for me. At least the first part did. I wanted to stay near home, so I went to Piketon College, as it was then called. As you said, I got top grades, the same way I had in high school. I got a four-year degree and was trying to decide between a number of very good job offers when I ran into one of my old friends. He had gone off to college on the East Coast on a scholarship, and I hadn't heard from him after that. He told me that he had flunked out with a D average after two semesters. It turned out that on the day he left town, about the time the bus reached the highway, he lost the ability to read minds. Without that, he never had a chance in college. After all, none of us had actually had to learn anything in high school. We just picked the correct answers from other people's minds."

"What happened when he came back home?"

Martinson smiled slyly. "The same thing that happened to you, Max. You were unable to read minds in Phoenix, weren't you? And it all came back when you returned to Piketon, didn't it?"

Max sat frozen in astonishment and fear. Had Martinson actually been eavesdropping on his thoughts all along? He wanted to look around for danger, but he was afraid to move.

"Would you like another?" Martinson asked, holding up his glass.

"I—I'm still working on this one."

"Hmm." Martinson pushed himself to his feet, went over to the bar, and poured himself a second glass of brandy. He went back to his chair, set the glass down carefully on the table beside it, and lowered himself slowly into his seat, supporting himself with his hands on the arms of the chair.

"I wish mindreading could fix these damn knees of mine," he said. "Ah, well." He picked up his glass, sipped appreciatively, and stared at Max again. "You're wondering how I knew that about you?"

"Yes. I know you're not reading my mind."

I hope you're not reading my mind, he thought.

"I'm not. You've shut me out very effectively. And, um... I suppose I might as well tell you. I'll have to eventually. My powers have weakened with age. Sometimes, I'm back to where I used to be at the beginning, able to hear someone's thoughts only when the person is in the grip of some strong emotion. Perhaps you'll be lucky and that won't happen to you. From the start, you seem to have been stronger than any one of us, and perhaps that will protect you. In any case, it's happened to all of us, to every member of the group."

"The group?"

"Of friends. The friends I mentioned before. After I met the friend who had flunked out of college, I put my job search aside and tracked the rest of the old gang down. I was the only one who had gone to college here at home. All the others had flunked out of college. They couldn't read minds when they were away from Piketon. They all ended up in trouble, down on their luck—no college, no jobs, nothing. I persuaded most of them to come back home. When they returned, they could read minds again."

"Most of them? What about the ones who didn't come back here? They're still out there, and they know what you can do."

"There were only two of them, and they both...passed on prematurely." Martinson stared into his brandy and smiled.

"Jesus! You had your own friends murdered to protect your secret?"

Martinson shrugged. "They had proven that they weren't really my friends, hadn't they? But that's all water under the bridge. Those of us who remained formed a closer bond than ever. We worked in harmony and became very rich."

"How?"

"You don't know? I'm surprised. We have a lot to teach you. We knew the secrets of the corporate world. We knew where, when, and how to invest. Most lucrative of all, we knew personal secrets."

"Blackmail?"

"Of course. In most cases, we use that knowledge to extort very large sums of money from our— Oh, I won't call them victims. They're people who have done things they really should not have done. They thought no one could possibly find out. We showed them better. We've also used our knowledge of personal secrets to acquire a team of tough and unscrupulous men to protect us."

"Krakowski."

"Yes. He was terrified of us because of what we knew about him."

"He's no longer terrified of you?"

Martinson chuckled. "He's no longer terrified of anyone. After you left for Phoenix, I deemed it safe to come home again. I found Krakowski lying on the ground outside the house, moaning in agony. That was a nice touch, by the way—running over his leg and then leaving him here. It would not have occurred to me."

"It wasn't intentional," Max said.

"Oh? Well. I'm disappointed. In any case, the pain and terror made his mind an open book to me despite my somewhat weakened state. I saw his plan to help you and then switch sides again, his dreams of taking over from me, and so on. Of course, he's always been that sort of man, filled with envy and resentment. But in the past, we could keep him in line easily. No longer, clearly. I shot him myself." He looked pleased. "I wasn't sure I was still capable of that. My friends came over, and we buried him," he gestured vaguely, "out there in the back somewhere. You'll meet all of them soon. They wanted me to run point."

"They wanted you to take all the risks in case I turned out to be dangerous."

Martinson raised his glass in salute. "Very good! You'll fit right in."

"I still don't know what you mean."

"Back when my friends and I were young, some of them got married and had children. We thought we'd raise another generation of mindreaders and keep growing, create an organization and keep building our wealth and influence. But none of the children inherited our ability to read minds. Apparently it's not genetic. We finally realized that we were all born and grew up near the military research center I told you about, the one that used to be where this house now sits. We're all within a year of each other in age. The place was top secret in those days. Fences, guards, all that. You couldn't get close to it. They must have been doing some kind of experiment here that affected us when we were in the womb, or perhaps even when we were being conceived."

"So what about me?"

"Yes. That's a bit mysterious. Anyway, when we realized that the children were worthless, we removed them and their mothers."

"Removed them? What does that mean?"

"You know what it means."

"Jesus!"

"You would have done the same."

Max said nothing. This was a place of violent death, and his temporary feelings of safety had faded away.

Martinson smiled. "Exactly. You can see it. Well, the original research center was gone, but we thought it likely that the same experiment, whatever it was, was continuing elsewhere. Time passed. We aged and weakened. Some of us died. We spent decades listening for an awakening child mind, someone we could recruit to carry on our work and protect us in case the day came when we lost our mindreading ability entirely."

"If it was someone just like you, how could you trust him?"

"Enlightened self-interest, partially. But more to the point, we would know his thoughts while he was growing and maturing. We would find some way to get control of his upbringing. We would shape him properly. Or her. Or them. Preferably them."

"And that's me?"

"No. That's not you. You're an anomaly. We have no idea why you can do what we can. We never did detect such children. Perhaps they don't exist. Or perhaps they do, but far away from here. The farther we are from this house, the weaker our ability."

"The base point. That's what that means."

"Correct. We call this the base point. It was the site of the experiment that we think started it all, and its influence persists somehow. Something remains here from the original experiment, and it powers us. I'm not entirely sure that's it. We've also found that we need to be near each other for our mindreading to be effective. We think that we reinforce each other, that we create some kind of mindreading field that we have to be surrounded by. When the others join us, you should notice your own strength increasing—perhaps greatly, since you're already so much stronger than the rest of us."

"So we're all vampires feeding on each other."

Martinson looked uncomfortable. "I wouldn't put it that way. In any case, we don't really understand what's behind all of this, how it all works. We're not scientists."

"I wonder what happened to the scientists involved in the original project," Max said.

"Who knows? They'd be older than me, so most of them are probably dead. I suspect that any who survive are locked away safely, so they can't tell anyone about what they did here. That's what I'd do with them."

"Uh huh. You said you think there might be other projects, experiments, like the one you assume was being conducted here," Max said. "Maybe in this country? Maybe in others?"

"Yes."

"If you could find one of those places, you could get in

touch with them. They'd probably have a lot of insights into how this works."

Martinson looked surprised. "Why would we do that? We don't really care about the mechanism. We just want to continue being able to do it."

"And you're afraid of what the government would do if they knew you and your group existed and what you've been doing for decades."

"Exactly. You keep confirming my judgment of you. I'm so glad we've come to this understanding. But you did put your finger on something important. If there are or were other base points, then there could well be others like us, just possibly including children who can read minds. But where are they? We don't know, and we can't travel all over the country or the world looking for them. You could. For whatever reason, you're just like us, except that you're still young and fit. You could be our agent, recruit those children and bring them back here—if they exist. In return, you'd be one of us, and we'd make you very, very rich."

"That's it? Travel around the world, all expenses paid, and kidnap children for you?"

"Recruit, not kidnap. Those who are unwilling, well, they'll know too much by the time you present our offer to them, so you'll have to make sure that neither they nor their families will be a danger to us."

"Sounds like fun."

"You've killed already. Misgivings at this point ring false."

"Perhaps so." I killed in self-defense, Max thought. Or close enough to self-defense. You're a cold-blooded killer. I'm not.

Even as he thought that, he wondered if it was true. He had killed in self-defense, but he couldn't pretend that he had felt any emotions while doing so. He had absorbed not only the skills of the killers he had killed but also their detachment.

"But if I go away from the, uh, base point, I'll lose my mindreading ability. I won't be able to detect those children, even if they exist."

"Let's hope that the base point phenomenon is duplicated in those other locations. If so, you'll find your mindreading returning as soon as you're in the vicinity of one. That's how you'll know."

"If so," Max repeated. "Well, I already have a pretty good job, and it doesn't require killing people."

"Working for Grady Jacobs. We know all about that, of course. You must know you can't keep doing that. Sooner or later, there would inevitably be a conflict. Someone in that office would find out what you've been up to. Why, you'd probably have to kill them to keep them quiet."

Max grunted and sipped his brandy, not knowing how to respond.

"Even without being able to read my mind, you can tell how open and frank I'm being with you," Martinson said. "And I can tell how reluctant you are to accept my offer. Take some time. Think about it. In the meantime, while your job lasts, you can be our eyes and ears in the DA's office."

"Your spy."

"Our source. Think about our offer, but don't take too long. As I said, your position with Jacobs is bound to come to an end, and even if it doesn't, our patience is not limitless. Join us, and your parents will be safe."

"You already promised me they'd be safe."

"I did, but I believe I made it clear that my promise was contingent on you joining us. Perhaps you didn't understand that. To clarify, if you become one of us, your parents will be safe for the rest of their lives."

"Their natural lives."

Martinson smiled. "I'm not trying to trick you. Very well. Their natural lives."

"I'll think about it." Max put down the brandy and stood. "I have to say, this day did not turn out the way I expected it to."

"Hmm. I think that's been true for me almost every day since my ability to read minds first manifested itself. Our lives are much more interesting than those of lesser people. Become one of us, and you'll see what I mean."

20

The next morning, Max strolled into the office as if nothing unusual had happened since he was last there. Before he could sit down, Grady Jacobs was standing beside him.

"Jesus Christ, Max! What the hell happened to you? Where've you been? I thought the bastards got you."

"I was in Phoenix visiting my folks. I needed a break after all that excitement. Sorry. I guess I should have let you know and submitted some kind of paperwork to HR."

"No shit! Never mind, though. I'll take care of it. I'm just glad you're okay. All I knew was you killed one of the assailants at the safe house and then went off like some kind of vigilante. With a gun."

"Well, yeah, I was pretty angry. I thought better of it. I'm no vigilante. I didn't know I killed that guy. I thought I just knocked him out. Adrenaline, I guess. Am I in legal trouble? Am I a murderer?"

"I think you'll be okay."

"God, I hope so. Anyway, I calmed down, changed my mind, and went to Phoenix."

"And the gun?"

"I dumped it in a trash can at the airport. The TSA people are used to finding guns in those trash cans. People think they'll get their gun through security, but then they chicken out and chuck it in the trash."

"So I hear."

The words were one thing. The roiling uncertainty and suspicion in Jacobs' mind were another.

"You know," Jacobs said, "we got a call from someone at your apartment building. He said he saw you there and heard a gunshot from inside your place. We found a mess inside there, and a dead man. How did that happen?"

"A dead man? Christ!"

"That's right. Well?"

"I don't know anything about it. I was in Phoenix."

Too late, Max caught the thought in Jacobs' mind about checking with the airlines to find out whether Max had really flown to Phoenix, and if so, exactly when he had left and when he had returned.

"Oh, was that Joey?" Max said. "The person who called you about a gunshot in my apartment?"

"I can't share the name with you."

Max nodded. "Of course, but I bet it was. I went back there to grab a few things on my way to the airport, and he was there in the hallway." He chuckled. "Joey's okay, but he has trouble keeping things straight. I got my stuff and went to the airport, but I had to wait around for hours for a flight. Joey probably got confused about the time. A gunshot and a dead man, though..." He shook his head. "Maybe the bad guys know where I live and sent someone after me. Maybe there were two of them, and they had a disagreement. Does that make sense?"

Reluctantly, Jacobs said, "Maybe it does. All right. I'm glad you're okay."

"Is Lynnette okay? She was a mess when I last saw her."

"She's been out since that day. She has a lot of accumulated sick leave and vacation time."

"I bet she never takes it."

"She's dedicated to this office." Jacobs turned away and walked back to his office, thinking, I'm glad he's okay. I need the guy. I'm going to check with the airlines.

She's dedicated to you, not this office, Max thought.

He was relieved by her absence, though. He didn't think he could deal with her loud broadcasting of anger and hatred at that moment.

At least I won't have to deal with Grady's suspicions, too, he thought. He'll see that my story about the airline flight checks out. That will buy me some time.

"I'm going out," Max announced to no one in particular.

He left the building and wandered through the downtown streets, not knowing what to do. If he picked up thoughts about minor crimes, he could do nothing with them. Jacobs wasn't interested in spending resources on the small stuff now that he had tasted fame and was hungering for higher office. If Max picked up information about major crimes, he couldn't tell Jacobs about them in case investigating those crimes led Jacobs to Martinson or a member of his group. Martinson would assume that Max had fed that information to Jacobs, and that would put Max's parents in danger.

As he strolled, lost in thought, Max suddenly caught his own image in someone's thoughts again. Someone was looking at him and then at his picture on their phone, comparing the two.

He was jerked from his reverie. He looked around, trying to find the source of the thought, but it became obscured by the mental hum and buzz of the downtown crowd. He caught the thought again, a fading whisper from the mind of someone hurrying away, and then it was lost.

Weird, Max thought. One of Martinson's people, assigned to keep an eye on me? No. Martinson knows I'd detect that. Grady? There was no hint of it in his mind. Who, then?

More to the point, did this represent danger? He had no way of knowing.

I can't waste time on it, Max thought. I have to find a way to keep Grady pacified for now. Most of all, I have to come up with an answer for Martinson ASAP.

As if Max's thoughts had summoned the demon, his phone rang, and it was Martinson.

"I need more time," Max said.

"I would have given you more time, but then you sicced your girlfriend on us."

"What are you talking about?"

"Don't play innocent." There was a cold, hard edge in Martinson's voice. Max knew this was the real man showing through, not the mild, charming front Martinson had assumed during their meeting.

"I'm not. I don't have a girlfriend, and I don't know what you're talking about."

"Lynnette Salzmann. She works for Jacobs, which means that she works with you. She knew about you coming here. Clearly you're working together. She came here and started asking questions. We've got her."

"You've—? Don't hurt her!"

Martinson snickered.

"Look, I don't why she's there, but you can read everything in her mind. She's an open book. You can tell that I'm not working with her. Let her go."

"Open book? Hell, her mind is screaming all the time. None of us can read her. It's painful to even try. It's painful to be anywhere near her. She won't shut up. It will take a bullet in her head to do that. But we don't need to read her. We know who she is, and we know she works for Jacobs. That's enough for me. Give me your answer right away. And it better be the right one, or your parents are dead."

"All right! I'll join you. Let her go."

"The deal only covers your parents. Be here tonight. Eight o'clock. The others are eager to meet you. We have things to discuss. Oh, and you'll have to drop your guard. Be prepared for that. We'll be reading everything you're thinking. We have to be sure we can trust you."

"If you hurt Lynnette, you'll have Grady Jacobs coming after you with everything he's got. Just let her go."

"If we let her go, we'll still have Jacobs coming after us." There was a long pause, and then Martinson said, "We'll talk about it tonight. We'll keep her alive until then."

He hung up.

21

For a moment, Max considered returning to the office and telling Jacobs about Lynnette's situation, but he quickly dismissed that idea. It would do no good. The authorities could do nothing to rescue her. As soon as they came within mental range of Martinson's mansion, she would be killed. Even worse, Martinson would know who was responsible for a rescue attempt, and he would order the murder of Max's parents.

Instead, Max wandered around downtown Piketon, trying to devise a course of action that would end up with him, Lynnette, and his parents alive.

Nothing came to him.

He passed one of his favorite downtown restaurants and paused. It was past lunchtime, but he had no desire for food.

I'm on Death Row, he thought. Tonight, I'll have to open my mind to them, and as soon as I do that, they'll have me killed. Lynnette and Mom and Dad, too.

What if I refuse to open my mind? The result will be the same.

He wondered if condemned men really ordered special last dinners, and if so, if they were able to eat them. The thought of eating anything right now, special or not, made him ill.

He wondered, too, why he was so determined to save

Lynnette's life, why he placed it on a par with his own and that of his parents. She was a hateful person who had been hateful to him. Her obsession with Grady Jacobs and hatred of his wife were likely to disrupt Jacobs' life and derail a promising career, and Max had come to respect Jacobs and wish him well. Wouldn't Lynnette's death in fact be beneficial? But he found that he couldn't think about her in such a cold, detached way. There was a connection of some sort between them—not a sexual or romantic attraction, not even professional respect, but something else. He had felt it from the beginning. He had no idea what it was, and the fact that it existed unnerved him, but it was there. He couldn't ignore it, and he felt obligated by it to try to save her life.

He was drained. There was no point in going back to the office and pretending to be doing anything there. His time was almost up, so why bother pretending?

My time, and Lynnette's, and my parents', he thought. At least they don't know it's coming. Although Lynnette might have guessed by now.

He thought he could sense her terror from miles away, but he was sure that was just his imagination.

He went to his usual bus stop and went home. When he reached his apartment, he thought again of eating something or making himself a drink but decided against both.

"The condemned man declined a hearty meal," he said aloud.

He wondered if he should call his parents and tell them to head for parts unknown, change their names, live new lives...

No, there was no point in that. They would think he had lost his mind. They certainly wouldn't flee to safety.

They're as doomed as me, he thought.

He set his alarm for 7 a.m. and lay down on his bed fully

clothed.

The condemned man decided to waste his few remaining hours by taking a nap, he thought. Except that I won't be able to sleep.

He was wrong. The 7 a.m. news on his clock radio woke him.

He was fully awake immediately, his mind clear and filled with the thoughts of the other people in the building. Methodically, he began to shut them out one by one. Eventually, there was only one mental sound left, and that one he couldn't block. It was a distant sound, a faraway, high–pitched scream. He felt the beginnings of a headache. He focused, concentrated with all of his will, but the best he could do was mute the sound.

What the hell is it? he wondered. Lynnette? No, that's impossible. She's too far away.

It was an intriguing mystery, but one he would have no time to solve.

He drank some water and headed out. He drove robotically, his mind almost blank. He wondered if this was the way condemned men felt as they walked that last mile. He ignored the transitory thoughts of others that impinged on him as he drove. The scream was still there, though, and it grew louder as he went.

The gate at the entrance to Martinson's estate was open and as unattended as before. Max wondered if the place was empty again.

You mean you hope it is, he told himself.

The mental scream was penetratingly loud, impossible to ignore. It must be Lynnette. Max felt sure of it now.

He drove slowly, cautiously down the driveway and parked in front of the house. No one appeared to challenge him.

The scream was constant and close to unbearable.

Max sat in his car, his eyes squeezed shut, and concentrated on blocking her. He managed only to muffle the sound a bit.

Then he realized that he could sense no one else. Either the house really was empty except for Lynnette, which seemed unlikely, or those in it had shut down their minds just as he had.

It's the scream, he thought. That's the only way they can bear it this close up.

What about the non-mindreaders who worked for Martinson and his group?

Cautiously, Max opened up slightly, trying to feel any unblocked minds that might be in the house. He thought he sensed some, but he couldn't be sure because of the terrible mental scream. Opening his mind made the sound that much worse. He definitely had a headache now, and it was intensifying steadily. He closed up again.

No point in delay, he told himself.

He got out of the car and climbed the steps to the big double door.

It opened as he approached.

Martinson stood there, looking shriveled, old, and in pain.

The old man spoke, using only his voice. "Come in, come in. We'll have to limit ourselves to speaking. We can't open our minds to each other until that bitch is dead."

Max stepped inside, and Martinson closed the door behind him.

"I thought we were going to discuss what to do with her," Max said.

"We've already discussed it. She's intolerable. None of us can get close enough to her because of that damned screaming. The men who work for us can't do it, either. They say they get headaches so bad that they can't function."

"So let her go. Let her get far away from us."

"Don't be ridiculous," Martinson snapped. "You know that's not possible. You're stronger mentally than the rest of us. Maybe you can get close to her and end it. Then we'll get on with the test."

"Where is she?"

"In the basement. Do you have a pistol? No? Well, I'll give you one. That way, you won't have to get right next to her. You can shoot her from the basement stairs."

"I've never fired a gun of any kind," Max lied. "I doubt if I could hit her from a distance."

Martinson glared at him. "That's your problem. Probably all you'll have to do is wound her to make her stop screaming. Then you'll be able to put the pistol against her head and finish her. Consider it part of the test."

This is okay, Max told himself. It buys me time. Maybe I'll be able to figure something out. Maybe I'll survive the night.

Martinson led the way through the foyer and into the room where the two of them had sat before, sipping brandy and pretending to be convivial.

The room made Max think of Krakowski and his dangerously big dreams.

This is the lifestyle he wanted, Max thought, the lifestyle they're offering me.

This time, they were not alone in the room. Four of the armchairs were occupied by frail old men who looked like a breeze would blow them away. Max recognized one of them as the driver of the car that had been waiting outside the safe house. The man looked even frailer and wispier now than he had then.

"This is the group?" Max asked. "This is everyone?"

The four winced at his voice. He thought that of the five, only Martinson had the strength to stand. Martinson was the only one he had to worry about. Cautiously, he opened his mind the slightest amount, hoping he'd be able to read them, but Lynnette's piercing mental scream cut into his brain like a knife, and he shut down again quickly.

"She really is intolerable," he said conversationally and in a louder voice than necessary.

Again, the four seated old men winced.

Martinson looked uncomfortable but stood straight and kept his expression neutral. "She is," he said, "and she's keeping us from making progress. Go down there and take care of her now."

Max nodded. "Of course."

He hoped he was doing as good a job of not showing his discomfort as Martinson was. The old man impressed and frightened him.

You're the real danger here, aren't you? Max thought. Not those four old fossils.

"Where's my weapon?" he asked Martinson.

Martinson went to the end table next to one of the empty armchairs. It was the largest armchair in the room and the same one he had sat in when Max was there before. He pressed something on the end table—a button, Max assumed, not visible from where he stood.

A much younger man entered the room. He was tall and muscular, but his shoulders were hunched, and his face wore the same look of pain as the faces of the four old men. Based on what Martinson had said before, the newcomer was too young to be a mindreader, but Max assumed he was being affected by Lynnette in much the same way as the rest of them.

"George," Martinson said, "take Mr. Iverson down to the basement where we're keeping our guest. When you get there, give him your pistol and show him how to use it."

"Yes, sir." He turned to Max. "Please follow me."

Max followed him from the room and down a hallway. George walked slowly, his path wavering. He touched the wall from time to time.

"I think you need to take some aspirin and go to bed," Max said. "Why don't you just give me your gun and point me in the right direction? I'll know what to do."

"Orders are orders," George said, and Max could detect the fear in his voice.

The hallway ended in a staircase heading down. George led the way, gripping the railing as he went slowly down the stairs.

With each step, the mental scream grew louder. Max had to exert more effort to keep moving, to keep thinking. George walked ever more slowly, groaning softly from time to time.

It was a long flight of stairs. By the time they reached the bottom, George's face was white and his eyes were wide, staring into space. Max wasn't sure if the man was entirely conscious.

The stairs ended at a closed door. There was a light switch on the wall beside it.

George leaned against it. "Through there," he gasped. "I can't..."

Thoughts were not attenuated by doors, so opening this one wouldn't make Lynnette's scream any louder. Nonetheless, Max braced himself for a moment. Then he pulled George away from the door and opened it.

There was blackness beyond.

Max snarled. "You're keeping her in the dark? Bastards." He thought of Lynnette's terror and was surprised by the wave of sympathy that rose in him.

"Here." George held his pistol out in a hand that shook. "Do it."

"You first." Max grabbed the man and pushed him ahead

into the dark opening.

George moaned and twisted in Max's grasp, but he was too weak to resist. Max had the back of his shirt bunched in his left hand and held the pistol in his right. He slipped the gun into his pants pocket and flipped the switch next to the door to the up position.

The blackness of the basement changed to bright white. Ahead of him was a small metal landing and then metal stairs descending into the basement. The lights were everywhere, bathing the entire big space in brilliance.

Lynnette stood at the foot of the stairs, staring up, squinting against the sudden light. Her mouth was open, but she made no sound. The scream continued, louder than ever, but it was entirely mental. The blankness of her face made Max wonder if the scream was all that was left of her mind.

George groaned and clapped his hands to his head. He pulled himself from Max's grasp and stumbled forward. He stepped off the landing and tumbled down the staircase, landing at Lynnette's feet. He tried to rise, rolled onto his back, and lay still, eyes open, face frozen in an expression of pain.

Lynnette screamed with her voice. Her mental scream grew even stronger.

Max felt as though his head would explode.

"Stop it!" he shouted. "I'm here to rescue you!"

His words had no effect. Both her vocal and mental screams increased in power.

He turned and ran back up the stairs, desperate to put distance between himself and Lynnette.

He burst into the library. Martinson and the other old mindreaders were on the floor. The others were unconscious, their minds blank. Martinson was awake, writhing in pain, his mental defenses down, blown apart by Lynnette's scream.

Martinson's mind was laid bare—his evil, his lies, his memories, and most of all, his lie about the origin of Max's mindreading and what he knew about Lynnette.

As he rifled through the old man's memories, Max was temporarily immune to Lynnette's scream. The rage induced in him by what he saw blocked even that.

22

After Martinson and the others gave up on finding babies with capabilities like their own, they experimented with trying to create such capabilities in babies still in the womb. They connected with those new minds and tried to force their thoughts into them, hopeful that they could do so with an unformed, unborn mind and that that would spur the development of mindreading. They failed uniformly. In most cases, their efforts had no effect. But sometimes, the children died suddenly, their brains overwhelmed.

"I think we're too far away," Felix Martinson told the others. "We need to be nearby during the birth. That's what I think."

"How?" one of other men asked. "We can't go to a hospital and stand outside the maternity ward. We're supposed to avoid drawing attention to ourselves. That's what you always say."

Martinson glared at him. "Christ, Harry, stop rejecting everything I propose." But in fact, he had no answer to Harry's objection.

John Drew said, "You remember that midwife in the old neighborhood?"

"I do, Johnny," Martinson said. "What about her?"

"She's still there. Still practicing."

"So?"

"She does home births. I'll try to find out when and where the next one is. We can all go there and give it a shot as the baby is being born."

"That's good, Johnny. That's very good. But we can't all go there. It's the same problem—drawing attention to ourselves. You'll go there. By yourself. Get as close as you can, but make sure no one sees you."

"Just one man?" Harry asked. "That won't work. We need the field in order to be strong enough."

"Fortunately, that one man is Johnny, not you," Martinson said. "We'll try it this way first. Let's see what happens." He was thinking that something needed to happen to Harry.

A week later, after dark, Johnny was leaning against the outside wall of a small, shabby house not far from the one he had grown up in. The midwife was inside. It was summer. Every window in the house was open, and a woman inside the house was crying out in pain.

Johnny grimaced and wished Felix had sent someone else on this mission.

He closed his eyes and focused. The woman was screaming nonstop. There was a jumble of thoughts. The woman's mind contained nothing but agony. Her husband's was filled with worry and fear. The baby's was confused and half-formed. The midwife's was focused, professional, and the smallest bit bored by something she had done innumerable times.

Johnny was rattled. He could feel the woman's pain inside his own body. He wanted to leave, but he feared Felix's anger, so he stayed. He kept trying to make some sort of mental contact with the baby, but as with all of the group's previous experiments, the child seemed unaware of him.

Suddenly the baby's mind responded. The response was a blast of fear and anger that made him stagger backwards.

The birth was over. The midwife was cutting and tying the cord. The mother, father, and midwife were of no interest to Johnny, but this baby was. There was disturbing power in that little brain.

I did it! Johnny thought. Felix will be pleased. I have to get closer.

He hesitated. He had to fulfill this mission, or Felix would be angry.

He could tell that no one was in the house other than the three adults and the newborn baby. He took a deep breath, then walked in through the unlocked front door.

Thinking mostly of the child, trying to make contact again with its mind, Johnny walked into the bedroom.

He stopped, horrified by the sight and smell of the blood soaking the bed and shocked by the exhausted woman lying there, her groin covered with blood.

The husband jumped to his feet. "Who the hell are you?" He rushed at Johnny, a huge, threatening figure.

Panicked, Johnny pulled his gun from his pants pocket and fired a bullet into the man's face.

The two women screamed, and Johnny shot them both. The midwife managed to put the baby gently on the bed. Then she slid to the floor and lay still.

Johnny stood frozen, not quite realizing what he had done. He stared at the baby, the only other living being in the room. The baby's eyes were squeezed shut. Its mouth was open, making weak little sounds, but its mind screamed at him.

Unnerved, terrified, Johnny turned and fled, leaving the two bodies lying on the floor, the dead mother on the bloody bed, and the baby lying beside, crying out with its mind.

Johnny returned to the mansion and told the assembled group of his failure. The others glared at him, but Martinson said nothing.

Johnny held his breath, waiting for the explosion. Thank God he had said only that he had failed. He hadn't mentioned that the infant seemed promising.

He need not have feared. Fetuses die in the womb, babies die during birth, mothers die in childbirth, newborns die in their cribs, people are murdered—tragic but not uncommon, and certainly of no importance to Felix Martinson.

"Oh, well," Martinson said. "That's all right, Johnny. Better luck next time."

Then Martinson frowned in concentration. "Hold on. I think I'm detecting something good. All of you, drop your guard and join me."

They did so. The field strengthened. Joined, their power grew.

On a highway not far away, a car was stopped at a red light. The driver was a heavily pregnant woman, and the mind of her unborn child was radiating its dreamlike thoughts strongly.

That child's mind! Martinson thought. Focus on that!

Together, their minds joined to become the shaft of a spear with Martinson's thoughts the spearhead, aimed at the brain of the fetus in the car.

The woman driving the car jerked as though she had been impaled by a physical spear. Her weak heart gave way, and she fainted, falling forward onto the steering wheel, her foot slipping off the brake and onto the accelerator.

The car rolled forward into the busy intersection. A speeding pickup truck in the cross street slammed into the car on the driver's side. The door caved in on the pregnant woman. The two vehicles spun into a third. Amid breaking glass and squealing brakes, already dying from her injuries and her failing heart, the woman felt powerful contractions in her abdomen.

Never mind her! Martinson commanded. Hold onto the baby's mind.

But they're both dying, Johnny thought.

Obey me, Martinson replied, his thoughts cold and terrible.

They could feel the bewildered child's mind opening to them even as the mother's contractions were pushing him headfirst into the opening of her womb. The mother's mind was fading away.

Johnny was suddenly reminded of the bloody scene he had left behind just a short time before. The image of the terrified, furious newborn girl screaming at him with her mind intruded. He managed to stifle it almost immediately, hoping desperately that Felix hadn't caught it.

Martinson was otherwise occupied. Another mind had intruded, distracting him. This mind was strong, filled with urgency. It was the mind of a man, a focused professional, who was trying to save the baby.

Stop! Martinson yelled at him. Leave us alone!

Martinson was beset by a vivid memory of his pregnant mother accusing his father of infidelity and of his drunken father striking her, knocking her backwards over a chair.

Felix had yelled at his father, "Stop! Leave us alone!"

His father had backhanded him, flinging him across the room. The man's murderous thoughts had washed over the boy. Felix had curled into a protective ball, moaning in terror. His father had lost interest and staggered from the room.

Shaking, Martinson forced himself to focus on the task at hand, but it was too late. His connection to the baby faltered, and then the baby himself shut them all out. In an instant, his infant, untrained mind erected an impenetrable barrier.

They sat back in their chairs, exhausted.

"Can we try again?" Johnny asked. "Give the boy time to recover, then maybe we can contact him again in a few months."

Martinson shook his head. "The brat's gone. I don't know what he did, but we'll never get through that wall. He'll be undetectable behind it for the rest of his life, I think—a short life, I hope, the little shit."

"But we'll try again, won't we? We'll keep trying to recruit minds, right?"

Martinson sighed. "I suppose we'll have to keep on trying. What else can we do?"

23

"You murdered my mother," Max said aloud. "You made me hate my parents. You stole my life from me. You stole them from me."

Martinson stared up at him. Through his pain, the old man was trying to focus his mind, to shut out Max.

"You took everything!" Max shouted.

He knelt beside Martinson, his hands reaching for the man's neck. Then he stopped. He wanted to do this with his mind, to destroy the mind that had destroyed his love for his parents. He let his anger pour out of him.

Martinson fought back, but weakly. Max felt himself in control, growing more dominant.

The other old mindreaders began to wake up. They sensed the battle and added their minds to Martinson's.

Max wavered. Combined, they were too much for him. Weakness spread throughout his body.

I'll kill you, boy, Martinson thought. You should have died on that highway along with your mother.

There was a burst of mental energy from him, of hatred, that knocked Max off his knees and onto his side on the floor.

Then Lynnette's rage invaded Max's mind. She screamed her hatred and anger at Martinson and the others. Her fury was a knife slicing through his mind and into the minds of the five old men.

Their rage merged. The two crippled children shouted mentally at the men who had destroyed their lives.

My parents! Max screamed. *My love for them!*

My parents! Lynnette screamed. *My need for their love!*

They screamed with their minds and their voices.

Martinson and the other old men screamed, too, but very weakly.

Something exploded in Max's head, and then there was nothing.

24

His head ached. He was lying on his back. He couldn't seem to open his eyes. There was a loud beeping. People talked loudly and incomprehensibly. They poked and prodded him. He moaned and drifted away.

The next time Max awoke, he was still lying on his back, but he was able to open his eyes.

He was alone. The beeping was gone. His head no longer hurt. He was aware of how quiet everything was to both his ears and his mind.

He was too weak to sit up. He rolled his head from side to side, looking around. He seemed to be in a hospital room, hooked up to equipment he couldn't turn his head enough to see.

What happened to me? he wondered.

He closed his eyes and searched for nearby minds, hoping to glean information about himself. He could hear nothing.

Am I alone in the building? he wondered. How could he be the only person in a hospital?

A middle-aged woman in nurse's scrubs entered the room. "Ah, you're awake again," she said.

Why couldn't he sense her thoughts? He tried to say something, but only a hoarse, wordless sound came from him.

"Oh, don't try to speak," she said. "You've had a tube in your throat for the last two months. It just came out this morning. It will take you a while."

"Two months!" he tried to say, but again nothing came from him but the same hoarse sound.

Eventually he recovered the ability to speak, although his voice sounded weak to him. After weeks of physical therapy, he could walk again, but when he looked at himself in the mirror, he was shocked at how wasted he looked, at how much of the muscle mass he had worked so hard and for so long to build had wilted away.

But most of all, he was shocked and frightened by the mental silence that shrouded him. No matter how hard he tried, the thoughts of others were closed off to him.

Who was sneaking up on him? How would he know?

He fought panic constantly.

He became aware of the disrepair of the place, of how overworked the staff were, how limited the resources. He wondered who was paying for his care. Whoever it was, they were not spending a lot on him. He suspected it was Martinson, and that thought bewildered him.

Four weeks after he awoke from his coma, he had a visitor. It was Grady Jacobs.

Jacobs was ill at ease. His heartiness was overdone, and his glance darted about the room, avoiding resting for long on Max's face.

Max hauled himself from his bed and onto his feet. He shook Jacobs' hand.

"Up and about!" Jacobs said. "That's great to see. We were worried about you."

"I'm ready to leave, but they won't let me. What happened? I don't know anything. I don't even have my phone. No one will give it back to me. I don't know what the hell is going on."

"Your doctors want to make sure you're well enough first."

"Well enough to use my phone? That makes no sense."

Jacobs hesitated. "Well enough to read your messages and access your voicemail."

"That's ridiculous!"

Max's knees buckled, and he sat down on the edge of the bed, grabbing frantically at the sheet to keep himself from sliding off onto the floor.

I'm so weak, he thought. Getting angry knocks me off my feet. Maybe they're right about me staying here. But I want my phone. I need to talk to Mom and Dad.

"I have to call my parents. They must be worried. They're used to regular phone calls. Hell, if they know I'm in the hospital, they'll be frantic by now."

"Yeah, I know, I know." Jacobs looked still more uncomfortable and avoided Max's eyes again.

Max stared at him, frowning with effort, trying to penetrate that skull, trying to read what Jacobs was obviously hiding from him.

"What's going on, Grady?"

Jacobs sighed. "I should leave this to your doctors. They know how to handle this stuff. I don't want to set you back. They say you're making progress."

"Thanks for visiting. I'm going to crawl out of this place on my hands and knees now."

Jacobs held up his hand. "Okay. Ask me questions, and I'll answer."

"You're avoiding taking the initiative. This is some kind of lawyerly self-protection, isn't it?"

"Kind of. What do you want to know?"

"How did I get here?"

Jacobs looked relieved. This was clearly something he was happy to talk about.

"You can thank Lynnette for that. There was an email from her. I didn't see it at first. I was in meetings in the morning. It had documentation on Felix Martinson, his connections with some crimes, weird stuff. Not really convincing. But she said you were part of it, and she was going to his home to confront him." He shook his head. "It's that damned girl detective thing of hers. I think she must have read too many of those books when she was a kid."

"So you went to Martinson's estate and found me there?"

"Not exactly. What she sent me was just a bunch of speculation. That's not like her. She's normally meticulous. I was surprised. I was worried about her safety, but that's about it. Then she phoned me. She said she was there in Martinson's home, that they had tried to kill her, and that there were a lot of dead people, including you. Also, you had tried to rescue her, so you're one of the good guys."

"That's nice to know."

"I called the cops. They went out there to check. I went with them."

"You went because of Lynnette."

"And you. I was hoping you weren't actually dead."

"Thanks."

"And you weren't. You were unconscious. There were a

bunch of unconscious old guys there, too. It's was a very weird scene. The ambulances came and took everyone to the hospital. The old guys didn't make it. You did, obviously, although the doctors weren't sure you'd ever come out of your coma. They didn't even know why you were in one. Everything looked normal. Same thing for the old guys. Their brains were normal, just old and dead."

"How's Lynnette?"

Jacobs sighed and shook his head. "When we got there, she was standing in the middle of the unconscious men, screaming. I could hear her as we drove up the house. She hasn't stopped. She screams constantly except when she's asleep, which is only for short periods. No one can communicate with her. She's being cared for. The attendants keep quitting because her screaming gives them terrible headaches, or so they say. I went to see her, but she didn't even recognize me. I don't suppose you'd be willing to give it a try?"

Max shivered and shook his head. "But she was able to call you."

"I know. It's very strange."

What an astonishing effort that must have been for her, Max thought. In her state, after what we had both gone through, to be able to make that phone call before lapsing into that mindless state. Or is it mindless? Maybe I should go to see her, try to get through to her. Martinson and his cabal created some kind of connection between us on the day we were both born. She's aware of it now. I bet she's screaming mentally, too. Maybe her scream would bring my mindreading ability back again. Then maybe I could communicate with her.

He shivered again, knowing he lacked the strength and will to do it.

Jacobs was talking. Max forced himself to pay attention.

"Those old men… Odd coincidence, isn't it?"

"Very odd."

"Hmm. Okay. We got a search warrant. We found bodies buried on the grounds. We found paperwork tying Felix Martinson and his friends to some big-time felonies all over the state for decades. Fortunately for us, the man was a meticulous record-keeper. They would have spent the rest of their lives in prison if they had survived. What a bust! It was huge. This clears up so much. The news media haven't left me alone. Not just local. National, too."

"Sounds good for you."

"All's well that ends well."

Except for Lynnette, Max thought. Did I misread your interest in her, Grady, or does the bright light ahead of you blind you to everything else?

Max was sure there was more, something Jacobs was avoiding. Again he stared at Jacobs' head, focusing, concentrating, hoping to pick something up, a stray thought, a briefly unhidden secret. Again, there was nothing. There was an impenetrable barrier between his mind and the other man's.

It's a barrier made up of two layers of hard bone, Max thought, the bone of my skull and his.

"And all of this is being paid for by the medical insurance I have through working for you?" Max asked.

"That only paid for the first few days. Then we had you moved here. It's not a very good insurance plan," Jacobs said in a tone of confession. "I've been trying to get my staff moved to something better, but it's a budget quest—"

"Who's paying for this place, then?"

Jacobs sighed and said nothing.

"Grady, come on."

"All right. You are. It's your money. I chose this place based on cost and what you had available."

"What I had available? I don't have any money."

"You do now. Or you did. There's not much left. It's your...inheritance."

Max stared at him, trying to understand.

Jacobs rushed ahead as though trying to get through with it as quickly as possible.

"I called your parents to tell them what had happened to you—as much as I knew at the time, anyway. I told them you were in the hospital in a coma and the doctors didn't know what was wrong with you or what your odds were. Apparently, right after I hung up, your mother had a heart attack."

"Stepmother," Max said, automatically, mindlessly.

"Stepmother. Your father called 911, and they took both of them to the emergency room. Your stepmother died on the way. Your father died in the hospital a few hours later. I'm really sorry, Max."

Max sat motionless, dazed, numb with grief.

"The state appointed someone to oversee your care. The state's paying for this, but you'll be paying them back from what you inherit. There won't be much left."

Max said nothing.

Mom and Dad, he thought. Mom and Dad.

He had lost his chance to reconcile with them. He wasn't sure when he had last told them he loved them.

"I tried to get you on extended unpaid leave," Jacobs said. "Couldn't do it. But don't worry about it. I'll get you back on the payroll as soon as you're up to it."

Max stared at him. Jacobs thought it was a hostile, angry look. In truth, it was a look of intense concentration as Max tried one last time to read Jacobs' thoughts.

There was nothing. He knew that his grief was both for his

parents and for the loss of that wholly involving, intimate contact with others that had been his gift for such a short time.

"We'll see," Max said, knowing he was lying. He had nothing to offer Jacobs now. He was cut off, isolated within himself, and he wanted to crawl even deeper, even further away from the outside world.

I wish I could buy Martinson's mansion, he thought. In a way, that's my real birthplace. I could hide away from everything there.

He shivered again, thinking of the mansion with a mixture of fascination and fear. "What about Martinson's home? What happens to that?"

"RICO. The state's seizing it. I'm not sure what will happen next."

There was a strained silence.

"Well," Jacobs said with a return to his earlier false heartiness, "I'd better get back to the office. Crime never sleeps. You'll let me know what you decide about coming back to work for me, right? You've got my number." He laughed too loudly.

"Right."

They shook hands awkwardly, and Jacobs left quickly, clearly relieved.

Max sat on his bed wondering about his future and seeing only a blank space. His future was empty, and so was he.

25

It was a busy night, and a noisy one. Most of the noise came from a large group of customers sitting around some tables they had pushed together.

They had finished their food a couple of hours earlier, and now they were concentrating on toasts to the man of the hour, the newly elected mayor of Piketon. As they toasted more and drank more, the volume of their celebration increased, and so did the alcohol spilled on the table and the floor.

More work for me, Max thought as he glanced their way while bussing other tables.

Other diners looked annoyed, finished their meals quickly, and left. Carl, the restaurant owner, looked annoyed, too, but Max knew he was happily counting in his mind the profits from the stream of bottles going to the table full and leaving empty. Max wished he could read his mind to see just how big those profits were.

Doesn't matter, he thought. I'll never see any part of that money.

He recognized a few of the people at the table from his time in the DA's office. They had been more reserved then. This was a very different side of them, and again he wished he could tap into their thoughts to understand how they could be so different now.

He walked over to Carl and said, "It's getting late."

Carl nodded. "Yeah. Past closing time. Start cleaning up as much as you can. I'll send Kev and Ray to help you. Maybe that gang will finally get the idea. But be careful. I voted for the other guy, but we're going to want to stay on this man's good side for the next four years."

"Maybe eight."

Carl made a face. "Bite your tongue."

Max, Kev, and Ray started clearing away what they could, trying to be unobtrusive while dodging the clumsy movements of uncoordinated drunks.

Max's back had been bothering him ever since he'd left the hospital. He straightened and stretched, hoping the ache would lessen. The movement caught the attention of the man who was the center of attention, the only slightly drunk mayor-elect, Grady Jacobs.

Their gazes locked. Max smiled and nodded. Jacobs' gaze didn't leave Max's face, but he said something urgent to the woman who was dozing with her head on his shoulder. She sat up, blinking, trying to wake up. She finally understood what Jacobs was saying and looked at Max.

She was thin, with a pale, drawn face. Max recognized her from newspaper photographs as Karen Jacobs, wife of the mayor elect. He stared at her with interest, trying to reconcile this tired, nervous wraith with the virago he had seen in Lynnette Salzmann's mind.

Karen squinted, trying to focus her eyes and attention. Finally, she smiled tentatively at Max.

He smiled back.

She said something to her husband and stood up. He grabbed her arm and shook his head. There was a brief, intense exchange, and then she shook off his arm and headed for Max. She walked carefully. She had a forearm crutch on her right arm and paused occasionally.

She stopped in front of Max, looking up at him, and held out her left hand.

He shook it awkwardly.

"You're the mysterious Max. My husband has told me about you. He owes you a lot, doesn't he?" She smiled warmly.

Max nodded. "Oh, yes. Quite a lot."

She laughed. "I guessed as much. Why don't you come back to work for him? He could really use your help now."

"I'm sorry, Karen. I wish I could, but it's no longer possible."

She frowned. "I don't understand that. Why should it no longer be possible?"

"It's complicated, and I don't really understand it myself. You knew I was in a coma for a while?"

She nodded.

"Something happened to me during that time, and I lost the ability to do what I did for him before."

"That's very strange."

"I wish I could tell you more." He did wish it. He liked this woman and wished he could tell her everything—the strange thing he had been able to do, the cataclysmic events in Martinson's mansion—but he knew there would be no point in doing so. She would think him mad.

"There's nothing we can say? Is there anything Grady can offer you to change your mind?"

He shook his head. "I'm afraid not."

She sensed the finality in his tone, said a few regretful words, and turned to leave—surprised, perhaps, that her charm had not worked.

Max watched her make her way back slowly and painfully

to her husband's side and wondered what the next four years would bring the city. He wished he could be part of it. Instead, he waited until the large group finally weaved their way out of the restaurant—Grady Jacobs giving him a quick, embarrassed nod on the way—and then set about bussing their tables.

I never could have been part of that world, anyway, he thought. It's better this way. Maybe Lynnette will return to normal. She'll be more help to him than I ever could.

Lynnette, he assumed, was still locked up somewhere, still screaming constantly with her voice and her mind, still giving intense headaches to everyone near her. He wondered if she would ever return to normal.

At least I can no longer hear her mind screaming, he thought. Or anyone's mind thinking anything, at any volume.

He missed it and he didn't. He missed the feeling of being intimately connected to others for the first time in his life, but he didn't miss knowing the horrors that writhed and snarled behind the bland faces. He was trapped in his skull with his own horrors, and that was enough.

Thank God no one can ever know what my own horrors are, he thought.

Or can they?

How did he know that his bony refuge was secure? He had lost his ability to read minds, and the mindreading old men who had made him one of them were dead, but how could he be sure there were no others? Their talent had been given to them in some manner by a secret government research establishment—or so they had thought. Martinson had speculated that there might be other such research centers, and that speculation resonated with Max. What if there were or had been others just like it across the country, having the same effects on newborns in their proximity? There might be other old men like Martinson and his cabal. The other research centers might not have been shut down. They might still be operating, and they could have been creating new mindreaders everywhere for decades.

And if in America, why not elsewhere? How many countries had been conducting the same kind of research? How many mindreaders were there in the world? And what were they up to?

Are you reading my mind right now? he shouted.

He sensed nothing.

But I wouldn't, would I? he thought. No more than the people whose minds I read before were aware that I was doing it.

Am I a danger to them? Are they coming for me right now? Even if I can't read minds, I know that the ability to read minds exists. Maybe they consider me dangerous because of that.

For my safety, I must stop thinking about reading minds.

He couldn't do it. His mind was a beacon for assassins.

He tried to close his mind, the way he had learned to do from Martinson, but that knowledge had vanished along with his strange talent itself.

I can't stop them from detecting me, he thought. They'll come for me. I have to be able to protect myself.

He searched within himself for the deadly physical skills that had saved him before. He couldn't find them. They, too, had vanished.

Terrified, he strained his remaining senses, but they felt useless to him now.

He shivered. He wanted to hide, to crawl into a hole and pull it closed around himself.

There's nothing, he tried to reassure himself. There is no threat. If there were, you'd be dead already. There's just you, cut off from the world again.

Everything was muffled, muted, distant from him. Nothing outside himself seemed real. He was shut away inside his skull, trapped in his cage of bone.

About the Author

David Dvorkin was born in 1943 in Reading, England. His family moved to South Africa after World War II, and then to the United States when David was a teenager. After attending college in Indiana, he worked at NASA in Houston on the Apollo Project, then at Martin Marietta in Denver on the Viking Mars lander project. His aerospace career ended in 1974. Thereafter, until 2009, he worked as a software developer and technical writer. He and his wife, Leonore, and their son, Daniel, have lived in Denver since 1971.

In addition to non-fiction, David has published many science fiction, horror, and mystery novels. For details, as well as quite a bit of nonfiction reading material, please see David's website: http://www.dvorkin.com/

David is on Facebook at
http://www.facebook.com/DavidDvorkin
and on Twitter at http://twitter.com/David_Dvorkin
His blog is http://eyeblister.blogspot.com/

For information about the editing and self-publishing service that David operates with his wife, please see https://www.dldbooks.com/

David in 2019

www.ingramcontent.com/pod-product-compliance
Lightning Source LLC
Chambersburg PA
CBHW060556310726
48982CB00008B/1145/J
9781736288658